Also by Asia Mackay

KILLING IT
THE NURSERY
A SERIAL KILLER'S GUIDE TO MARRIAGE

Praise for Asia Mackay

'Sexy, stylish, thrilling and funny. Asia Mackay rips up the rulebook
in this wildly original, razor-sharp tale of marriage and
murder, mundanity and mayhem. I loved it'
Chris Whitaker

'Murder has never been so funny. If you liked *Mr & Mrs Smith*,
you'll love this original and darkly funny thriller'
Clare Mackintosh

'An invaluable manual that I return to again and again'
Hugh Grant

'I ABSOLUTELY LOVED IT!!! It's so new and different and
refreshing and I found it such fun (also loved the feminist message)'
Marian Keyes

'Certain to be your sassy, twisted must-read of 2025'
Janice Hallett

'I absolutely gobbled up this darkly funny and clever thriller
about one of the most dysfunctional marriages to
ever make it onto the page. Loved it'
Katy Brent

'Huge fun with a dark beating heart, a game of cat and mouse with
sharpened tooth and claw. You won't dare to put it down'
Harriet Tyce

'A riotously fun read. Asia Mackay puts the sass in
assassin as it's never been done before'
L. S. Hilton

'With a slick plot, pin-sharp prose and an authentic feel, this
fiercely feminist and witty thriller will keep you gripped . . . and
rooting for a rather wonderful heroine'
Sunday Mirror

'Funny, fast and full-tilt!'
James Swallow

'Mackay's debut is fresh and fun, and adroitly combines social
and parenting comedy with detail-rich derring-do'
Sunday Times

'With dark humour, a twisty plot and a healthy dose of genuine
emotion, this unique novel is a thrilling ride'
Heat

'I loved it. Really entertaining, good fun and captures
the mum juggle/guilt perfectly'
The Unmumsy Mum

'Witty . . . fun . . . clever. BRILLIANT!'
Sophie Ellis-Bextor

'This might be the best fun I've ever had reading a book. Funny,
observant and proper adrenalin-inducing thrills'
Georgia Tennant

'What new mother can't relate to murder? This is the funny
and thrilling story of how one woman does what all women do all
the time – manage every single thing – and throws in a bit of
efficient killing. Brilliant, wish I'd done more of that . . .'
Arabella Weir

'I really think it deserves to be read as a feminist
rallying cry to all of those mothers doing such a lot of emotional,
as well as physical, work to keep their families happy'
Stephanie Butland

'This fiercely feminist and witty thriller will keep you gripped – and
rooting for the really rather wonderful heroine'
Sunday People

'Hilarious, clever and refreshingly original'
Lancashire Evening Post

'Exciting and very funny'
http://bookoxygen.com

'*Killing It* is lighthearted, funny and very easy to
read . . . I couldn't put this one down'
The L Space

'Smart, funny and pacy'
Better Read Than Dead

NOT LIKE THE OTHER PARENTS

ASIA MACKAY

WILDFIRE

First published in 2026 by Wildfire,
an imprint of Headline Publishing Group Limited

1

Cataloguing in Publication Data is available from the British Library

Paperback ISBN 978 1 0354 1849 7

Typeset in 11/13.75pt Sabon LT Pro by Six Red Marbles UK, Thetford, Norfolk

Printed and bound in Great Britain by Clays Ltd, Elcograf S.p.A.

Headline's policy is to use papers that are natural, renewable and recyclable
products and made from wood grown in well-managed forests and other
controlled sources. The logging and manufacturing processes are expected
to conform to the environmental regulations of the country of origin.

Headline Publishing Group Limited
An Hachette UK Company
Carmelite House
50 Victoria Embankment
London EC4Y 0DZ

The authorised representative in the EEA is Hachette Ireland,
8 Castlecourt Centre, Dublin 15, D15 XTP3, Ireland (email: info@hbgi.ie)

www.headline.co.uk
www.hachette.co.uk

Part 1
Preparation

'Parenting is a job. The most important job in the world! And you need to approach it like one – be prepared, plan, anticipate, get ahead of the problems and they won't be problems.'

Bells Brightley, parenting blogger (MommaKnowsBest) and bestselling author of *Reason for Being: Blessed to Be a Mom!*

'Prepare for kids like you'd prepare for a nuclear bomb. Fucking hide and hope the fallout doesn't kill you.'

Hazel Matthews, mother

1

Haze

'The wheels on the bus go round and round, round and round.'

The song had been playing on repeat for the last half hour. Fox turned off the engine and it went blissfully quiet. We were parked inside an empty petrol station forecourt off the A329. It was 12.27am on a rainy Tuesday night and sensible people were tucked up at home.

'I'm telling you this is crazy.' Fox shook his head.

'We have to do this.'

He gripped the steering wheel. 'It's just a poo.'

'It's a poonami. Look at him!'

Fox turned round and glanced at our four-month-old son, who was strapped into his car seat and staring at us wide-eyed. A tell-tale brown stain darkened the whole front of his white Baby-gro. If it was like that at the front, I shuddered to think how annihilated the back was going to be.

'He seems fine with it.'

'He is now, but how long for? What if he kicks off when we're right in the middle of it?'

'There must be a spare nappy in there?' Fox gestured to the black holdall by my feet.

3

I rifled through it. A large knife, duct tape, a blowtorch, three screwdrivers of varying sizes, a roll of bin bags.

'It's only an hour round trip; I didn't think he'd need one.' I briefly considered fashioning something together out of a bin bag and duct tape.

'This is your fault for trying to multitask.' Fox put on an annoyingly good English accent. *'He loves the car. He'll settle in the car.'*

'He was screaming when we dropped Bibi at Jenny's. I couldn't ask her to look after him like that.'

'I think she, of anyone, would've understood.'

'I can be in and out of there in five minutes. Eight, tops.'

Fox sighed and looked around the empty forecourt. 'Okay. Do it. I'll try and fix it tomorrow.'

I paused with my hand on the car door handle. 'Tomorrow? Shouldn't you fix it tonight?'

'As it is, we'll be lucky to be in bed by 2am. And we'll get maybe an hour and half before he kicks off again. You seriously—'

'I just thought, if you were being so paranoid, you'd want to fix it as soon as possible.'

Fox rubbed his right eye. 'I do. I just . . . I don't think I can. I'm so tired I can barely see straight.'

I took a breath. 'We always knew this was going to be tough . . .'

'. . . But it's worth it.' Fox finished what had been our mantra for the last few months. He reached over and squeezed my hand. I squeezed back and got out of the car. I caught a glimpse of myself in the wing mirror and winced. My hair was piled up on my head in a knotty mum bun and I had panda eyes from where my mascara had smudged. I'd pulled on Fox's old hoodie as we were leaving the house, and could now see it had a large spit-up stain on the right shoulder.

I unstrapped Reggie from his car seat while breathing only through my mouth and held him in my outstretched arms as I walked briskly towards the petrol station shop.

Fox

It was going to be fine. I was overreacting. It was a small detour. The chances of anyone noticing us, anyone even interacting with us, were tiny. A one per cent chance.

I looked out as a white car pulled into the forecourt. I blinked several times. I was getting myself so worked up I was clearly hallucinating, because that car looked like it had blue and yellow checks along the side of it. And blue lights on top. I blinked again. The word 'POLICE' was printed across the bonnet. It was there. Definitely.

Okay, calm. Think calm thoughts.

I tried to ignore my rising heart rate. We were just a normal couple. Out for a drive at midnight. With a baby.

The police car parked right next to us. Would a normal man with nothing to hide turn and look at it? My mind wasn't working properly. I just kept staring straight ahead. Out the corner of my eye, I saw two police officers get out of the car. I gripped the steering wheel. Was I about to get a knock on the window? What could they know?

They hovered. I could feel them standing there looking at me. I leaned over and twiddled with the radio. When I sat back upright, both men were walking towards the petrol station shop.

Haze's mobile was still in the car. It didn't matter. She would see them soon enough.

2

Haze

I'd used nearly half a packet of baby wipes, but Reggie was finally clean and once again sweet-smelling. I binned the destroyed Baby-gro. Reggie was now rocking nothing but a clean nappy and a cardigan. I stuffed the pack of nappies and baby wipes back into the plastic shopping bag.

I walked back into the shop and past the refrigerated section. That reminded me – milk. We'd run out. I picked up a large carton, and then headed towards the counter, grabbing a loaf of bread, a handful of chocolate bars and a bag of crisps on the way.

Reggie was balanced on my hip. The cashier beeped everything through. I turned to the sound of the petrol station door opening. Two police officers walked in.

Fuck.

Fucking.

Fuck.

I could picture just how freaked out Fox must be right now. When you failed to prepare, prepare to fail. I gritted my teeth and tried not to think about how ridiculous it would be if, after everything, it was a poo explosion that ruined us.

Reggie, no doubt sensing the difference in tension in my grip, wriggled and let out a little cry. I jigged him up and down on my hip. 'Shhhh, shhhh, now.'

I swiped my card.

'Do you want another bag?' The cashier was talking to me.

'No. It's fine.' I scooped everything off the counter into my bag with the wipes and nappies.

I spun round and gave a small nod to the police officers. Just a normal mother. Grocery shopping after midnight. With a partially dressed baby.

I walked out of the door and tried to not run to the car.

As I got closer, I saw it. The back of the boot had a small smear of what looked like a red handprint. How had we missed that? The forecourt's lighting was illuminating it. It shone out like a beacon. I reached into the bag and pulled out the baby wipes.

I was two metres from the car when I heard a loud voice behind me.

'Excuse me! Madam?'

I stopped and spun round on my heel, fixed grin in place. 'Yes?'

The police officer took a step towards me. 'You forgot your card.' He held out my debit card.

'Thank you, officer.' I took it from him and looked up at his face. As long as he kept looking at me and not the car, my hope was he wouldn't spot the handprint shining out from our minivan's silver bodywork.

'You're out late with a little one.'

'Teething. He just won't settle unless we're in the car. It's messed up his whole bedtime routine. And I know he should be self-soothing, but it's just so tricky to not give in.' I wanted to bore the officer with such inane baby chat that he'd be begging me to leave. 'The car just rocks them so perfectly, and when they're teething they're total monsters. It's just—'

'Tell me about it! I've got one the same age. Our first. It's amazing, isn't it? Exhausting, but amazing. Have you tried the teething granules? I think they're much better at soothing than the gels.'

'I . . . Yes. You're right. Definitely much better.'

'And Sophie the Giraffe. She's been a lifesaver for our little one.'

How the hell did I manage to get stopped by a proud first-time father?

'Good old Sophie!' I jigged Reggie on my hip. He let out a little squawk. 'I'd better get him in.'

The police officer looked at Reggie. 'Poor little lad is probably cold.' Was he now looking at me with actual judgement? Assessing my parenting? He leaned to look over my shoulder at our minivan.

'Poonami!' I cried out, trying to turn his attention back to me. 'Annihilated his clothes.'

'Of course.' His face relaxed. 'Unbelievable how much can come out of them.' The second police officer was now out of the shop and heading towards their car.

'Is he about four months? How many hours is he managing between feeds?'

I gritted my teeth. 'Three, sometimes four. I'm too tired to count.'

'We need to go!' shouted the other officer. He looked a good fifteen years older than the proud dad.

'Just comparing nightly routines!'

The other officer muttered something under his breath as he got into the driver's seat.

'We're on four to five hours now,' the man said. 'And once he even slept through the night. I—'

Reggie let out a small cry at the fact I'd stopped jigging him. 'I'd better get him home.' I turned towards our van. 'Have a good night!'

I had to hope the officer wasn't watching me leave – or that, if he was, my body was blocking his view of the blood smear. 'You too!'

As I got to our boot, I pulled a baby wipe out of the pack and swiped at the blood smear, standing in a way that would shield it from view.

I heard the slam of a car door and the sound of the engine starting. I stood perfectly still, head down staring into the shopping bag on the crook of my arm. Reggie on my hip let out a little gurgle. I kissed his head as I heard the car passing behind us. I waited a beat and then looked up to see them joining the motorway. I slumped back against the boot and took several deep breaths, then put the bag on the ground as I opened the door to the back seat.

Fox leaned round to look at me. His face was ashen. 'What the hell was he talking to you about?'

'New father.' I strapped Reggie back into his car seat.

'Do you think he suspected anything?'

I held up the bloodied baby wipe that I'd hidden in my sleeve. 'This was streaked on the back of the boot. I just cleaned it off. They didn't see.'

'How did that get there? God, what's happened to us? You'd better check there's not any more of it.'

I shut the door and went round to the boot. Looking it over, there were no other marks, tiny or otherwise. I opened the boot slowly and peered inside. Most of the space was taken up by a tightly rolled black tarpaulin. The top had come a little loose. It had been a windy road. The very top of Clark Dixon's bloodied head was now visible. I pushed it back inside the tarp. It didn't look like anything had been dripping on to the interior. That was a relief – it had only been reupholstered last month. I dropped the petrol station bag into the boot next to him and slammed it shut.

'All clear,' I said, climbing into the passenger seat. I shook my head. 'We must've been distracted loading him in and not noticed his hand had smeared on the boot. We had a lot to think about.'

I glanced back at Reggie.

'This is exactly why we should never bring a baby to dump a body!' grumbled Fox as he started the engine. The sounds of 'Wheels on the Bus' once again pained our ears.

'We're working parents doing the best we can.' I took a Twix out of my hoodie pocket and ripped it open. I handed him one finger and kept the other. 'Now, let's get this fucker buried so we can get to bed.'

We both took a bite of chocolate as Fox pulled out onto a quiet motorway.

3

28th February

7.35am: Male subject came out of the back door of his house wheeling a large black bin. Male was approached by white male in his 60s (confirmed ID Barry Fenton, next-door neighbour, head of Neighbourhood Watch). Microphone picked up below exchange:

BF: I trust there are no recyclable items inside?
Male: Of course!
BF: So no wine bottles in there? There weren't any last week either and that's unusual for your house.
Male: I've really cut back on drinking.
BF: Your wife certainly hasn't. When I informed her yesterday that your grass had grown past regulation height, she was sloshing back a large glass of red when she asked me to 'Go measure my dick, not her lawn.'
Male: (Laughter) She has a great sense of humour.
BF: I'm keeping my eye on you both.

Previous investigation of their bin confirmed household waste (including two empty boxes of Maltesers, one empty Ben and Jerry's Phish Food carton and four wine bottles.)

Note – BF spotted observing their house on three different occasions and writing notes in black notepad. Potential problem.

4

Haze

Life is busy.

We're trying to have it all.

Our baby son, Reggie, is a smiley beautiful bundle of fun who thinks sleep is for losers. Our four-year-old daughter, Bibi, loves penguins, our dog Sausage and testing our patience.

If you'd asked me last year how we made it work, I'd have told you that, like any successful partnership, my husband and I divided the labour: we took it in turns and did whatever we could to make it work.

He took out the bins; I cleaned. He cooked; I washed up. He did playground; I did homework.

We were a couple that shared everything. From home, to kids, to work – we were a team.

We did bathtime together.

And we killed together.

Yes, killed.

Slice, dice, cut, stab, bash, slit, hit, bury, burn. Whatever it took to get the job done.

Our marriage wasn't like our people's marriages.

And our little work sideline wasn't either.

13

We made the world a better place by ending the lives of bad men.

We were not your garden-variety, run-of-the-mill serial killers. We were killers with consciences and a strict moral code. A self-appointed vigilante power couple.

We were good people enacting a service no one else was willing or able to provide. If we were ever caught, we shouldn't be prosecuted; we should be celebrated. We were doing everything right, and nothing wrong. Not really.

Some might consider it a crime how much we enjoyed the act itself. But that could just be down to the fact that vengeance gave us a wholesome thrill, rather than the actual watching-someone-bleed-out part. Give us the benefit of the doubt.

A year ago, I would've said that we were doing great.

Recently, it hadn't been going so well.

It had been going pretty fucking terribly, actually.

Overworked, overwhelmed and over it.

Clark Dixon was my first foray back into killing after a self-imposed maternity leave, and I had let myself down.

We were not in the habit of having our children join us on body-dump missions. Any exposure – even as an oblivious four-month old – to that side of our life was something we worked hard to avoid. Tonight was an exception – I normally wouldn't have crumbled, but Reggie was teething and being a particularly clingy nightmare. I couldn't put Jenny through that while she was also trying to get her son Felix and our Bibi settled in for their sleepover.

I should've foreseen the poonami. I should've had nappies with me. Now Fox was going to have to work his magic on making sure our presence at that petrol station was scrubbed from their CCTV. We had learned from our mistakes.

We would always err on the side of overcaution rather than risk being caught.

The dead man in the boot was not going to be the one that finally got us put away. He was in no way a big enough deal, a big enough prize, to warrant our downfall.

There was, however, no doubt that Clark Dixon deserved to die. A wife-beater and rapist, he'd been on our radar for a while. Jenny, my best friend and a serving police detective, had found him for us. A woman from her gym had the misfortune of being married to him. Jenny had tried to get him through the courts, but he had slithered out of their reach, so she'd marked him as one of ours.

Jenny had become an invaluable part of our little operation. Like most mum friends, we'd met at a toddler group. Unlike most mum friends, we'd had a little deviation from the normal route, by way of me killing her deadbeat ex, framing him for the European killing sprees Fox and I had enjoyed, and agreeing to Jenny joining us in our wholesome mission of tracking down and killing bad guys. But that was a whole other story.

Jenny might have only been in my life a couple of years but I couldn't imagine existing without her. The word 'soulmate' had always made me want to hurl. But I did believe I had found my perfect man in Fox, and my perfect woman in Jenny. Having been so profoundly let down by all the people in my life in childhood, it felt only right that I now had not one, but two people who were everything to me.

Stepping in with childcare help was never meant to be part of Jenny's remit, but at present we had no other options. Our children had no loving grandparents to lend a hand. Fox's parents were poisonous fuckwits who lived in New York. My mother was dead – and she was as much use to me like that as she had been when she was alive. My father was dead to me, due to the whole issue of me having no idea who he even was.

We used to have a nanny. Helga had brought order and peace and ironed sheets to our lives. It was beautiful while it lasted – right up until she fell in love with a butcher named Tibor and followed her heart all the way back to Hungary. In bleaker moments, Fox had entertained the idea of us doing a deep dive into Tibor's background in the hope of finding some tenuous reason to justify killing him. If it wasn't for the risk that her heartbreak at his untimely demise might ruin her nannying skills, we might have pulled the trigger off the back of nothing more than an unpaid speeding fine.

When it came to raising kids, I knew the familiar phrase: 'It takes a village.' These days, our village was comprised of Jenny and her parents, Sandy and Frank. We'd looked for a suitable replacement for Helga, but it was hard finding someone we could trust with the safety of our children, especially when we were so well versed with just how depraved human beings could be. Reggie was still so small that we both struggled with the idea of trusting a stranger to look after him, let alone trusting that they'd also be capable of protecting him from hardened criminals out for blood. Luckily for us, Sandy had been a midwife and, while Frank might be hitting seventy, he was still a retired police detective who knew his way around a gun. Even the size of him would make someone think twice.

Part of the reason we were stretched so thin was that killing wasn't our only work. It might make the world a better place, but it didn't pay our bills – our day jobs had to do that. Fox had started his own investment management company a couple of years ago, and, while it was never going to be a passion for him, the big money helped ease the pain. I was an artist. A London gallery exhibited my large, heartfelt canvases, and sold them to people who would never truly know what had inspired them.

Our spare bedroom was a makeshift studio. I was always trying to paint, but recently I'd been so tired my mind zoned out the minute I sat down. I'd found myself spending more time staring out of the window than putting brush to canvas. I had a good view of our street. It was helping me really get to know our neighbours.

I had fought Fox on moving to an affluent neighbourhood in Berkshire, but he had been adamant. If we were going to be parents, we needed to go all in on the proper suburban dream. I still missed London – its bright lights, glut of designer shops and beloved anonymity – but being here was gradually becoming tolerable. I had realised there were benefits to the slower pace of life. I didn't feel guilty for staying home. Without the lure of the capital's newest and hottest restaurants, I didn't see the point in shoehorning myself into a beautiful dress. I could kick back in my dressing gown, watch Netflix and be in bed by 10pm. Rock and fucking roll.

I'd also learned that, when it came down to it, when you stripped everything back, we were not that different from the nice middle-class families surrounding us. All of us sitting pretty in our big, detached houses. All of us with our secrets.

It hadn't escaped my attention that the Thompsons at number nine had a strapping twenty-two-year-old gardener who every Monday spent more time inside, with the lady of the house, than outside in the garden. Or that the Hudsons, three doors down, never recycled. The blank space where their bin should have been on recycling days was a big middle finger to the status quo. It was quite something to ignore the guilt of not doing your bit to save the planet – I couldn't work out if it was admirable or despicable. I was, however, a little more clear cut in my view on Cynthia from number thirteen. Last week, she drove away without leaving a note when her car scraped a badly parked Range Rover: a crime to which she thought there were no witnesses. Naïve, really, for someone who lived in a neighbourhood where everyone was watching each other. Judging. Competing. Hiding.

Walking up and down our street, saying hello to our neighbours, it had become clear to me: we all played nice, we smiled, we presented as good people. But no one really knew anyone. No one really knew what we were all capable of.

Fox and I really were no different to those upstanding members of the public we lived right alongside.

Killing bad men was a public service, but it was one we were forced to keep as a dirty secret. People were so squeamish, so narrow-minded.

Why couldn't everyone see that killing a Mr Wrong was totally right?

After what happened last year in Italy, lesser killers would've stopped, just hung up their knives and retired. But not us. We were trying to get back into some kind of routine. Work, kids, kills. Doing the best we could to pretend it was business as usual.

I knew better than most that life was unpredictable. I braced for the bad, brushed it off and kept going. I'd had a childhood of coping, of adapting to whatever was thrown at me. Fox, coming from his sheltered, privileged, Upper East Side bubble, found it harder. I didn't think any less of him for it. He was tougher than most and if he was struggling after what had happened, it was understandable. I was understanding, but also impatient.

I needed the old Fox back.

5

Fox

'And how did that make you feel?' Sally Bridgers looked at me over her notepad.

'Vulnerable.' I'd been seeing Sally for a few weeks now, and had become rather good at using different words to encapsulate my feelings of distress. I needed help. I knew that. Italy had sparked my downward spiral. I didn't feel in control of my life any more. The transition from family of three to family of four was joyous, wonderful, debilitating and exhausting. Our house was a mess. My mind was a mess.

Some nights I woke up in a cold sweat, the smell of oranges would fill the room and I'd deep-breathe until my heart rate returned to normal. Sometimes Haze would roll over and hold me tight. I never knew if she was awake or doing it in her sleep.

Sally's office was painted completely yellow: the walls, the ceiling, the skirting boards. She'd clearly wanted it to feel like a warm, inviting place, but sometimes it felt like you'd stepped inside the sun. The minimalist white furniture formed little clouds. The two chairs we'd sit in, facing each other, were deep and comfortable. She sat in front of a wall of her diplomas. The only item on her white desk was a large plug-in water fountain shaped like a tree. It was also a diffuser, so as well as the permanent sound of trickling water, it also emitted cinnamon-smelling steam. It was a strange sensory overload. I was sure it was all part of some psych trick to make you open up more. Or maybe she just had really bad taste.

'Do you have any worries about going abroad again?'

Sally had blonde hair and a hardened face that was difficult to age. My best guess being she was maybe a couple of years younger than me. She wore large tortoiseshell glasses that I had a strong feeling were just for appearance.

'No, not at all. I understand it could've happened anywhere. My only worry now would be travelling with two young children instead of one.'

Sally nodded. I didn't know if she had children. Haze had often complained about sitting next to a man at a neighbourhood dinner who only talked about himself and never asked questions. It had made me extra vigilant in my social interactions, which meant that only talking about myself with Sally had taken a little adjusting. Now that I had got used to it, there was no denying that it was also quite enjoyable.

'Your second child is only a few months old. It can't be easy handling a toddler and a newborn. How are you coping with that pressure?'

'It's not been easy. Juggling it all with work.'

'But you're managing?'

'Oh my god! Oh god! Bibi! No!' Haze was shouting.

I'd rushed into the kitchen to find Reggie, our sweet baby, sitting in his bouncy chair, seemingly unfazed by the duct tape wrapped round his whole head.

'I just went for a pee! How are we going to get it off? It's going to rip out his baby hair!'

Bibi was smiling next to him, gripping the roll of tape. Where had she got it from? We only kept duct tape in . . . our kill kit. I scanned the kitchen, and there was the familiar black case, open on the floor. We could at least be grateful she hadn't used the rope, bleach or industrial bin bags.

'There are moments where it feels . . . too much. If I was feeling better, then maybe things would be easier. It's why I'm so desperate to go back to normal, to how I was.'

Sally tilted her head. 'Nathaniel, I feel like we still haven't got to the crux of why you're here.'

I blinked at her. 'I've told you. Many times. I was the victim of a violent mugging, and it's been hard for me to move on from it.'

I'd told Sally this fabricated mugging had occurred in Italy. I'd been vague about where. Ivrea was a small town in the north-west. What had happened there had been covered on the news for a couple of days.

Sally leaned forward. 'What's the rush? You know that getting over trauma takes time, but you're clearly wanting a quick fix. Why?'

It was comforting to know she was a good enough therapist to spot this. She was right: I was in a rush. I couldn't carry on like this. My mental health could affect our physical health, and that's why I needed to fix this. Fix me.

I took a deep breath. 'I was having a moment with my wife, and I found it difficult to . . .' I trailed off.

'An intimate moment?' Sally tapped her pen against her notepad.

The two of us, standing over a squirming Clark Dixon.
'Very intimate.'

'And you had trouble performing?'

Gripping the knife in my hand: a hand that wouldn't move.

I dropped my head. 'I couldn't get it up.'

Sally nodded. 'Impotence is a common side effect post-trauma. How did Haze react?'

'She pretended she hadn't noticed.'

Haze gently taking the knife from my hand and walking towards Dixon.

'I felt bad that I wasn't there for her. That I let her down. I hate her doing it alone.'

Sally dropped her pen. 'There is nothing shameful about masturbation.'

'Mastur— What? Oh. Right. No, I'm all for it. Of course. I just meant I felt bad that I let her down.'

Sally snorted. 'Women usually find masturbation more satisfying. More likely to get the job done.' She looked up to see me staring at her.

What on earth? Was that true? Did all women think that?

'Sorry,' she said. 'I mean, interesting you feel that way.' She cleared her throat. 'Anyway, thank you for telling me. I understand how important this is for you to resolve. I'm sure, with all the good work we're doing here, we'll soon have you back at it in no time.'

'I just want to be back to what I once was.'

I left Sally's office feeling a little better. I wasn't totally sure how much pretending my issues were a mugging and impotence would affect her ability to help me – but it wasn't like I could horrify her with the truth. There was no little pill that could cure killer-instinct dysfunction.

I caught a glimpse of myself as I passed a shop window. Forty-five.

Did I look it? Did I look like I was losing it? Like I was past my peak?

I had to fight it. Train harder. Sweat more. Do what I could to compensate for my advancing years. Haze kept telling me to get a grip, to just be grateful that my hairline hadn't receded and that I didn't wobble when I jogged. But I had higher standards for myself. I had to be better than okay. I had to be invincible.

I tried to work out every day. Running. Weight training. Boxing. Whatever free time I had was spent working on myself.

It was tough fitting it all in, especially on pitiful amounts of sleep. But every time I thought back to last year it gave me the kick I needed.

Haze observed this new me with the same tact and understanding my wife was so famous for. *'Will you just chill the fuck out and have a drink?'*

She was right. But winners didn't give in to the easy option. I had stopped drinking. I couldn't afford the extra body fat. Empty calories.

And it wasn't just my body I was trying to shake up. It was my mind too. I had started writing poetry. I was trying to philosophise on life, to make sense of it all. I was trying to believe that I could be creative too, not just the practical, spreadsheet-filling list-maker who kept our lives ticking over. I hadn't shown the poetry to anyone. Especially not Haze. She was the type to make retching noises whenever there was a sappy part in a movie. She loved hard, but there was no softness. No space for grand gestures and over-the-top declarations. And definitely not for my rhyming couplets debating the meaning of our existence.

I was doing everything I could to keep us safe. I had to

protect myself. I had to protect my family. I knew firsthand how easily we could be attacked. Ambushed.

I had a fear now that had never been there before.

My children. My sweet, innocent, small children. I loved them so much it hurt. Dropping Bibi at the school gates each morning tore at me. How could I protect her if I wasn't right by her side? We were meant to be okay with letting them navigate the world without us – but how? How could we do that when bad things could happen at any moment?

And now I'd lost my power. I'd had a bad man before me, and I couldn't finish the job. I'd had my knife in hand, but I hadn't been able to use it. What use was I to my family if I couldn't protect them? How long until Haze thought the same? Maybe she already did?

When I thought of the me before last year, I realised I'd been living my life with blinkers on. Strutting around, feeling powerful, oblivious to just how quickly things could go wrong. I'd had my eyes forcefully opened – and I hated it. This bottled-up fear I carried around with me now, weighing me down, affected everything. If a bad thing could happen to me, it could happen to them.

I wanted to believe that kids were tough. I kept reminding myself of what Haze had gone through when she was young – and she'd come out the other side the best woman I'd ever known. Even looking back on my own childhood, I knew I had managed to survive 'affluent neglect'. Yes, I had a name for it now. Sally Bridgers had helped me understand the abuse my brother, Julian, and I had experienced at the hands of our incredibly wealthy parents. They had over-provided for every material need, forced us into extensive tutoring and used us as show ponies – all while being cold, emotionally distant and devoid of morality. We weren't children to them, just assets and heirs.

I knew it obviously wasn't the same as what Haze had gone through – I could still barely control myself when I thought of all she'd suffered – but, as Sally had pointed out, my trauma was valid too. Confronting it and reacting to it was part of the healing process. I did this by making absolutely sure I would never repeat any of my parents' mistakes.

I made sure my children felt loved. I laughed with them. I played with them. I was present for them. Not just because I knew I should be, but because I wanted to be. They were magnificent and they were mine. Every beautiful moment we'd ever shared had made me think about how devoid of regular humanity both mine and Haze's parents had to have been to walk away from us – literally in Haze's case, emotionally in mine.

Was this experience of abandonment the reason why we could disassociate from murder? Or had this innate ability to take a bad life with no guilt always been within us? The nature-or-nurture debate could perhaps be answered by what our children grew up to do. They might have inherited our killing genes, but we were going to give them the most goddamn boring upbringing we could and see if we could normal the bloodlust out of them. If they, too, ended up killing with abandon, the only trauma they could blame it on was that of being forced to eat broccoli.

Calming the demons within myself, hunting the demons out in the world, it was no wonder I'd been feeling so tortured and unsure of myself. Maybe this was my equivalent of a midlife crisis. Maybe because I'd had it all and done it all, it was always going to hit me harder.

I was Nathaniel Foxton Cabot II. A tall, attractive, well-dressed white man with a platinum credit card. When I walked into a room, women looked at me and men nodded at me. I'd travelled the world, stayed in the finest hotels, eaten at the very best restaurants. And I'd killed a large slew of men, all of whom had deserved it. I'd done everything I'd ever wanted to do. Things had always come easily to me.

Until they hadn't.

I'd got out alive – but at what cost?

Now I couldn't appreciate everything I had, as I was scared of what could go wrong next.

I knew I had to fight this insecurity. Fight my fears. I wanted to be the best me I could be. But how could I do that when my body was on a downward incline? Middle age was not kind.

Haze was more than six years younger than me. She had barely aged a day since the night we'd first met in Paris twelve years before. She still had that red dress. She still looked incredible in it. Did she look at me differently now? Could she see that I wasn't infallible? Did that make her love me less?

Sometimes, my thoughts could be my biggest enemy. And I couldn't escape from myself. When I was trying to drift off to sleep at night, they shouted the loudest.

I was getting older, slower, weaker.

I'd always thought I had it all figured out: kill bad guys, raise good kids. But recently it was all becoming a little more shaky.

In the months leading up to Italy, we'd upscaled our operation. Using Jenny's police resources, we'd aimed higher than we ever had before: tearing apart sex-trafficking rings by eliminating their key supplier; going after an influential bad man who'd used his embassy contacts to escape prosecution for putting several women in hospital. For a while, we were really making an impact. No more chance encounters with drunken would-be rapists. No more just flirting with being superheroes; we were bona fide gamechangers.

And then everything had fallen apart.

I thought of the postcard from Ivrea that was still pinned to our fridge. It had arrived a year ago, the day after we got back. In case it wasn't enough of a warning that they had our home address, the scrawled '*Stay out of our business*' made it clear.

We'd gone from being our most efficient, our most effective, to only fitting in one bad man in a year. And I couldn't even perform for that one. My wife had to do it for me. No wonder I was feeling crushed and overwhelmed. I was tired all the time. I wasn't putting in enough time at the office, so my investment fund wasn't where it should be. And then there was the nagging guilt that Reggie was not getting the same level of attention Bibi had. Just because he was the second born didn't mean he should be a second-class citizen. Where was *his* perfectly put together baby book with marked milestones and photo evidence? But then, when was the last time I'd run through phonics with Bibi? And Haze, when had we last had a proper date night, time to reconnect, rather than just rowing over whose turn it was to get up for Reggie?

Father of two. Husband. Killer. I wasn't *having it all*. I wasn't *killing it*. I wasn't killing anyone.

A full house of failure.

6

Haze

'Mrs Cabot!' Mr McCabe, Bibi's ridiculously attractive twenty-something-year-old new teacher, was waving at me from the classroom door. I'd been hovering by the school gates, waiting for Bibi to be dispatched to me. I now understood why I hadn't yet seen her in the throng of children rushing out of the door. I was being summoned inside.

Fox had insisted Bibi attend the exclusive private school fifteen minutes from us because of its excellent academic record, although I think he was equally charmed by the straw boater hats they had to wear. '*So charmingly English!*' Despite my scoffing, it did seem like the school was the right choice: she enjoyed going, they had good parking and her teachers' fixed grins were near believable.

I strode towards the teacher. 'It's just Haze!' I said this every time he addressed me, and still he refused to take it onboard. I had to hope it was down to an insistence on parental politeness and not due to the fact I was ten years older than him. 'Everything okay?'

'Bibi's fine. She's with Miss Dutton next door. I just need a quick word with you.'

He led me through to his classroom and motioned to one of the small plastic chairs. I squeezed into one as he sat down next to me.

I had a feeling I knew what it might be about.

We compensated for our nerves about leaving Bibi for so long by embedding trackers in her school shoes. It gave us the security of always knowing where she was and, as an added bonus, it helped us find her shoes during the morning scramble to get out the door. The events of last year might have shaken us enough to justify the need to use a tracker, but, judging by the amount of online rave reviews these devices had, we weren't the only nervous parents out there. There was the occasional rant from someone whining about them being an invasion of a child's privacy, but, let's face it, she was four. She shouldn't have anything private from us. It was our job as her parents to make sure we knew everything – including exactly where she was.

I didn't know how these fancy schools worked, but if they'd discovered she had trackers planted on her I imagined it might constitute some kind of rule breach. Mostly because they didn't want anyone to know that despite their brochure advertising an hour and a half a day of 'daily play and outdoor activities in the expansive park opposite', I'd clocked the most they ever managed was an hour and five minutes.

'There's been a common theme in Bibi's drawings this last week.' Mr McCabe moved a pile of papers towards me.

On the top was a picture of a stick figure with long hair and a dress. Next to her was a little stick figure in what looked like penguin pyjamas. Bibi had drawn herself and me. It would be adorable, except for the fact I was covered in red crayon. I looked like I'd bathed in blood.

I flicked through the pile. All varied in setting, and artistic talent, but all featured me, covered in red.

'Have you been in an accident? That perhaps Bibi witnessed?'

The Clark Dixon murder had been a disaster from start to finish.

My aim had been off. I'd sliced his femoral artery. The spray had got me. Really got me. Bibi had walked in on me in the utility room as I was stripping down. She'd screamed at the sight of her bloodied, half-naked mother.

'Gosh no! Nothing like that at all.'

Bibi had woken because of a bad dream and heard me talking to Jenny downstairs. Just after Jenny had left, she'd come to find me. I'd calmed her down by laughing off the mess I was in. I knew she didn't believe the excuse about a red paint can exploding while I was working. But having shown her that I wasn't injured anywhere, she seemed reassured that I wasn't hurt. She knew the story wasn't quite right, but she didn't know the truth.

By the time Fox had returned from doing a sweep of the street cameras, Bibi was back tucked up in bed, fast asleep. I was showered and clean.

I picked up a couple of Bibi's drawings as Mr McCabe watched me. She had talent. And, like her mother, blood spill clearly inspired art.

'I don't know why she drew these. I do like red dresses.' Breezy. Cool. Normal.

Mr McCabe frowned. 'She said, "Mama hurt," when I asked her about them. Clearly she's using her art to express her worries.' I saw his earnest expression and realised he really wasn't going to drop this. He cared about kids' wellbeing too much. I was both delighted and inconvenienced by this.

'Now that I think about it, Bibi did walk in on me as I was in the middle of changing my tampon, which had leaked all over my white nightdress.'

Mr McCabe gulped.

'I guess it must've been a shock. I tried to explain about women's monthly burden and how I wasn't hurt, that it was all natural. But you know it's hard to explain to a four-year-old you can be gushing blood and it—'

'Okay! Got it. Right. Okay.' Mr McCabe shuffled the papers together. He looked even more adorable when flustered.

'I'll talk more to her about it.' I leaned forward. 'Thank you for bringing it to my attention. I had no idea it'd had such an impact on her.'

I hadn't told Fox that Bibi had seen me post-kill, covered in blood.

I couldn't now drop that news, along with the further bombshell that it had traumatised her to such a degree she was drawing pictures about it. I knew keeping secrets from your other half was bad, but what about when it was for their own good? Fox had his own issues to deal with. I could handle this. Kids saw things they shouldn't all the time. There were plenty of four-year-olds who might have walked in on their parents having sex. Bibi had just walked in on me covered in a dead man's blood. It wasn't like she saw the man. Or me killing him. In the grand scheme of parenting fails, it wasn't that big a deal, was it?

Clark Dixon was meant to be an attempt to prove that we were getting back to normal. That even though life was getting busier, more pressured, we were still us, and we could do anything we wanted to.

But all it had done was show how far we'd fallen.

Fox was too jittery. So many worries about the abandoned warehouse Jenny had selected. Were the CCTV cameras really offline? Had we factored in the high wind speed, as that might carry noise further?

I had hoped that getting back to it would've triggered a

primal reaction. Reminded him of what he'd once been. But there was no spark in his eye when the knife came out. No joy at the blood spurt. And when I handed over to him to finish he couldn't. My man froze. He couldn't perform. I pretended that I hadn't noticed, that he was being gracious when he said, 'No, darling, you do it.' But we both knew. He'd lost his mojo, his killer instinct.

Not only was my husband not pulling his weight at home, but he wasn't pulling it at work either. Day to day, he looked off mournfully into the distance, questioning life. How nice to have the time to be so introspective. I was taking on the brunt of night feeds, laundry, nap-time logistics, household shopping. And now I was having to do it alone out in the field too.

It was why I'd been off with my kill strike. I'd been so worried about Fox, I hadn't aimed properly. I'd forgotten my training and I'd messed up my clothes – and also, apparently, my daughter's head.

People don't say it enough: marriage is hard. You sign up to it in the throes of love, full of hope and promises and doe-eyed enthusiasm. And then the years and years go by, and the spark is dulled. Throw in becoming new parents and, as beautiful and life-affirming as this cherished new life is, it makes you miss your old one. You say goodbye to passion, spontaneity, fun, and welcome in sacrifice, compromise, boredom.

Love is still there. It has to be, right? It's just that everything else has changed. You've changed. For the better *and* the worse. It takes time to realise all this. You let it fester: the disappointment, the anger, the—holy shit! Is this it?

It can all bubble up to one monumental showdown – and then guess what? It's the reset you needed.

That's what worked for us. We had an all-time low before we found our way back. We no longer wanted to kill each other, our marriage was back on track and we were daring to be happy, happier than we'd ever been. We were winning at marriage, winning at parenting.

But since The Incident in Italy a year ago, it had all gone to shit.

I still remembered the silent flight home, with us gripping each other's hands.

In the months that followed, everything was a blur. We were busy trying to recover, trying to forget. I didn't even notice when I missed a period. And then another.

Reginald Matty Cabot was a happy accident. A blessed mistake. By the time I took a test, I was already nine weeks pregnant.

Pregnancy coinciding with our self-imposed exile from the killing game seemed fortuitous timing – we didn't want to risk further antagonising whoever wanted us dead, and the whole getting out and about to end a man was definitely less appealing when heavily pregnant with a toddler in tow.

We had worked hard to set up this vigilante sideline, and as long as we stuck to the run-of-the-mill scumbags we could carry on doing it. Even though there was an element of risk to our business model, we knew we could keep our family safe. And, in a way, if you ignored the killing bit, and focused on the 'chasing your dreams' part, we were setting a good example to our children. Reach for the stars, baby! Win that gold medal! Be a top barrister! Climb that big mountain! Kill that bad man!

'*Mama hurt.*'

I just needed to work on that separation between work life and home life, make sure Bibi wasn't emotionally scarred forever, help my husband be fighting fit and get my baby to sleep through the night, and everything would be perfect.

7

Fox

I knew keeping secrets from Haze was a bad idea. We had both learned from past mistakes.

I loved my wife. I wanted her to be happy more than anything.

And it was while thinking of her happiness I did something a little crazy.

When Haze was pregnant with Reggie, I was having trouble sleeping. A combination of being kicked repeatedly by my darling wife in her sleep, nightmares that felt too real and waking up in a panic over whether the front door was double-locked. Some nights, I'd give up trying to fall back asleep and go down to the kitchen and scroll the internet. News articles. YouTube videos. Anything that caught my interest and kept my mind busy.

One of those nights, I happened to come across a video clip about a woman who'd been reunited with her birth father in adulthood. She spoke very movingly about how finding him had helped her sense of self. This woman, who even looked a little bit like Haze, said knowing where she'd come from and understanding her heritage had given her a peace she'd never felt before. It was all very emotional.

I was not in the best place mentally. I think this was why the beauty of their reunion scene tipped me over the edge. I felt like I was seeing it for a reason. The universe was telling me what I needed to do for my wife.

Before I could really think about it, I'd ordered a DNA kit from Find My Heritage.

Finding Haze's father was never something we'd talked about; she'd certainly never expressed any great yearning to meet the man whose name she didn't even know. But I started wondering whether, like that woman in the video, Haze could find a kind of peace in being able to have answers to all the questions she must have about herself. And really, wasn't it a responsible thing to do? What if our children one day needed a donor for something and blood relatives were the best chance? My parents were clearly a bust on that front. Besides, thinking about it from a health perspective, surely it would just be a good thing to know what potentially inherited genetic diseases our children could be prone to?

This was what I kept replaying over and over in my mind. As soon as the kit arrived two days later, I took one of Haze's hairs from her hairbrush and sent it off. I'd had no grand illusions of some Hallmark moment where Haze and her long-lost father would fall into each other's arms. She was not known for her open displays of emotion. But maybe even just a mildly awkward coffee would help her know a little more about her background. She'd always written him off as a deadbeat who'd abandoned her mother and left her to grow up with an array of awful foster families. But maybe he'd never even known she existed. Maybe he was a good man who'd just never got the chance to know her.

I might have had the presence of mind to take precautions by registering her under a fake name and with fake details, but, other than that, I wasn't thinking straight. Clearly, stealing my wife's DNA and secretly trying to track down her father was a truly terrible idea. So when I got the email saying there was no familial match on their database I was relieved. I'd tried opening a can of worms, but the lid was firmly screwed shut. I didn't need to make any difficult decisions, or even come clean to Haze, as there was nothing to say.

But then a few months ago, just a week after Reggie was born, I got a notification.

A parental match had entered the system. Haze's father was out there. He was alive.

This was perhaps when I should've come clean to Haze, but she was – and I say this with deep love and respect – batshit hormonal. One morning, she burst into tears when she discovered we had run out of bread. When I was out at the shop buying some, she screamed at me for not answering my phone on the first ring. Where was I really? Out having fun? Leaving her at home with a newborn, a four-year-old and a dog? What kind of irresponsible sadist was I to knock her up twice and then abandon her?

It would've been the worst time to reveal what I'd done behind her back. She was in no position to see that my actions were coming from a place of love.

Still, I hoped that finally meeting her father might help her understand more about herself – and who wouldn't want that opportunity?

I decided I should at least vet him before coming clean. I was in a hole and thought it was best to just keep digging. And that was how I, pretending to be one Harriet Smith, had ended up in a lengthy email correspondence with Mike Martin.

Mike was shocked to discover he had a daughter. He had met Haze's mother in a bar and they had spent a few nights together. But he had left one morning after discovering her going through his wallet when she thought he was asleep.

I had found out everything I could about Mike online, and he seemed like a stand-up guy. He was in his seventies. A retired accountant. He lived on a remote island in Scotland with his wife and two rescue dogs. He sounded like a kind of perfect long-lost grandfather. His home was even a converted lighthouse. I wished I could come clean to Jenny and ask her to give him a full police background check, but a part of me wanted to believe I was perfectly capable of vetting him myself. Before she'd come onboard, I'd always been the one who did all the research on targets – Jenny might have steamrolled into that role, but I was still more than capable. And, really, I knew I couldn't trust her to not go running to Haze as soon as she worked out who he was.

I'd taken my email chats with Mike as far as they could go. And now he'd started with the inevitable: 'Maybe it's time to meet?'

I was running out of excuses, both for Mike and myself. I needed to come clean to Haze, but it was hard finding the right time. Mostly because it would never be the right time. How could I explain to her that, due to a sudden overwhelming urge to try and make her life better, I'd gone behind her back and found her father? And that I'd been catfishing him for the last few months, pretending to be her?

I'd read repeatedly how exercise was great for your mental

health – it was an outlet for built-up tension and helped complete the stress cycle. I'd been pounding the treadmill harder than ever as I tried to both trigger my brain out of flight mode and think of a solution to my current predicament. Despite the impressive mileage I'd covered in the last month, I was no less stressed and no closer to an answer. Sally would at least be proud of me for realising I couldn't run away from my problems.

And so I had made a decision. This was it. I was going to catch Haze in a good mood and tell her everything.

8

Haze

'For fucking fuck's sake. It's your turn!' I whacked Fox in the back. How could he be oblivious to our son's wails?

Fox did a half-snore, half-snort and sat up with a start. 'What? Fire?'

Our bedroom light came on.

'What the—?' Fox and I looked at each other, squinting in the sudden brightness of our supposed sleep sanctuary. The clock told us it was 4.15am.

'He woke me up, and today is my ballet show.' Bibi appeared at our bedside, her hair in a messy bun on top of her head. She was standing with her hands on her hips. Only the penguins on her pyjamas were smiling. 'Did you not hear him? Why haven't you got him?'

Nothing like being parent-shamed by your four-year-old.

'You do it,' groaned Fox as he collapsed back into his pillow. 'You know he just wants boob,' he murmured. 'I don't have boob. I'll make up. Really make up . . .' He was already fading back to sleep.

This playing of the titless male card was getting very tiresome.

I got out of bed and stumbled to Reggie's room as Bibi stormed back to hers. I plucked a howling Reggie out of his cot and into my arms. I rocked him as he bobbed against my chest.

I sank into the chair next to his cot and closed my eyes as he latched on and the howling stopped. This was relentless. Fucking relentless.

And my husband was asleep.

It wasn't his body that had had to birth a whole human being. It wasn't his body that had to nourish a whole human being. How was this fair? He got to enjoy the conception and then sit back and watch me swell, pop and feed.

This was a woman's lot in life, and it made me furious.

I picked up my phone and scrolled through Instagram. Goddammit, I had to stop talking about my kids. My algorithm was ruined with parenting reels.

A perky mother invited me to 'see her morning routine!'. This lunatic started her day at 5am, not because a kid woke her, but so she could do an hour-long workout, a four-step skincare routine and write in her gratitude journal. All before making her kids gluten-free, sugar-free fruit muffins from scratch. I sent the reel to Jenny with a series of expletives.

Reggie finished and I put him on my shoulder and rocked him as I patted his back.

I needed to get a grip.

I shouldn't let some narcissist who needed online validation get to me. I didn't have a fucking gratitude journal – I had a kill list.

I didn't sit quietly counting out the good in my life. I went out and ended the bad.

I had enough to worry about without succumbing to the nagging guilt that I wasn't doing enough. Could we have killed more bad men these last couple of years if we were childless? Absolutely.

Could Bibi have, by now, grasped the basics of the French language if we hadn't spent all our free time researching, finding and eliminating targets? Potentially.

The relentless grind was further exacerbated by how both parenting and killing involved suffering through an unholy abundance of cleaning up other people's bodily fluids.

Yesterday after pick-up, I'd had a long chat with Bibi in the car about how she needed to find new artistic inspiration. I'd spoken in great detail about periods and had got her to look all over my body to show her, once again, that there wasn't a single cut on it.

Bibi had stared at me and poked me a bit, then shrugged. 'Okay.'

'So, no more pictures of me covered in red?'

'I like red.'

'Me too, baby. But just draw it on other things. Like in rainbows. Not all over me.'

'Okay.'

I had to hope that I'd got through to her.

Reggie was asleep on my shoulder. I staggered to my feet, gripping him close, and manoeuvred him into his cot. I held my breath to see if he would stir. One big stretch, and he stayed sleeping. The gods were on my side tonight.

I tiptoed to his door and slipped out. A litre of coffee down in the kitchen, and I'd be ready to face the world.

Our house was a war zone. There was mess on top of mess. The ordered regime of clearing away toys at the end of the day was long gone. What was the point when they were just going to come out again tomorrow? Random solo puzzle pieces seemed to be scattered throughout the house. The other day, I'd even found one inside my bra.

The kitchen was the heart of the house. And it was sticky. Everywhere. Even after we wiped down surfaces, the layer of ick seemed to reappear within days.

I could've used the quiet hour downstairs solo to prepare for the day. Empty the dishwasher. Load the dishwasher. Take the washing out of the tumble drier. Purée some carrots for Reggie's lunch. Whip up some homemade chia-seed pancakes for Bibi. I could've done all of that. But I just lay slumped on the sofa with my coffee and scrolled the internet, adding some self-hate to my morning ritual.

Bibi skipped downstairs at 7.02am, holding a large fluffy monkey. I brushed her hair as she munched through a bowl of Cheerios. The third time she asked for a refill, I told her she could go get the milk herself. All part of making sure she wasn't turning into a spoiled brat.

I stretched and put my arms behind my head, and felt a clump of my hair that was matted together. I grimaced and patted it. Then I remembered a breakfast going awry at some point this week.

Honey.

In my hair.

I wasn't sure how long it had been there. I had nothing to wash my hair for, so I rarely did. Our social life was as dead and buried as one of our victims.

It wasn't always like this.

Before Bibi had steamrolled her way out of me, we'd had a very different life. We were very different people. We weren't always fucking tired, we were always fucking fabulous. London's best restaurants always had a table for us. Our names were top of the invite lists for the parties to remember. We were the life and soul, shining bright in the spotlights, spinning across dancefloors. It didn't end there. We soaked up the glitz and the glamour of everything Europe had to offer. Five-star hotels. Yachts. Private jets. Total carefree abandonment, and a full focus on the pursuit of pleasure. For the haters who might call it a shallow life, it was not one without meaning – we fitted it all in while eliminating men who didn't deserve to walk this earth. Partying and purging. They went together hand in hand.

Then parenthood hit, and we went from being at the top of the Michelin-starred food chain to eating leftover fish-fingers and lights out by 10pm.

I missed it. But I was too tired to do anything about it.

Family life was overwhelming.

Fox might have been physically here day and night, but I felt alone in this. I wanted him to share with me everything he was going through, but that privilege seemed to be reserved for sodding Sally. I just got to see him sleepwalking through our life together and not pulling his weight. I kept waiting for him to crack and blitz the mess in this house. The old Fox wouldn't have been able to live like this. He'd have been scrubbing the floors, boxing up the mess, reorganising the fridge. Not shuffling downstairs in his dressing gown and shrugging his shoulders. This Fox could only focus on himself, his body, his mind, his thoughts. He couldn't stop to look around and fix everything else.

On the kitchen countertop was the pile of post I'd brought in yesterday. I picked up the *Vogue* as a card fluttered on to the table. The image on it was of three men wearing black masks and red tunics, several oranges flying through the air towards them. A matching postcard was already pinned to the fridge. I turned this one over and read the message.

I got to my feet, gripping the card.

Fox.

I stopped myself. More information was needed before I got his head a-spinning again. I reached for my phone.

9

Fox

I woke to the shrill rattle of curtains opening and light blasting into the bedroom.

'Why?' I howled.

'Get up!' I felt the bed wobble as my beloved wife jumped on it. I kept my eyes shut.

'Now, Fox!' shouted another voice I knew all too well.

I struggled to sit up and opened my eyes.

Jenny and Haze were on either side of me.

'You know, we should talk more about boundaries, Jen.'

She laughed. 'I have a key to your house, and every username and password for all your accounts and devices. What boundaries?'

I pulled up the duvet. Was I being paranoid, or did that sound a little chilling?

Haze handed me the Ivrea postcard from the fridge. I took it from her. 'Why do—'

'Turn it over.'

We warned you. We're watching.

A new postcard. A new threat. My constant worries were valid. They were coming for us again.

I looked between the two women. 'Clark was a random English finance guy. Why would they care?'

Jenny shrugged. 'It doesn't make sense. I ran due diligence on Clark, and he has no ties to anyone from that world. Apart from his crimes against his wife, he was squeaky clean.'

'Maybe it's just an empty threat? They just want to keep us on our toes?' I was reaching. Wanting to believe anything other than the clear truth.

Haze and Jenny looked at each other.

Jenny took a deep breath. 'I've done some checks. The Chameleon got to England a few days ago.'

So this was no empty threat.

Everything in me was screaming that we should get away. Far away! But then what about school? And, really, where in the world could we hide from a man like him?

10

One year ago
Ivrea, Italy

Haze

Things got bad fast.

We'd tracked our target to Ivrea.

And we had the perfect plan.

Every year Ivrea held the Battle of the Oranges to celebrate their liberation. According to thirteenth century legend, the evil duke that ruled the town was killed by a young woman he'd tried to force himself on. Using oranges to represent the stones thrown at his castle during the subsequent revolution, huge crowds of people would now pelt them at each other.

The roaring noise from this massive, organised food fight would mask any of our victim's screams, and the chaos would help us make an unnoticed escape.

Earpieces in. Guided by Jenny. We knew where he was staying. It was going to be a fast, efficient takedown.

But it was a trap.

An empty room and outside it five men coming for us.

'*The bedroom window,*' *Jenny said.* '*Jump and you're at the back of the restaurant!*'

I got out.

Fox didn't.

Fox

I felt hands pulling me back. I spun round and punched the man nearest to me. Then the second. I tried to turn back to the window, but several fists to the head dazed me enough to stop fighting back. I staggered as they slammed me to the ground. Three held me down as two pulled a black bag over my head.

I felt them carrying me down the stairs. I felt them lugging me into a cart. My hands were tied behind me. I tried to sit up and got kicked twice. The cart was moving. The noise from the crowd grew louder. People were chanting and cheering now. No one would hear me shout. I was powerless. Their prisoner. How the hell had this happened?

I was meant to be better than this.

Haze

We saved him.

Just in time.

It all happened so fast.

Jenny shouting at me to hold the phone steady. The map. Following the GPS tracker in Fox's watch.

The old factory.

'*In there!*'

The gunfight.

Dead men on the ground.

Sirens.

Jenny pulling me away from an unconscious Fox. Tying me to a post. *'We've got to fix the scene!'*

Shouting. People swarming everywhere.

I was cut free.

A clueless victim. Sitting wrapped in a foil blanket. I was there but my head wasn't. I couldn't think of anything but Fox. I needed to see him, hold him, hear him breathe.

The police were everywhere. I gave dazed answers to anyone who asked me a question.

One of them stood out. He was watching me. A tall man with dark skin and grey hair, dressed in a beautifully tailored blue suit with a crisp white shirt. He was smoking a slim cigarette. It was hard to clock his age, but I'd have placed him somewhere in his sixties.

He was coming towards me. He reached for my right hand and brought it to his nose.

'Alain Drake.' He announced with a slight French accent. 'I am with Interpol.' He let go of my hand. What the hell was that?

'When can I see my husband?'

'I can take you now.' Drake walked over to a moustached detective who nodded a few times as Drake spoke.

Drake motioned me over and then led me outside. More hurried conversations with other police we passed. And then we were in his car. An old black Mercedes-Benz.

Five minutes of silence until he spoke. 'Your hands smell of disinfectant.'

Jenny had scrubbed my hands to remove any gunshot residue in case I was tested for it.

'Someone gave me hand sanitiser. To get my husband's blood off.'

Drake took a drag of his cigarette. He was not like the

Italian detectives. He was trouble. 'The way we found your husband. It looked like an interrogation.' I had come to the same conclusion. 'He had information they wanted.'

I looked over at him. 'Fox works in finance. I can't imagine what a bunch of gangsters could want to know from him.'

'Your statement to the police said that a group of men took you and your husband from the carnival at gunpoint. Then another group of men attacked your kidnappers and got away before the police arrived.'

We had decided on the 'innocent tourists caught up in rival gang dispute' angle.

Drake wanted to trip me up. 'I was unconscious for quite a lot of my ordeal. I think that's what happened. Loud gunshots and—'

We had just passed our hotel. 'Stop!' I shouted without thinking.

Bibi.

I needed to see her. Drake seemed unphased as he turned the car round.

I ran into the hotel and rang Jenny from reception. She brought Bibi to me. I took her, pyjamaed and sleepy, into my arms. A hushed catch-up with Jenny as we hugged goodbye, and I was back at the car.

Drake helped Bibi into her seat. 'Hello, *ma chérie*. I'm Alain.' He reached behind her head. 'And what is this?' From behind her ear, he pulled out a purple-wrapped sweet. 'The fairies must like you. They only give presents to very special people.'

Bibi grinned at me and quickly unwrapped the sweet before popping it into her mouth.

I looked at him as he got back in the driver's seat. 'You have children? Grandchildren?'

'Some people aren't born to be parents.' He started the engine.

'Couldn't agree more.' I thought of my mother. Her blank face, the empty bottle.

Drake turned to look at me. 'You had bad ones?'

'Oh, no,' I lied. 'Wonderful.'

At the hospital he whisked us through different rooms to a waiting doctor. I listened as he talked, trying to only take in what I wanted to hear.

Fox was going to be okay.

That was all that mattered.

I couldn't bear to hear the list of his injuries.

I just needed to focus on the fact that he was going to be all right. I needed to focus on the good, because if I let myself take in the bad, the rage would take over.

Revenge would come another day.

Drake and the doctor took us through to Fox's room. I didn't notice them leave. I could only stare at my husband.

Fox's arms were bandaged. He had black eyes. A broken lip. He was half asleep now. Maxed out on painkillers, the doctor had explained.

I sat in the chair next to his bed, holding his hand, Bibi on my lap. 'Dada ouchie.' She leaned down and kissed his arm.

I didn't want to think about just how close I'd come to losing him.

Slumped in that chair, I must've drifted off. Shouting men, screams, shots, all peppered my dreams.

With a start, I woke.

Fox.

Bibi.

I looked around the hospital room. My husband was in the bed. My daughter was in my lap.

We were safe.

Bibi was playing with a shiny little ball, rolling it across the standing tray table that was next to us.

I stretched and stroked her hair. 'What you got there?'

'I think fairies give me.'

I picked it up and rolled it around in my hand. It looked like a cheap pendant. The chain must've broken off. 'It can be your lucky charm.'

'Yes!' Bibi kept rolling it between her hands.

I was grateful that she had something to focus her attention on. Something that wasn't the beeps of machinery, the sterile setting of a hospital room and her father's damaged face.

'Haze,' Fox croaked. His eyes were open.

'Dada's awake!' I smiled down at him.

Everything was going to be okay.

11

Present day

28th February

3.50pm: Male subject arrived at playground with daughter (BC).

Male approached by two unidentified women in their 40s. Microphone picked up below exchange:

Male: . . . Look at Bibi go! Better get to her. Have a great day!

(Male moves out of range of microphone.)

Woman One: Jesus, how is he so hot?

Woman Two: It's obscene, isn't it? That jawline.

Woman One: The way that shirt strains over his torso.

Woman Two: My husband has a beer belly he can rest a pint on.

Woman One: You ever spoken to his wife?

Woman Two: When she's here she sits alone on that bench with her sunglasses on, staring at her phone. Looks like a bit of a bitch.

Woman One: One lucky bitch, though. Imagine waking up to that every morning.

Woman Two: Oh, I wouldn't waste time sleeping. God, the things—

(Women continued to discuss FC's body. Nothing relevant.)

Male subject and daughter (BC) spent two hours at playground. Male told BC it was time to leave eight times. Male told BC she'd lost her walking-home snack for not listening. Stayed at playground further twenty minutes. Male gave BC snack as they walked home.

28th February

4.45pm: Female subject had an altercation with male driver in BMW who cut her off.

Microphone (and everyone in surrounding area) picked up the below exchange:

Female: Are you fucking blind? You saw I was going for that space!

BMW driver: Babe, it's every man for himself.

Female: Babe? Seriously?

Female exits vehicle and goes to BMW driver's open window. She leans through it. She speaks softly into his ear. Audio not picked up. BMW driver accelerates out of space and car park.

Obtained car park CCTV from several different angles. No confirmed line of sight of Female showing the driver a weapon.

12

Fox

'*You are in control of your destiny.*'

'*Life is not random.*'

Speaking daily affirmations aloud was a new technique I was trying out to keep my anxiety at bay. I hadn't shared this with Haze, as she'd either laugh at me until she cried, or have me sectioned.

It had been one of Sally's ideas to help me remain calm in between sessions. The low, steady voice uttering these nuggets of wisdom apparently belonged to Dr William Tipton, AKA Doc Willie, an American psychotherapist with a near cult-like following.

I parked outside Sally's office and paused the audio. I had felt no discernible positive effects from repeating these affirmations, but maybe repetition was the key. There was, however, a nagging feeling that Doc Willie was able to genuinely believe the phrase '*You are in control of your destiny*' because he had not met my wife.

As soon as I had sat down in the white cloud chair opposite her, Sally got straight to it.

'Let's revisit the event.'

Sally insisted on doing this every session. She had explained, citing several learned sources with long surnames I couldn't remember, that by constantly reliving my trauma, I would normalise it and get bored of it. This would solve me being triggered by it whenever my memory was unexpectedly prompted. I didn't want a repeat of what had happened last month when I was suit shopping: the fabric sample I was presented was exactly the same shade of blue as the rope I had been tied up with. It was hard pretending to Fabio that my hyperventilating was down to horror at the high percentage of polyester it contained.

I closed my eyes. 'I saw them coming towards me and knew they were trouble.'

The five men rushing into the apartment bedroom.

'I was able to tell Haze to run.'

I pushed her out of the window.

'They punched me several times and dragged me away.'

I was flung into the cart. The sound of the crowds surrounding us. The smell of oranges. The kicks to my stomach every time I tried to move.

'They took me to a cashpoint.'

The crowd noise got fainter and fainter as the cart left the main square. When it finally stopped, they pulled me out of the cart. Through the black bag they'd placed over my head, I could just make out a building. They dragged me inside and tied me to a chair.

'They kept shouting at me. "What's your code?"'

'Who are you working for?'

'They kept punching me because they didn't think I was telling the truth.'

'No one! It's just us! We're just us!'

I had felt the blows raining down on me. One of the men

got a little carried away with a knife and my right thigh. And so it went on and on. I kept blacking out and then being slapped back awake.

'I was lucky the police came across us.'

A burst of gunfire. I could barely see out of my blackened eyes, blood dripping down my forehead. But I knew it was her. I knew she'd come for me. They may have taken my knives, but they hadn't taken my GPS watch. Around me, the men fell to the ground.

I shook my head and opened my eyes. Sally was staring at me.

'Being saved by the police shouldn't make you feel emasculated. That's their job. To help people.'

I smiled at her. 'I know.'

But it wasn't the police that had saved me.

It was my wife and her best friend.

And there was the rub.

Despite being a man who understood that women were our equals, I couldn't help feeling embarrassed. Lesser, even. Did that make me a bad feminist?

'How has it been going with your performance issues?'

It was never far from my mind.

Clark Dixon.

I had choked.

Not him.

Just choked.

'I just don't understand why it happened. I was excited for it. And then, at the last moment, I couldn't do it!' I thought of my hand dropping to my side. The knife limp in my fingers. I wished I could explain to Sally how catastrophic it was to be a killer who couldn't kill.

'You have unresolved issues that are preventing you from being mentally in the moment.'

It wasn't that I couldn't get it up. I couldn't stick it in.

Sally tilted her head. 'How are the nightmares? And the panic attacks?'

'They're not panic attacks! They're just moments when it feels like the walls are caving in and I have trouble breathing.'

Sally let the silence linger.

'Okay, so I suppose some might say that is a panic attack. But I'd rather not have the label.'

Sally tapped her pencil against her notebook. 'You're taking the pills I gave you?'

At our last session, after Sally had listened to my particularly long monologue about the state of the world and how it was impossible for us to believe it was a good place when so many bad things happened every day, she had decreed it was time for medication. Anti-anxiety pills that she said would help me. I'd only started taking them in the last few days, and so far I'd noticed no change. But then, maybe I was too far gone for help. I chewed the inside of my cheek. I was having anxiety that the anti-anxiety pills weren't working. That was not a good sign.

'Yes, I'm taking them.'

'You still haven't told your wife about these not-panic-attacks?'

'I don't want to worry her.'

Haze needed to rely on me as a tough, capable partner in crime. We were a team. We each needed the other to pull their weight. She'd already had to save me once. I didn't want her to feel like she had to save me again.

'You shouldn't keep things from her.' Sally leaned forward and looked me in the eye. 'You need to be honest with her.'

I knew she was right. Healthy communication was important for any couple.

I just struggled to actually do it.

13

Haze

The problem with killing bad men, especially well-connected ones, was that when a carefully orchestrated hit was made on you, it was difficult working out exactly who was behind it. This was the problem we'd found in the aftermath of Ivrea.

We wanted names and addresses. But all Jenny and her extensive police resources were able to dig up was an alias: The Chameleon. One of the men caught alive had a text message on his phone showing off to a friend that he was doing a job for him.

The Chameleon was a somewhat infamous shadowy figure in the criminal underworld: a violent assassin who had not only managed to evade capture, but had also done so without leaving behind any hint as to his identity. Not even his nationality. We automatically referred to The Chameleon as a 'he': an assumption, but in our experience more often a correct one than not.

According to Jenny's many reputable sources, including Interpol, The Chameleon worked almost exclusively for The Corporation, a powerful secretive group with confirmed ties to high-profile Albanian and Italian gangs and a monopoly on organised crime throughout Europe.

'The Corporation' moniker came from the fact that they had big money behind them, and also operated more like a tightly run business than a shady criminal enterprise. The way Jenny described it had made me imagine criminals approaching them for a Dragons Den-type pitch where they outlined why their illegal start-ups were deserving of their investment.

Despite repeated attempts by European police forces working with Interpol, no one had got any closer to understanding who The Corporation were. Any violent activity they were involved in happened behind closed doors – no tacky shoot-outs in the street, no bodies branded with their gang sign. They kept under the radar through fear, respect and paying incredibly well.

The Corporation had links to two victims we'd killed before Ivrea. Their deaths were clearly what had attracted attention to our little enterprise, and explained why they'd enlisted The Chameleon to engineer our assassination. How could we possibly defend ourselves against an enemy about whom we knew nothing? They could be anyone. This was really not helping my trust issues.

I wasn't one to assign blame, but, really, it was clear Fox had fucked up. He had got too male with his aspirations of taking down big shots, forgetting that in the grand scheme of the big bad criminal underworld, we were just small fry. We might be a pretty efficient, exceptionally well-organised team of three, but we had no back-up, no network, no allies. It was just us.

The last year had been a blur. We were playing catch-up. If we were to be free from the threat of The Chameleon and

The Corporation, we had to find them. We needed more than the alias of a shadow. We needed more than the name of a gang of individuals unknown.

We had spent yesterday finding our own individual ways to cope with the news The Chameleon was back in our lives. Jenny had spent the day at the station using every contact and database she could think of to get more information. Fox had slunk off to see Stupid Sally. And I'd sharpened our knives while enjoying a particularly good bottle of Malbec.

This morning, the three of us had reconvened at our kitchen table. Bibi and Felix were transfixed by the television in the next room, and Reggie was gurgling on the floor in his bouncy chair. Our French bulldog, Sausage, was lying alongside him. A pile of both dog and baby toys lay between them. This life was real enough; it didn't seem like there could be a space in it for international gangs and assassination threats. But here we were.

I watched Fox as he took a sip of coffee. He looked wiped out. Although, recently, we both looked wiped out – all the time.

'Interpol are the ones that flagged The Chameleon. Now rumoured to be in the UK,' said Jenny.

'Interpol? You mean Alain Drake?' I thought of the man I'd met in Italy. Sharp eyes and softly spoken. He was trouble.

Jenny nodded. 'Drake's received intelligence that The Chameleon is retiring after this UK visit. He's spent decades trying to find him, and he wants to bring him to justice before the trail goes cold.'

We had to escape both the assassin who was trying to get to us, and the Interpol agent who was trying to catch the assassin. It was going to be the biggest challenge we'd ever faced – and I had a husband in therapy and a baby that wouldn't sleep.

Was it too early to start drinking? Champagne breakfasts were socially acceptable but belonged at five-star hotels with the thrill of being away. Not for drowning out sorrows with a bowl of Shreddies at a kitchen table in Berkshire.

'The postcard implies The Chameleon is here for us.' Fox was gripping his coffee mug so hard his knuckles were white.

I nodded. 'We need to find him before he gets to us.' I could feel it bubbling up within me: this desperate need to find this man or woman. If there was ever someone I'd break our 'no women' rule for, it'd be this bitch.

'I've got one lead. Balgray Hall.' Jenny looked between our blank faces. 'It's a National Trust house in Oxfordshire.'

Fox frowned. 'The Chameleon has an interest in English heritage?'

'My contact at Interpol said they had been monitoring online chatter and had found two mentions to it in association with The Chameleon before they were quickly deleted.'

I tried to process this. We finally had a lead. And it made no sense.

'No police force here has any interest in Balgray,' Jenny said. 'I'll do more digging when I get into the office.'

Fox huffed. 'We can't just sit here waiting for news. We need to—'

Jenny stood up. 'You know what families like to do for fun on Saturdays? They go and look around National Trust houses. Expand young minds. Appreciate the architecture. Enjoy the landscaped gardens and fresh air. Try and find out what interest a master criminal might have in such a place.'

Fox and I looked at each other. I nodded.

He drained his mug of coffee. 'Let's get the kids and pack up the van.'

Last year, my Range Rover had been written off for the greater good – that is, disposing of Jenny's ex, Bill Grundy's body. I had presumed I'd just go down to the dealership and choose a brand sparkling new one, but Fox had insisted we use this opportunity to rethink our choices. He'd found a Volvo minivan with an impeccable safety record and declared it the perfect family car, considering we would often be transporting two children, a dog, a pram and the occasional body. The boot space of a family van was very much underrated.

For Fox, it was the missing piece of the perfect-suburban-life jigsaw. For me, it was the final nail in the old-life coffin.

An hour and a half later, we arrived at Balgray Hall.

Reggie was asleep in his car seat, while Bibi was plugged into Fox's old iPad and her eighteenth episode of *Bluey*. I turned to Fox. Bibi had headphones on, but I still spoke softly.

'Are we making a mistake? What if he's here and he spots us?'

The car park was busy. Fox pulled into one of the last remaining slots.

'He clearly doesn't want us dead right now.' Fox turned off the engine. 'If he did, he wouldn't have announced his arrival with a postcard. He'd have killed us in our sleep.'

I nodded. That made sense. 'Good pep talk. Thanks.'

We made slow progress from the car park to the entrance, with Bibi walking at a snail's pace and repeatedly changing her mind over which stick she wanted to pick up. The over-enthusiastic lady at the counter asked if we wanted a National

Trust membership. My response of 'God, no,' made her face fall, and Fox elbowed me. According to her advice, we should start with a walk around the grounds before we headed into the turreted Jacobean hall.

'I don't get why somewhere like this would catch the attention of The Chameleon.' Fox looked at the crowd of people exclaiming over an ancient oak tree. 'Jenny said the family who own it have no criminal ties. Boring broke aristocrats.'

'Is it bad that I don't give a shit about trees?' I watched as several fawning people took photos of the oak. I fingered the small device in my pocket.

We walked slowly, painfully slowly, towards the Estate Office, which, we'd learned from the leaflet handed over with our tickets, was part of the Stable Block. I handed Fox the assortment of sticks I'd been instructed by Bibi to look after. 'Give me five minutes.'

I sidestepped the 'Private' notice hanging in front of a small courtyard and walked alongside the wall. The office had a large window. I peered inside. It was empty. The benefit of getting here at lunchtime. I opened the door and stepped in. A large whiteboard hung at the back of the room, covered with scrawled writing describing where they were with a fundraising target. It wasn't going well – which would explain the threadbare carpet. There were three desks, all with computers that looked at least ten years old. They should prove no problem for Jenny's hacking skills. At the back of the room was another door next to a huge printer.

I had never worked in an office. I looked around, trying to imagine coming in here every day, sitting at a well-worn office chair, the place silent except for the batting of keyboards. I shuddered.

The largest desk up against the wall held several photos of a large black Labrador. Underneath it, I could see the flashing lights of the router. I reached down and, taking the small device out of my pocket, placed it just behind the router. Mission accomplished.

The desk next to it held a half-eaten sandwich. I needed to move. I walked back towards the main door just as the rear one by the printer opened.

'What are you doing here?' A short lady with a bob and thickset glasses was staring at me.

'I'm so sorry! I'm looking for my daughter; she came running through here.'

'There's a sign.'

'I know, I know. I'm—'

'Mama!'

We both turned to look. There was Bibi, out in the courtyard. She stood next to Fox, who was gripping the pram, the nappy bag slung over his shoulder.

'There you are!' I smiled at Bibi and turned back to the woman. 'I really am so sorry.'

'Yes, so sorry!' Fox called. 'We've told her, no more hide and seek!'

The woman's shoulders loosened as she looked between us. 'Just keep an eye on your children.'

'Of course!' I rushed back towards my family. I took Bibi's hand as we returned to the authorised area of the grounds.

Bibi looked up at me. 'Why did you say I ran off? I didn't run off.'

'I took a wrong turn and thought it was better to give a little excuse like that rather than getting into trouble.'

'It's bad to lie,' said Bibi as she chewed her lip.

'Yes, it is. But sometimes a small little lie is okay.'

Fox gave me a look. *Shit*. Why didn't kids come with a handbook?

'So I can lie?' Bibi smiled.

'No,' Fox said, at the same time as I said, 'Yes.'

14

14

Fox

To make the most of the entrance fee we'd paid, I'd insisted we walk around Balgray's expansive grounds.

'Shall we go?' It had been ten minutes, and Haze was already bored. Sometimes she was harder to entertain than a toddler.

'Dada, look!' Bibi pointed at a couple of ducks waddling by the lake up ahead.

'We could give it a few more minutes. She's happy.'

'I need the loo. I'll meet you by the house.' Haze rushed off before I could respond. She'd once made the mistake of telling me how even a trip to the toilets without a child in tow felt like a taste of freedom. I'd soon realised it didn't actually take fifteen minutes to put in a tampon, and that it was just an excuse she used to enjoy a locked door and an Instagram scroll.

Reggie thankfully remained zonked out in the pram while I took a painfully long time to extricate Bibi from her determined pursuit of her duck friends.

We walked on towards the house. Balgray Hall came into view at the end of the path. It was an impressive building.

I came round the corner to see Haze, just at the bottom of the Hall's sweeping front steps, talking to a tall, attractive man I'd never seen before. She had her back to me, so I couldn't see her face. A stranger hitting on her? Typical men. Racing up to someone they'd never met and thinking they could—

Haze was laughing. The man touched her shoulder as he stared down at her. They knew each other. Definitely.

I quickened my pace. 'Come on, Bibi!' She was a few steps behind, picking a daisy. I'd nearly reached them when the man checked his watch, pulled Haze in for a hug, and walked up the large steps.

Haze turned round as I reached her.

'Who was that?' I tried to keep my voice level. Aloof. Nonchalant. Totally uninterested.

'Danny something. I used to know him. You know, back in the day.'

'You mean he was an ex?' So much for trying to keep it casual.

Haze shrugged as she reached into the nappy bag. 'Just junk food.'

'What?'

She pulled out Bibi's water bottle. 'You know, someone you gorge on for a bit even though you know it's bad for you.'

I gritted my teeth. *Gorge?* Images of a naked Haze and the man pawing at each other were playing in my mind in bright technicolour. 'Do you compare all men to food?'

'You're fillet steak.' Haze smiled. 'Okay?' She handed Bibi her water bottle.

I watched Danny as he reached the front door. I took a few deep breaths. I was a weapon. A carefully controlled weapon. I only took out bad men. Men who didn't deserve to live because of the things they'd done to women – and not because of the consensual things they'd done with *my* woman.

I was a modern man. I was better than this primal jealousy. I knew what Haze and I had. I knew I was the first man she'd ever loved. He was nothing. Nobody. I tried to remember a mantra Sally had made me repeat. What was it?

I control my feelings. My feelings do not control me.

Danny turned back to look at Haze just before he went in. Haze was bending over, adjusting Bibi's cardigan, and didn't notice. Danny clocked me, and our eyes met. He smirked at me and walked inside.

What a prick.

I felt the rage roaring up inside me. Deep breaths.

I control my feelings. My feelings do not control me.

Haze leaned over. 'I think I know why Balgray Hall was mentioned.'

I tried to focus.

'Danny works for an events company, and next month they're organising a big flashy charity event here. He said it would be quite a gathering. Big hitters from the UK, and also a lot of rich, dodgy Europeans. That kind of clientele sound exactly like people The Chameleon would be interested in.'

I looked around the grounds. A father was shouting at a snotty-nosed boy. 'Caspar! I said stop wiping it on my trousers!'

It did seem like an international assassin would be more interested in a flashy party rather than families on a day out.

'How do we get access to the guest list?'

'I said I'd meet Danny for coffee next week.'

Bibi handed Haze her water bottle back.

'You're meeting up with Danny?' I stared at Haze.

'I can try and find out more about the event and have a snoop around his office.'

An image of Haze and Danny up against his desk flashed into my mind. What the hell was wrong with me?

'I don't think there's any need for that. There's no guarantee the party will have anything to do with The Chameleon.'

'You heard what Jenny said. His name has been mentioned along with this place more than once. A party here with other dodgy people is what he's surfaced for, clearly. It could be a handover, a hit – anything!'

I tried to think logically, to pretend Danny was a useful contact and not just a guy from my wife's past. In truth, this was a breakthrough of sorts. I should be feeling more in control now that we finally had a lead, now that we were getting one step closer to locating The Chameleon. But all I could feel was the panic rising in my chest. Fight or flight. I'd always stood my ground, raised my weapon and chased down any threat that faced me. So how come all I wanted to do was pack up, take my family and run?

Haze seemed oblivious. 'We need to find The Chameleon, and we need to end him.' She stormed ahead with Bibi skipping alongside her. All fight, no flight.

I pushed the pram behind them and chewed on my lip. I was fine. It was all going to be fine.

15

Haze

Fox was clearly pissed about Danny, even though he refused to admit it. How could he be jealous of an ex and try to ban me from seeing him? I could understand if Danny was uncharted territory. But as if I would ever do anything with someone I'd already tried, tested and rejected. When I'd told Fox there was no one before him, I meant it. No one relevant; no one worth remembering.

Men and their egos. It was exhausting. Fox knew I had a history, just as I knew he did. But I wasn't going to start griping at him if I had the misfortune of bumping into one of his blonde, perma-tanned, long-limbed sorority exes. I would've dealt with it the mature way and just made retching noises and told him how lucky he was to have upgraded.

I knew he wasn't himself and that everything seemed to be hitting him harder than it should. I just wished he could move forward, move back to what he once was.

My husband and his blessed life had never faced hardship. He had grown up not wanting for anything, materially at least. Big houses, plural. Staff for the staff. Always turning left on a plane – that was if he was roughing it enough to share one with the public. And, beyond his money, he had the looks, the brains and the brawn. He always won a fight. He always had a plan go exactly as expected. He was part of the privileged echelons of every society. He was used to getting everything he wanted. He was used to people treating him with respect. He was used to being invincible – or, at the very least, to everyone thinking he was.

He had drifted through life always getting his own way. Always having people wanting to be his friend, to make him happy, to meet his every need.

My childhood had taught me to always expect the worst; his had taught him to always get the best. I could fare in any situation. He could not.

For all of this, I understood why he was struggling. He was falling from a great height. Bad dreams, paranoia, indecision, blank staring off into the distance. It was why I let him do insufferable things like going to see a therapist. He didn't want to open up to me, but he was happy paying to do it with another woman. I was the one there holding him at night, but I wasn't a safe enough space for him to talk through his trauma.

He'd also started going to yoga classes. I wanted to believe this was because his yoga teacher was really hot, and not because he actually wanted to limber up and centre his chakra or whatever. Watching him slope off, gripping his rolled-up yoga mat was really not working for me. Neither was having to suffer through his attempts to learn the guitar. He'd taken Bibi with him to buy one and come back with an additional purchase. If ever there was a sure sign he wasn't thinking straight – it was buying a four-year-old a drum kit.

Within an hour of their first band practice, I had Amazon one-clicked a pair of noise-cancelling headphones. Fox hadn't worked out how to use the amp properly and, in case the crackle of feedback wasn't enough, the smashing of Bibi's cymbal added to the headache-inducing hell. Why did his mid-life crisis have to be so noisy? Did being a good wife mean having to suffer through noise pollution so that he could feel better about himself? Not for the first time, I thought about how wedding vows really didn't cover all the shit you needed to put up with.

I had signed up for the emotionally reticent preppy American who felt most at home in a collared shirt and a loafer. A practical, no-nonsense, blue-eyed, man-killing, spreadsheet-filling machine. And now he was wearing yoga pants, strumming on a guitar and talking about his feelings to a stranger.

Whenever he muttered to me about the importance of self-help it was hard to not lose it. I didn't need self-help. I needed a full-team-of-people-help. A cook, nanny, night nurse, driver, cleaner, personal trainer, PA-to-deal-with-all-the-school-emails . . . That was what I needed to find my Zen. Lighting a candle and humming really wasn't going to cut it. How was I meant to clear my mind when I had so much on it?

I was trying to be patient with him. But we were flailing here. Barely holding it together. I didn't want to be in this alone. Feeding the baby. Tidying the house. Killing the man. He needed to pull himself back together.

We needed to find The Chameleon above all, because if there was ever a victim that could get him back to the bloodlust, back to enjoying what he was born to do, it was the one who'd orchestrated the trauma that had taken it away from him.

The drive back to London was quiet: Bibi plugged into the

iPad, her parents plugged into thoughts they didn't want to share.

The traffic was bad. We made it to Bibi's dance school with seconds to spare before her lesson started. There was a big practice before her recital. We had just enough time to get home, get some food into Reggie and head back out to watch it.

I was just puréeing some carrots on high speed when Jenny rang.

'We've got a problem. You know where you said goodbye to our friend?' That was Jenny's code for 'where you buried your last victim'.

After the scare at the petrol station, Clark Dixon had finally been laid to rest inside a water tank at an old crisp factory. Jenny had starred it as an 'excellent' dump site location with a small chance of discovery.

One rainy Sunday afternoon, she'd compiled a detailed spreadsheet on all the best places in a thirty-mile radius. Looking at her in her faded dungarees with a biro stuck through her mum bun, tapping away at her laptop with Felix watching Bluey next to her, you'd never have guessed she was working on where to hide a body, and not a school class contacts list. I'd under-estimated her the first time we met, and had never again since.

Before Jenny came onboard, Fox had insisted that we stick to the golden rule of never killing on our own doorstep. We could fly high when in Europe, but in England we needed to live our cover stories. But that had all changed with Jenny. Also, in fairness, with becoming parents. The logistics of organising trips abroad with kids, sorting childcare and being able to track down and eliminate targets was a lot of work. We'd had to rethink our model and decided that the added security and efficiency of having Jenny meant we could finally kill on home territory. It really was much easier to fit in the stalking, researching and abducting when we didn't have to deal with different time zones and attempting to hack foreign street cams.

'There's a report of a fire on that road.'

Clark being discovered now would be big trouble for us. The chemicals we had poured in with him to make sure he couldn't be identified, as well as to destroy any potential evidence we might have left on the body, needed time to do their job.

Clark was meant to be festering in there for at least weeks, if not months or years.

It had only been eight days.

'You both need to get out there and see what's going on. I just—' Jenny's voice went muffled. I could hear her faintly, speaking to someone else. 'Sure, coming back in now.'

I looked at my watch. We had an hour and a half until Bibi's recital.

'I've got to go.' Jenny came back on the line. 'Text me what needs to be done from my end.'

If it looked like Clark was about to be discovered, Jenny needed to be briefed so she could prepare for damage control. The dump site was within her police force's area, another reason why we had picked it.

I abandoned the carrots and grabbed a readymade pouch from the larder.

'Fox!' I shouted up the stairs to him. 'Problem with Clark! We've got to go.' I plucked Reggie out of his bouncy chair.

Fox came rushing into the kitchen, gripping a leatherbound

journal in which I knew he liked to write incredibly bad poetry. He could expertly wield a knife, but not a pen.

'Jenny rang. A fire's been reported close to the dump site.' His eyes widened. I flung the car keys at him. 'You drive. I've got to feed Reg.'

16

Fox

By the time we were arriving at our destination, Reggie had smeared green purée all over him. Haze had discovered trying to shovel it into him with a plastic spoon in the back of a car was not a good idea. I figured the odds were he must've got at least some of it down him.

I drove slowly down the road the factory was on. It actually looked quite nice around here in daylight. There were two commercial buildings on the same road, all a good distance apart. One was a furniture company and the other a storage facility. The factory was at the end of the road. It was a starred dump site due to the fact there was never anyone around in the evening, and there was no CCTV outside the factory. Jenny had looked into it and the owners of the building had no plans to develop the site. It had lain empty for five years since a variety of health infractions had closed it down.

We were halfway down the road when we saw the flashing lights of a parked fire engine ahead.

I turned to Haze. 'What's our plan?'

'Dog?'

I drove slowly down the road until we were parallel with the fire engine. I stopped and rolled down my window.

A tall fireman spotted us and came over. 'You okay?'

'Sorry, I'm sure you're busy, but we're looking for our dog. I don't suppose you've seen a small black French bulldog cross-breed? She slipped her collar chasing a rabbit and someone said they saw her running down this road.'

The fireman shook his head. 'We've only been here an hour and haven't seen any dogs.'

'What's going on? The usual teens causing trouble?' I motioned towards the smoking pile of embers just outside the factory.

'Looks like it.'

'You guys here for a while? Our dog is a nervous little thing. She could be scared of all the lights and be hiding until you've gone.'

'We're just waiting to get hold of who owns the building.'

I chuckled. 'That place has been abandoned for so long, doubt they'd even notice if damage has been done to it.'

'You locals?'

'It's a favourite walking route. Are we okay to park up and look for her?'

The fireman shrugged. 'No problem.' He walked back to his colleagues. Judging from the ash pile, it hadn't been that large a fire.

'Kind of overkill, isn't it?' Haze stared over at the four men walking around the site.

'Must be a quiet afternoon. You stay with Reggie. I'll go for a walk around.' I got out of the car and made a big show of calling out 'Sausage!' as I traipsed up and down the road, only risking the occasional glance at the factory. Bibi had chosen the name Sausage. It had been embarrassing at first, shouting it out in the park, but now I was as oblivious to its ridiculousness as I was to her neon-pink diamante collar and lead.

After a suitably dedicated performance of a good five minutes, I returned to the car and got back into the driver's seat. 'It looks like they're packing up. I think we're okay.'

'They're not going round the back?' The water tower was just behind the factory.

'If they haven't already, I don't think they will.'

Crisis averted. We could let Jenny know she needed to keep an eye on things, but it seemed we were going to be okay.

Just as I started the engine, the tall fireman came rushing up to our car. 'Your dog was lost where, exactly?'

Haze leaned forward. 'Just around here somewhere. We're going to keep driving. We can't lose her – she's everything to us.' She clasped a hand to her chest.

'I don't want to get your hopes up, but I think your dog has been found.'

Sausage was safely tucked up at home with her favourite bone.

'Wow!' That was all I could say. 'You've found a lost black French bulldog cross? Really?'

'It's a small black female dog, no collar. The individual who found her wasn't sure what breed it was. But they're bringing her here, as it's on their way to the shelter.'

I checked my watch. 'We actually need—'

'Great!' Haze tapped my shoulder. 'Would be amazing if it really is her. We've been so worried.'

'Just hold tight. She'll be here soon.' He gave us a smile and crossed his fingers, then walked back to his colleagues.

'We're going to be late for Bibi!' I looked at Haze.

'We said we'd lost our beloved dog. It would look pretty

suspicious if we didn't bother hanging around to see if it was her.'

She was right. We were cutting it fine, but we had to protect our cover story.

Ten minutes later, there was no sign of the rescued dog.

Twenty minutes later, I told the fireman that our neighbour had called to say they thought they'd found our dog. Happy days! The fireman said we should still wait to check, as wasn't this where we'd lost the dog? And if she didn't have a collar, how could our neighbour be sure?

Haze had tried frantically searching her photo gallery for a picture of Sausage not wearing her collar so we could assure him she'd been correctly located.

Thirty-two minutes later, a car arrived with an over-excited black female dog in the back. Adorable, lost, but – surprise, surprise – not our dog. We thanked all the assembled people for their assistance and finally left.

For the first ten minutes of driving, we still had hope we could make it to Bibi's recital. We'd be okay. Missing-the-beginning-but-creeping-in-at-the-back-type okay.

That was right up until we pulled to a halt behind a lorry and a man in a hi-vis vest standing in the road, telling us it was closed and there were diversions in place.

We looked at each other.

We weren't going to make it.

17

Haze

We were total failures. We had missed Bibi's big moment. Protecting our family meant protecting our secret life. We knew we'd had no choice. But it didn't make the sting any less painful.

Fox had tried to give us both a pep talk. *There will be plenty more big moments. Life can disappoint us sometimes. She knows we love her. We will make it up to her.* But his heart wasn't really in it.

We were parked up outside the ballet school. The recital had ended three minutes ago. We were bracing ourselves for having to do the walk of shame, for going inside and facing her.

It hit me like a wave. I imagined her tearstained face. Thought of her looking out and not seeing us. It crushed me. It didn't matter what excuse we had. It wasn't good enough.

It was different for me when I was growing up. I'd never had any expectations of seeing someone there for me, in the crowd. But Bibi had got used to it. We turned up to everything we could. A wave and a smile and a happy nod from her. We showed up. Right up until we hadn't.

We walked inside the reception, Fox holding the car seat with a sleeping Reggie inside. Kids and their smiling parents were leaving the main hall. We pushed past those streaming out to look for Bibi.

I didn't know how to play it. Should we grovel? Or would that play it up and make her care even more? Should we try being dismissive? *It's not a big deal, darling? Why do you even care? No one cares!* I shook that off. Gaslighting a four-year-old seemed too twisted. We all had lines we couldn't cross.

We spotted her by the stage, standing next to her teacher.

I got to her first and crouched down next to her. 'Darling, we're so sorry we missed it. There was awful traffic and we got stuck.'

Fox put the car seat down next to us. 'We drove as fast as we could.'

Bibi observed us both. 'I was looking for you.'

'I know, and I hate that we weren't there for you.' I squidged her cheek.

'We've already checked, and they recorded it, so we can get the video,' said Fox

'And we can watch it all together,' I added.

'And you can re-enact your performance for us.'

Bibi nodded. She looked between the two of us. 'Ice cream?'

I said, 'Of course!', just as Fox said, 'Absolutely!'

We exchanged a look over the top of her ballet-bunned head. She was okay. It was all okay. Yes, we'd potentially overkilled it and now opened ourselves up to being manipulated into endless treats. But that was fine.

As we walked to the car, Bibi announced: 'Ted pulled my hair today.'

Fox gritted his teeth. 'Ted who? Where does he live? I will go—'

I glanced at Fox. He stopped talking.

'Did you tell your teacher?' I asked.

Bibi nodded. 'She said it was an accident. But it wasn't.'

Fox looked at me. 'Should we go in? Talk to the teacher? Ask for CCTV footage to be checked? Threaten to sue?'

I touched Fox's arm. 'She needs to learn to handle this herself.'

'She's four.'

'You're never too young.' It was a big, bad world out there, and it owed you no favours. Despite my commitment to giving them loving, easy lives, I couldn't let my kids be brought up too soft. They needed to learn to help themselves too. 'Bibi, if he hurts you again, you hurt him right back. Harder.'

Bibi frowned. 'Isn't it bad to hurt?'

'Yes,' said Fox, just as I said, 'No.'

I leaned down to Bibi. 'You can hurt people if they hurt you, or if they're about to hurt someone and you want to stop them. There are certain situations where it's acceptable.' It was good to let her know the conventions we lived by. The whole world was our playground, and we knew when to step in and punish the ones not playing by the rules.

Bibi nodded. 'Okay.'

We watched her as she skipped ahead to the car. Parenting was always second-guessing yourself and what you were teaching them. We wanted our children to know the difference between right and wrong. We wanted to raise them to be good people. And although we might believe strongly in the work we did it was not the life we wanted for them. Do as we say, not as we do.

My phone beeped. I took it out. An unknown number.

*Hello Haze. You get my postcard? Stop trying
to find me. I will let you know when
it's time for us to finally meet.*

I read it twice and held it out for Fox.

'What does he mean?' Fox ran a hand through his hair.

The Chameleon didn't want to kill us; he wanted to play with us. This sounded tiresome. I tapped out a message as Fox paced next to me.

> *Enough with the dramatics. What the*
> *fuck do you want?*

'Did you just send something? What did you—?'

I showed him my phone.

'Hazel! That is not a good idea!'

He replied immediately.

> *Didn't your parents teach you patience?'*

> *They taught me sod all. You're showing more interest*
> *in me than they ever did. Are you here to kill us?*

> *You sound like a troubled soul, Haze.*
> *Things will be clear soon.*

> *Can't wait, babe.*

I even added a blowing-kiss emoji.

Fox was reading everything over my shoulder while chewing on his thumbnail.

I found the messages strangely reassuring. This shadowy unknown figure wasn't so special. He was flesh and bone, like us. He had a mobile phone. He was into texting cryptic shit, like some annoying fuckboy who couldn't just say what he meant.

All of this, it made him human. And that made him killable.

18

Fox

'Everyone dies!' The freckled barista smiled as she handed me my coffee.

'Sorry? What did you . . .?'

'Enjoy your latte!'

'Right. Thank you.' I walked off and looked back at her. She was still smiling.

I didn't have time for an existential crisis right now. I needed to focus on the actual crisis we were facing. I was not handling The Chameleon's reappearance well.

This morning, I had woken up at the kitchen table. It took me a few minutes to work out where I was. It was 5.04am and I was in my pyjamas. They were striped with a collar, and were the ones Haze said made me 'deeply unshaggable'. They were what I'd been wearing when I went to sleep last night. I'd tried to remember getting up in the night and coming down here. But nothing.

I'd never sleepwalked before. Maybe I was thirsty and had been on autopilot, coming down for a cold glass of water. Fine. People did that. But then I'd looked down at my feet and seen they were dirty. I'd followed a trail of mud sprinkles from the table to the back door. I must've got up in the night, come down to the kitchen for water and then – what? Gone to check on the plants outside? That sounded like a totally normal thing to do. Or maybe I'd seen a fox and gone to shoo it away?

I was sure it was a one-off. My body manifesting the stress with a little night-time wander.

Haze had seemed totally unfazed about now being text buddies with the man who'd tried to kill us in Italy. She'd told me to get to my office and focus on making us money – she'd get Jenny on the case of tracking down The Chameleon through the number he was using.

Jenny and Haze. The two of them were becoming increasingly inseparable. I was happy my wife was happy. Of course I was. Haze had always been suspicious and closed off to everyone she came into contact with. I'd only made it through her inbuilt defences so swiftly due to – in her words – my 'insane hotness and cool knife'.

We'd met in an alleyway in Paris. I'd come rushing to this beautiful stranger's rescue, but had quickly realised she was the hunter, not the prey – which made her even more alluring. Ours was a love affair that had started over the bloodied body of a bad man – a perfect start to what had been a perfect match.

We were the original duo. It was just that my other half now had another other half. Did that leave me with only a third?

I did, of course, have friends of my own. Neighbours whom I'd sometimes meet for a drink, or to play a round of golf, or to hang out watching whatever sporting event was considered essential viewing. But female friendship was a different beast. There was this constant updating on daily life, a confessing of deepest, darkest fears and unpleasant health concerns. I wasn't threatened. Of course not. Just a tad disconcerted.

Our killing mission had always been our secret. We were

bonded together by this love of doing the right thing to the wrong men. But now Jenny had even muscled in on that.

I had, until recently, always preferred being out of the office. Doing fieldwork, so to speak. Now, I felt more comfortable being base camp. Sitting behind my desk. Doing research. I'd always enjoyed working, but it had never been as vital as it was now. My paycheque was actually needed for us to live the life to which we'd become accustomed.

I had grown up in a bubble, protected from the horrors of real life by my family's money and privilege. When my brother and I had finally stood up to our parents, ganged up to throw them out of the family business, the fallout had been the dissolving of our trust fund.

The security net that had been there my whole life, to be plundered as and when I saw fit, was now gone. Thankfully, I had squirrelled away enough that money was still in plentiful supply. I just had to be a little more cautious than before. Especially as I'd now realised how expensive private-school fees were.

My company, Cabot Matthews Investments, was based out of a Mayfair townhouse that we'd converted into offices. Haze was only really involved to the extent that her surname was there alongside mine. I wanted her to feel a part of everything I did. 'CMI' was embossed on a small, discreet sign above a large mahogany reception desk that was always manned by my assistant, Richard, a short, well-built man who'd dabbled in professional rugby before one accident too many had made him rethink his choices. He had four kids with his childhood sweetheart and was very motivated to be out of the house as much as possible, and to make as much money as possible. He might have had the least experience of all the candidates I'd interviewed, but he had a steeliness I respected. I was bored of the well-spoken, suited-and-booted graduates who were too green to understand exactly what high stakes really were. Richard was also good at turning a blind eye. He never had any questions about what exactly my wife, her best friend and I were plotting when we booked out the meeting room for two-hour-long stints. He also never questioned exactly how I'd previously been so good at predicting what companies were about to tank or skyrocket.

Our business model for ending bad men had always had the added bonus of helping with our finances too. Our targets always fit a certain criteria that Haze had insisted on from the start of our little enterprise. Straight white men who were culpable of many a terrible act were, thankfully, easy to find. We targeted them because of the things they'd done. Making sure we focused on those who might also have certain knowledge that would help our investments was something we'd now zeroed back in on.

I had acknowledged that last year, I'd gotten too ambitious with my choice of targets. Suddenly having Jenny in our corner had given me the overconfidence to go for bad men who were part of big, bad networks. I wanted to turn the needle enough to really make a difference to the world.

I had thought we were different, that we didn't need to rein in ambitions just because we had a family. Somehow, I'd been idiotic enough to believe we were immune from the pressures of trying to have it all. I had been out there working hard to hit our peak professionally – and at what cost? Whatever we'd done that year had brought The Chameleon to our door.

My phone pinged. A new email from Mike Martin, sharing his mobile number in case I – 'Harriet' – wanted to call him to arrange our first meeting. I knew using the reappearance of The Chameleon was not a good enough reason to put off talking to Haze about her father. But, really, I was grasping for any excuse to not come clean to her about what I'd done.

19

Haze

Killing Clark Dixon had sparked our creative outlets again – for Fox, that spark was about how best to invest. For me, it was about how best to paint. I was currently working on a raw, uncompromising canvas titled *Pressure Cooker*. We'd had another baby, and now we were getting back to work. It was business as usual for this suburban family.

But now The Chameleon was here.

On our home turf. There had been a long line of those I deemed total shit stains not worthy of life, but right now there was no one I hated more than the one who was making us look over our shoulders. The one who had tried to end our lives, and was now encroaching on the life we'd built for ourselves here.

It had taken time for me to adjust to living here. If it was all to end, I wanted it to be on my terms, to be because I'd reached the limit of how much I could take of normal suburban existence. Choosing to pull the plug and start over elsewhere. Sometimes I entertained thoughts of being one of those cool travelling families I'd seen on Instagram. Tie-dyed, bed-haired, upscaling an old campervan and driving around Europe. Our kids being free-range, homeschooled: #theworldisourplayground.

But Fox was far too rigid to ever roll with the 'take each day as it comes' itinerary, neither of us had the patience to teach our kids anything other than manners (even that was a push – why can't you fucking remember 'please'?), and I liked the nice things in life too much to ever want to wash my hair in a weak RV shower. And all that was before you factored in how you couldn't exactly paint huge canvases or make financial trades crammed into a van with no Wi-Fi and dodgy phone reception.

We could've moved abroad. Somewhere, anywhere. But who could be bothered with trying to get yourself understood in a foreign language, or being made to feel like an arrogant English waste of space for not trying to? America was out, because the thought of being in the same country as Fox's parents was deeply unsettling.

We were here because we'd chosen it, mostly due to a lack of other options. And we were, for the most part, happy.

That was what it came down to. The idea of starting again somewhere else was not an option. We had put down roots. We'd got the house, the 2.4 kids (Sausage the dog made up the 0.4), the minivan. Bibi had started primary school and was enjoying it. And I had Jenny nearby – there was no way I was giving up having my best friend in close proximity.

When Jenny had asked me once what the other mums at Bibi's school were like, I'd looked at her blankly.

'You must've talked to them?' she said. 'Done some coffee mornings?'

'Why would I talk to them? I just drop her off and go. And those coffee mornings aren't mandatory, are they? I'd rather drink coffee with you.'

I spoke to Jenny every day through several different mediums – WhatsApp, emails, Instagram reels, weblinks to designer items I was considering buying, voice notes. I'd become reliant on her counsel in every aspect of my life. Our messages never said hello or goodbye, as we were always in the middle of a conversation that never ended.

Rather than be touched by my fidelity to our friendship, Jenny had sighed and rattled on about how I needed to make an effort and find some allies. Ever since she'd mentioned it, I had started to notice how, at pick-up, the other parents – okay, well, mothers with the occasional lesser-spotted father mixed in – were always standing in different clusters, deep in conversation.

No one ever tried to speak to me, and it wasn't like I didn't try. I mean, did I ever make eye contact with anyone? No. Did I ever attempt a smile? God, no. But I was there, wasn't I? Every day I was there, sunglasses on, staring at my phone, keeping one eye out for Bibi and her pigtails to come bouncing out of the school gate.

This morning, I was one of the last to arrive at drop-off. I hugged Bibi goodbye and headed back to the car with my head down, staring at my phone. A gaggle of mothers, deep in conversation, was still hovering by the gates.

'Hazel!'

I kept staring at my phone.

'Oh, Hazel!'

I looked up to see Frederica walking towards me.

Frederica's daughter had only started this term, but Frederica had quickly become a prominent figure at the gates. She was an influencer. I knew this from the way the other mothers would shout over to her about how much they'd loved her latest post. Frederica wore leather trousers and flicked her hair a lot. I'm not big on tips to make life easier, but 'Don't wear clothes that are dry-clean only around kids' seemed a pretty obvious one. At least her job helped explain why she was making the effort to look that perfect every day – she was a walking #ad. I managed to force out a 'Hi'.

'Congratulations on Bibi getting the part of Gretel.'

The cast list for the end-of-term school play had just been announced in a letter home. We'd asked Bibi about it and how she'd got the main part, and she'd just shrugged and said it was because she was really good.

'Thanks. And congratulations to your child on who they are.'

'I'm going to start a WhatsApp chat for the party planning.'

I looked at her blankly.

'It's kind of an unspoken thing that whichever children have the main parts, it's their mothers that organise the after-party.'

This woman had been here five minutes, and she already knew the unspoken things?

'The first meeting needs to happen asap, as we've got so much to decide on.'

My phone pinged. I looked down at it as Frederica rattled on about whether commissioning a life-sized gingerbread house would be overkill.

Danny.

*Hello sexy, want to see my office and
have a catch-up coffee?*

Perfect.

'Sorry, I've got to go. Just text me.' I rushed towards the sanctity of my car.

'But no one seems to have your number!' Frederica called after me.

20

Haze

The offices for Unique Events were on the top floor of a warehouse in Islington.

When the lift doors opened, Danny was waiting for me.

'Haze!' He held out his arms and drew me into a tight hug. His scent of Hugo Boss and cigarettes triggered memories of times I'd rather forget.

I patted his back and waited for him to release me.

'Follow me,' he said. Danny was wearing a pale blue fitted shirt and chinos. His brightly coloured garish trainers were, perhaps, an attempt to fit in with the much younger staff members who were buzzing around the office. 'Pretty cool place, huh?'

The only way to get one up on The Chameleon was to be one step ahead of him. We needed to know what he had planned for us. And this dipshit was currently the best chance we had of finding out.

Danny led me down a series of corridors until we got to a large corner office with 'Brainstormin'' on the door. He ushered me inside. In front of the large window was a metal sideboard filled with cans of energy drinks and a large cafetiere of coffee. On the rectangular glass meeting table was a laptop and a few A4 booklets. He settled me into a neon plastic chair and then took the one next to me.

The door opened and a woman with cropped pink hair popped her head around the door. 'Hi! I'm Razia.' She stared at Danny and then me.

'Haze,' I offered.

'Can I—'

Danny cut her off. 'We're okay for drinks, so we're good.'

'Okay, shall I—'

'Thanks, Razia, bye!'

Razia nodded and closed the door.

Danny rolled his eyes at me. 'My PA. She's annoying, but she's got a great typing speed.'

I tried to remember if Danny was always a prick to people to whom he felt superior. I was struggling to recall anything about the nights out we'd had together other than there being a lot of alcohol. I liked to think that his rudeness was one of the many reasons I'd never particularly liked him.

'Working in events must suit you,' I said. 'You were always the party boy.'

'I turned doing what I love into a job!'

'How's it going with the big Balgray Hall event?'

'Pretty much sorted!' Danny tapped the pile of booklets on the table. 'The Balgray Hall lot are, like, a hundred years old and only ever want printouts. They don't give a shit about the environment.'

'Do you?' I tried not to stare at the booklets. I needed one.

'Fuck, no. It's just annoying having to print everything.'

'It's a charity event, right?'

Danny shrugged. 'Yeah, something about saving old posh houses.'

I got up and went to the sideboard to pour myself a coffee. I felt him stand up and lean behind me.

'You're looking good, Haze.' He ran a hand down my back. 'Considering.'

I turned round to face him. 'Umm . . . considering what?'

'You know what I mean. You're older. Had a kid.'

I gritted my teeth. 'Two, actually.'

'Cool.' He stared down at me.

I was already three steps ahead. When he finally reached out and grabbed my right breast, I kneed him hard in the balls. When he keeled over, groaning, I slammed my elbow into his back and had the satisfaction of him letting out an actual squeal. I reached for one of the Balgray booklets on the table and headed for the door.

Even without him laying a non-consensual hand on me, I still would've hurt him for the 'considering' comment.

I wasn't an idiot. I knew what he'd been hoping for when he'd asked me here. I'd planned to lean into it enough to get me into the office. But he'd misread the signs so badly that he thought some teenage pawing at my breast was going to lead to me cheating on my husband, cheating on my family. Tragic.

I couldn't tell Fox. I wasn't in the mood for a resounding 'I told you so'. I was well aware of the weaknesses of men, but was it too much to ask that I could just plunder one for a bit of useful information without being sexually assaulted?

I thumbed through the booklet in the lift. A confirmed guest list, a running schedule and even a list of auction prizes. Not a bad prize for a tit grope.

I sent Jenny photos of everything.

My phone pinged. The Chameleon.

An envelope is waiting for you at home.

Jenny had been unable to get any trace on his mobile. It wasn't surprising. He was a professional. He wasn't going to risk texting me unless he knew it was completely safe.

> *Enough of this shit.*
> *What do you want with us?*

His reply was instant.

I like your bluntness.

> *Great, don't kill us then.*

I don't want to kill you.
But you're making it difficult.
My bosses want you dead.

A hired gun who couldn't own his actions. *I'm doing bad things, but it's not my fault!* Pathetic. If he was leaning into that, I'd lean into this.

> *We're just a family trying to live our lives as best we can.*

You aren't a normal family.

> *Lols. Who is? Everyone has their quirks.*
> *Everyone has their secrets.*

A pause.

That is very true. Maybe one day you'll find out mine.

You're actually a very nice assassin who's just misunderstood?

It was a bit of a thrill. Chit-chat with the man tasked to end us.

That sounds as realistic as a morally righteous serial killer.

I typed back with a smile.

I kill who I want to. Can you say the same?

Touché.

21

Fox

No one ever grows up dreaming of one day sitting in an office staring at four computer screens, watching stocks and shares lines go up and down. What we dreamed of was being happy and fulfilled. But the sad truth of it was, money helped us get there.

I stood up and stretched. I'd achieved very little in the two hours I'd been at my desk. I took my journal out of my briefcase. As I dropped it on to my desk, it opened to the last page I'd been writing.

> *Money makes the world go round*
> *In circles, a never-ending chase*
> *We follow it blindly*
> *And never think to stop*
> *To smell the flowers, breathe the air*
> *Money drives us and life passes us by.*

I could hear Haze's voice in my head: *Very deep for someone who's never had fewer than six digits in their bank balance.*

She was right. Money was as much a part of who I was as

my blond hair and size-fourteen feet. And I needed it to be happy. I wasn't so lacking in self-awareness I couldn't see that. We'd built a life for ourselves that required a constant stream of cash to keep it going. It was another reason I needed to find my way back to top form. Astute, informed decisions.

Fresh air and lunch. That should reset me enough to manage to make progress this afternoon.

I walked back from the local deli, gripping a flaccid salad. It was the healthiest remaining option post lunchtime rush. I stared down at it. A soggy, unappetising mess. Is that what Haze would be calling me right now? Was she wishing she'd stuck with her junk-food ex, Danny? Seeing the cocky man with whom she'd once shared a bed, was that making her notice how broken I now was?

Whiny git.

That's what Haze would be saying if she could hear me. I wanted to beat myself up. Kick some sense into myself. What could I do to make me feel like a man again? To make me forget about impending death and just live life?

I turned the corner and came face to face with the answer.

22

Haze

I had just got home when the call came from Bibi's headmistress announcing that our presence was required immediately. I was trying not to panic. What the hell had she drawn now? I wasn't sure which would make Fox flip out more – that I'd hidden how Bibi had come across me covered in Clark's blood, or that I'd hidden how it had traumatised her so much she'd been drawing about it.

Fox was going to meet me there. He had muttered something about wanting to leave the office early anyway. His dedication to his day job had been severely lacking recently. Trying to find himself had been taking priority over trying to find us big money. Our bank balance certainly wasn't what it had once been. It hadn't helped that I hadn't done a new painting in over a year. I needed to get my latest one finished and over to Hamish at the gallery to help gain yet more financial benefit from the Clark Dixon kill.

I was pulling into the school car park when a biker cut me off and sped ahead of me. He then had the audacity to wait for me next to the one empty parking space. Road rage was a recurring issue for me, and that was why Fox never let any sharp objects in the car when I was driving.

I flung open my car door and got out. 'What the hell is wrong with—'

The biker had pulled off his helmet.

Fox.

Of course.

He'd bought a motorbike.

We never hear about women having midlife crises, because we don't have time for this shit. How nice to be a man and have the luxury of being able to wallow and overcompensate with ridiculous purchases.

Fox was grinning at me. 'Look! I've always wanted one – and it's great for beating traffic.' He revved the engine. 'I got my motorbike licence when I was in college. I was always going to get one soon as I graduated, but you know my parents. They—'

'Can we just deal with Bibi first?'

I hadn't been inside a headteacher's office since my own schooldays. It felt the same. The stale air of files of paper-work and impending disappointment. Mrs Baring was short, with tightly pulled back hair, and she looked like she didn't know how to smile. She had not acknowledged Reggie even once, though he sat on my lap, resplendent in a Baby-gro that was designed to look like a suit and tie.

Next to me, Fox tried to get comfortable in his hardback chair, his new leather Belstaff jacket creaking every time he moved.

'Mr and Mrs Cabot, I'm afraid we've had to call you in because Bibi hit a boy in the face today.'

A mix of emotions. Relief that it wasn't another bloody drawing. Worry that she'd inherited our violent streak.

Mrs Baring leaned forward. 'Thankfully, no hospital treatment was required.'

Please. She was four. Her right hook was going to have to wait a while before it was able to hospitalise someone.

She clasped her hands to her chest. 'But there was blood.'

'Who was the boy?' asked Fox.

I knew who it was. 'It was Ted, right? He's the little shit that was pulling her hair yesterday. He probably started it. Doesn't she have a right to protect herself? Are you victim-blaming?'

'We can allow a certain amount of leeway for rough play, but she punched him, seemingly unprovoked, and called him . . .' Mrs Baring cleared her throat and looked down at her notepad. 'A f-u-c-k-i-n-g dirtbag.'

We took this in.

Fox cleared his throat. 'We know that that sort of talk isn't right for a four-year-old.'

Mrs Baring looked between us. 'I don't know what language she's exposed to at home.'

Fox did an admirable job of not looking at me.

'But we do expect a certain high standard of behaviour from our students.'

There was a knock on the door. Baring stood up. 'We have found that parents of the aggressor and the injured party meeting to discuss next steps is usually the most helpful course of action.'

The door opened and a tall woman stepped in. Her pale blonde bob was perfectly styled. She was unsmiling and wearing a blue trouser suit with a nipped waist that I'd been admiring on Net-a-Porter just last week.

'Mr and Mrs Cabot, please meet Ms Diana Morgan. Ted's mother.'

Diana swept to the empty chair next to us and sat down. She did not meet our eyes. 'This has come at a very inconvenient time. I have a big meeting to prepare for.' She checked her watch.

Mrs Baring looked at us. 'Ms Morgan is a managing partner at Backhouse Dunne.'

Backhouse Dunne was a big London law firm. This was why Baring was taking it so seriously. She was terrified of Ted's mother suing them for the bitch slap Bibi had given her little shit of a son.

Fox cleared his throat. 'We're very sorry about this unfortunate incident. We will—'

I elbowed him hard, and he went quiet. 'I think you'll find Ted and Bibi have not been getting on for a while. Just yesterday, Ted pulled her hair, which was very upsetting for her.'

Diana turned to look at me. 'Any evidence of that? Video? Witnesses?'

'No, but—'

'Your daughter thumped Ted in front of two of their peers and a teacher. There is no denying what she did.'

I took a breath. 'I'm explaining her motive.'

Diana snorted. 'She waited a day and then took her revenge? It's not exactly self-defence is it? She's clearly a savage.'

'You're a fu—'

Fox squeezed my thigh.

I stopped and tried to deep-breathe.

Fox leaned forward. 'Until we talk to Bibi, it's hard to understand the full situation.'

Mrs Baring cut in. 'Absolutely! But the main thing is everyone is very sorry this happened, and it won't happen again.'

'Children need boundaries,' sniffed Diana, 'and strong parental guidance to behave appropriately.'

This ice-queen bitch was questioning our parenting? How dare she? Only *we* were allowed to do that.

Fox spoke before I could, 'Bibi has excellent instincts and a strong sense of right and wrong.'

Diana snorted and ran a hand through her hair. She didn't get to sit there and judge our daughter, when look at how her kid had turned out.

'Ted is the one who's clearly trouble. It starts with hair-pulling, then a shove, then a punch – then, next thing you know, he's got zero respect for women's boundaries and understanding that no means no.'

Diana stared at me. 'Are you . . . Are you suggesting my four-year-old son is going to grow up to be a rapist?'

Mrs Baring paled.

'No!' Fox squeaked it out. 'Absolutely not.'

At the same time, I said, 'I think you should watch him carefully.'

23

Fox

I think it was fair to say we had made an enemy for life in Diana Morgan.

Mrs Baring had wrapped up the meeting with a shrill announcement that she had to leave. I think she needed to go and cry somewhere.

Diana and Haze had been death-staring each other to such a degree I didn't know where to look.

Bibi seemed unfazed by us both arriving to take her home two hours early. We got her into the car park before unleashing.

'Bibi, please tell us what happened.' I wanted her to explain in her own words.

'Why did you hit that boy?' Haze wanted to get straight to it.

Bibi shrugged. 'You said it was okay to hit if they were hurting someone.'

I breathed out. 'Who was he hitting?'

'No one.'

Haze and I looked at each other.

I spluttered 'Then why—?'

'He was looking at Savannah funny.'

I turned to Haze and hissed, 'I told you four was too young to understand the intricacies of when it's acceptable to hurt someone.'

'For all we know she has excellent instincts, and he was about to hit Savannah.'

Bibi started kicking a small stone around the car park, humming to herself.

'Or she wanted to hit him and came up with that as a cover for whacking him,' I said quietly.

Haze turned back to face Bibi. 'You're not old enough to know if someone is going to be bad before they've been bad, so how about you don't hit someone unless you can prove to an adult there's a good reason for it?'

'Okay.' Bibi carried on humming.

'Maybe the karate lessons were a mistake.' My motorbike was parked next to Haze's car. I walked up to it.

'Maybe they're what's stopping her from hitting more!' Haze unlocked the car. 'If she's anything like her parents, she needs an outlet.'

I pulled on my helmet as Bibi got into the back of the car. She looked between my bike and me. 'Cool dada!'

At least one of the women in my life was impressed by my new purchase.

Parenting on the same page was not easy. Trying to bring up your daughter so she was strong enough to protect herself, but not so strong she was picking fights, was not easy.

'In here!' shouted Jenny from the kitchen when we arrived back home. We'd driven in convoy. I could've raced ahead, but it was all part of showing Haze that I could be responsible on my new toy.

Haze plonked Bibi in the sitting room in front of a documentary on regenerative farming. We needed to talk without her being around, but seeing as she was only home because she'd punched someone we couldn't let her watch television she might actually enjoy.

I picked up the envelope that had been waiting for us on the doormat. Inside was a party invitation to the charity event at Balgray Hall. 'Haze and Fox' was written in neat print in the top-left corner. The 'only admits two' at the bottom was circled. The dress code was 'masquerade'. What a wonderfully glamorous way to make sure we couldn't even see the enemy approaching us.

I chucked it on the kitchen table. 'I get the feeling our attendance is non-negotiable.'

Jenny was staring at the 'only admits two'. 'They're making it clear you're not to get any help.' She turned to Haze. 'What else did he say in his messages?'

Haze took out her phone and placed it on the table. We scanned them together.

'This is good!' Jenny smiled. 'You're building a rapport with him and reminding him that he's just The Corporation's errand boy.'

'How is this good?' I shook my head. 'He's enjoying toying with you.' If Interpol's intel that The Chameleon was doing one final job before retiring from the killing game was correct, everything seemed to be leading towards us being a part of his grand finish.

If we could find him before the party, we had a chance of ruining whatever surprise he had planned for us. The only way to beat the threat was to get ahead of it. Come for him when he least expected it.

Haze tapped her chin. 'He's not going to expect us of having the party guest list.'

I frowned. 'How did you get that?'

'Danny.' Haze looked down at the table. 'I saw him this morning. I was going to tell you, but then all the Bibi punching drama kicked off.'

I went up to the coffee machine. 'You spent the morning with your ex. Sounds fabulous. Great. So great.' I struck the coffee portafilter three times against the knock box. Perhaps a little harder than was necessary.

'Shall I . . .?' Jenny half rose.

Haze pushed her back into her chair and stood up. 'Baby, if I was going to cheat on you, it wouldn't be with a tried-and-tested ex I'd already rejected. I'd go for someone new and exciting. Like, maybe the tattooed barista in that coffee shop. Or the football coach down at the kids' club, or the—'

'Okay, stop!' Jesus, was there anyone she hadn't considered nailing? I was a little, okay a lot, off my game, and she was eyeing up other men as I wasn't enough for her any more?

Haze came up behind me and wrapped her arms round my waist. 'You trust me, don't you?'

'Of course. It's him I don't trust. Did he try anything?'

I felt it. The slightest loosening of her touch. 'He wouldn't dare.' She let go as I spun round, wanting to look her in the eye. But she was walking back to the table.

'I got nothing helpful from Balgray's Hall computer system so the guest list has been a huge help.' Jenny looked at me. Ever the peacemaker. 'I've checked all of the names and it's clear something is going down at that party. A lot of recognisable names from the great and the good of Britain's criminal underworld.'

It did sound like The Chameleon's type of crowd.

'One name sticks out,' said Jenny. 'Joe Jones. There's nothing on him online, and the company he's supposedly from is bogus. It could be The Chameleon, or someone else going by a fake name.'

Despite the unappetising thought of Haze spending time with her smirking ex, there was no denying it felt like we were making progress.

'Even if it's an alias, it'll help us find him, right? It's a clue of sorts. If we could just find him, we could confront him when he least expects it.' Haze was rubbing her hands together.

She was celebrating. I was sweating.

We were getting closer to finally coming face to face with the man who'd engineered my kidnapping and torture. Where was my excited rage at getting to wreak my revenge?

I pressed the button on the coffee machine and let the grinding sound drown out my heartbeat. It was hammering so loud I was sure Haze and Jenny could hear it.

Fearful, not fearsome. Frightened, not frightening. I was a broken weapon.

I wished I could be honest with Haze about how much the events in Italy last year had changed me. I wished I could let myself be vulnerable with her.

I knew she loved me. But I also knew that she'd fallen in love with me when I was her equal. A love match. A kill match. We were together, flying high. The elite. If she started seeing me differently, if she started treating me differently, that would break me in a whole new way – and not one I thought I could ever come back from.

24

Haze

Tonight, I was facing an inescapable torture. An evening with Frederica and her friends planning the school play after-party. Frederica had somehow tracked down my carefully protected phone number and demanded my attendance at a wine bar in town. I had felt guilted into going only because I didn't want to ever be accused of letting Bibi down in any way – and, really, when you factored in all I'd already sacrificed for my children, you might as well add 'night out with a bunch of women I didn't know' to the list.

I scanned my wardrobe. What did I want to present as? What outfit said what I didn't want to have to say out loud? If Frederica opted for leather trousers when she was picking up her kid from school, I presumed her eveningwear would be even more over the top. Fuck it. I hadn't had a night out in ages. Who cared if it was with a bunch of mums in a naff wine bar to talk about how many bags of Kettle Chips to buy. I had clothes that deserved to be worn. I settled on a pale blue Stella McCartney jumpsuit and chunky heels. If I was going to be bored shitless, I could at least do it looking fabulous.

I stomped downstairs to the kitchen.

'Whoa! Look at you! We got plans tonight?' A sweaty Fox was in his gym kit, glugging a large glass of water.

'No, it's a school thing. With some of the other mums.'

Fox gave me another once-over. 'Really? Not a secret date with another man?'

I let the question hang in the air for a second as Fox's grin grew more and more fixed. He was trying, but the whole Danny thing had clearly knocked him.

'Are you going to be okay with Reggie?'

Fox blinked at me. 'Of course! I know what to do.' He counted on his fingers. 'Which bottle is best, what temperature to warm the breast milk to, how he only likes feeding when his head is on the left arm, the mid-feed burp, sit with him until it's empty, even if it takes an hour.'

I nodded. 'You know all this – just not at two in the morning?'

'I . . . I think that's when he just needs you. The boob is more comforting.'

'We're meant to be in this together.'

'And we are!'

'Really? When was the last time you did a grocery shop? Or made us dinner? Or practised Bibi's spellings?'

Fox ran a hand through his hair. 'I'm sorry. I've been all caught up in everything I had going on.'

'I let you indulge in all your me-time activities before Reggie was born, as I knew you needed to recover. But he's here now, and I can't do all this without you.'

Fox slumped back against the kitchen sink.

'I get that Italy was awful for you. But it wasn't exactly fun for me either, and you don't see me taking a day off to talk about my feelings.'

I was fed up with cutting him slack. It was time to tighten it.

'I'm trying to heal! Sally is—'

I cut him off. 'Sally is not the answer! You don't need therapy. You need to get back to doing what you do best. Throw yourself into your work, into your children, into me.'

I let him take this in.

'Live your life. Don't hide from it. You don't see me indulging in dumb shit to try and make myself feel better.'

'You can find new hobbies too!' He stared at me with the utter idiocy of a man who thought that if I took up knitting, life would get easier.

'I don't have time for hobbies! I'm a mother!'

My raised voice had him retreating.

'I'm sorry. Really sorry,' he said. 'I'm going to do better.'

'Please stop saying that you're going to do better, and start actually showing up.' His head dropped, but I wasn't done. 'I want to know I can rely on you. For holding the baby and holding the knife.'

We observed each other silently.

He was my partner in life, and my partner in death. I couldn't keep doing it all alone. The stakes were higher than they'd ever been. This time, we weren't chasing bad men – the bad men were chasing us.

'You need to get your shit together. We need you.'

Fox looked around the kitchen. 'I'll start with tidying up in here.'

This was encouraging.

'While you're out at this school thing. With just other mums.' He stared at me as he gave my outfit another once-over.

I put him out of his misery. 'The Leather Trousers Mum organised it.'

'Gotcha.' He knew how much she annoyed me. 'You're really showing her.'

I didn't know if it was good or bad that, despite everything I had going on, I could still find the time and inclination to one-up a woman from the school gates.

I watched as he downed the rest of his water. I felt better for having said everything that had been roaring around my head for the last few months. But had I got through to him?

25

Fox

Bibi and Reggie were finally both asleep. I walked back down to the kitchen and surveyed the mess. I knew I needed to be stricter with Bibi. The rule of 'put one toy back before you take out another' was consistently ignored. I moved a few things to a corner. I'd tidy up properly once I'd had something to drink. I poured a green juice into a whisky glass, added lots of ice, and tried to pretend it was something stronger.

I knew everything Haze had said was right. I'd been letting her down. I needed to get out of my funk and be the man I knew I could be. We both agreed I needed to get back to my normal self – we just disagreed on the methods to get there. She had been consistently scathing about my attempts to heal myself. '"*Self-help" sounds like a New Age way to describe wanking*'.

I cleared a space on the sofa and sank into it just as my phone rang. Jenny was calling me.

I answered with, 'I'm not with Haze.' Normally when Jenny rang me it was because Haze had managed to forget her phone was on silent or had left it in another room.

'Where is she? I've got a potentially really big—'

'At a school-mums thing.'

Jenny stopped talking. 'What? Really?'

'What's the big news?'

'Joe Jones has just checked into an Airbnb that's nine miles from you. If he's The Chameleon, he's bedding in pretty close by.'

I tried to take this in. The Chameleon. In our neighbourhood. I cleared my throat. 'So, are we going to go check it out?'

'I'm at work. I won't be out of here for another few hours. You need to go.'

'I can't leave the kids.'

'My dad can be over in ten minutes. They're already asleep, aren't they?'

'They just went down.' Haze. I needed Haze. 'I'll pick up—'

'No! If she's finally making an effort at school, you need to let her.' Jenny's voice went muffled as she spoke to someone with her.

'I've got to go. Call me if you need help. I mean, hah. As if you would. Just don't go too crazy. We need answers, remember. And deniability for how he ends up.'

Jenny clicked off.

I stared at my phone.

This could be it.

I could actually come face to face with The Chameleon. The man who'd arranged my would-be assassination. I should be rising to the challenge. Excited. Invigorated. Ready to enact unholy revenge. So why did I just feel sick? I went to the kitchen sink and splashed my face with water. Too much green juice. That was all.

I put together a few items in a small bag.

Don't choke.

I had been standing staring at myself in the hallway mirror for I'm not sure how long when the doorbell rang.

I opened the door to Jenny's father, Frank. He was a large man. A retired police detective and Jenny's idol. I'd met Frank a few times now. He seemed a very nice man. I watched the way he was, the way he spoke to Jenny, with a deep fascination. No acidic barbs. No not-so-subtle digs. Just warmth and love. It was pretty amazing to watch.

'Thanks so much for this, Frank.' I welcomed him in as I picked up my bag. 'Help yourself to anything in the fridge. TV is on, so watch whatever you want. Call me if you have any problems, but hopefully the kids will stay asleep. You're very kind for stepping in. Urgent work thing. Client landing from Heathrow. Only time to see him . . .' I trailed off. I wasn't sure what Jenny had told him.

'It's no bother. There's actually something I've been wanting to say to you for a while. Man to man.'

'Oh?'

'Jenny's never fully explained what part you and Haze played in helping her get her life together. But I want you to know Sandy and I are very grateful. Everything that happened with Bill was terrible, and it could've totally knocked her, but you two have really been there for her.'

'We didn't do much, Frank.'

'Sure, sure.' The big man smiled at me. 'Just saying, whatever you did do. Thank you. Never seen Jenny as happy as she is now.' He patted me on the shoulder and went through to the living room.

I walked out of the front door, resisting the urge to rush upstairs to give my children a final kiss goodbye. Just in case it was for the last time. I could hear Haze's voice in my head: *Don't be so fucking dramatic.*

I got into the car and put my seatbelt on. I tapped in the address Jenny had texted me.

An eighteen-minute drive.

It had to be him.

The Chameleon was going to a party at Balgray Hall. Joe Jones, with no digital footprint, was going to a party at Balgray Hall. Joe Jones had booked himself into a house eighteen minutes from ours.

I pressed play on an affirmations recording that Sally had recommended and started driving

'*Repeat after me: I am in control of my destiny. I make my own choices.*'

I took several deep breaths. I felt my shoulders relax. See? There was nothing to worry about. I was scoping out a house. That was all. Chances are that this Joe Jones wasn't even there. I could check it out and then come back tomorrow with Haze.

God, listen to me. Needing my wife to come with me and hold my hand. I gripped the steering wheel tighter. I was my own man.

I took a deep breath and repeated: 'I am in control of my destiny. I make my own choices.'

Seven minutes to my destination. Wherever this house was, it was very close to Fobney Island Nature Reserve. I zoomed in on the GPS. A house at the end of a dead end in a remote location. Not at all concerning. It was mostly commercial addresses out here, which would explain why I hadn't seen any other cars.

I checked my phone reception. At least there were five solid bars. I stared out at the dark night. I looked over at the bag on the passenger seat. I was going to be fine. I was always fine. Apart from that one time . . . But I didn't need to think about that now. Definitely not now.

I turned up the volume on the recording. 'Try and repeat those two phrases every morning. I want you to reinforce to yourself your own personal strength. Here are some more to repeat to yourself throughout the day.'

I hummed to myself as I turned into Joe Jones's road.

Three minutes to my destination. There was a passing place just up ahead. I could pull in there behind a large oak tree and walk up to the house undetected.

'*I set my own path. I follow my own rules.*'

I took a breath. 'I set my own path . . . I follow my own rules.'

My headlights lit up a man in a cap standing right beside the large oak tree up ahead. What was he . . .? Gun! I saw the unmistakable flash of black as he raised it towards me. I didn't have time to think. I slammed my foot down on the accelerator and crouched down by the steering wheel.

There was a loud clunk, and a few seconds later the car bumped over an object. A large object.

I kept driving, only pulling to a halt a few feet down the road.

'*I am in charge of my destiny.*' The recording continued oblivious. '*I have faith in myself to make the right choices.*'

I jabbed at my iPhone screen until the voice went quiet.

I must've hit him. Oh, god, I hit him. Was he okay? Did I actually *want* him to be okay? He was, after all, trying to kill me.

I looked in the rearview mirror. The road behind was dark. I put the car into reverse and slowly backed up. The reversing lights illuminated the road. A few seconds of nothing but road, and then a man, lying face down on the ground, was caught in their beam. He was not moving.

I stopped the car and turned off the engine. I took a few deep breaths.

I must've hit him, and then he slid off my bonnet. And then I ran him over.

It wasn't an accident. It wasn't murder. It was self-defence! He had a gun.

Was it definitely a gun?

Or did my nerves make me think it was one?

Christ. What if it was just a mobile phone? Or a dog lead?

I didn't want to go and check on him.

He was dead. I knew he was dead.

What if I didn't find the gun?

I couldn't move. I had to move. Another car could turn up at any moment. There was no talking my way out of this one. Police would be called. Questions would be asked about what, exactly, I was doing here. I took a torch from my bag on the passenger seat and got out of the car.

I walked up to the man. He was tall with dark hair. Leaning down, I felt his neck for a pulse. Nothing. Unsurprising, considering the large amount of blood that was pooling onto the road. I reached for his right shoulder and tugged him over on to his back.

I stared down at the man's face, and stepped back with a start. I recognised him. I took a deep breath and pinched the bridge of my nose.

I'd just run over my wife's ex-boyfriend.

Part 2
Sacrifice

'Whatever I've lost isn't a sacrifice, as the minute I became a momma, I didn't care about anything else. I don't mourn "past me", as she didn't have the love and light of children. She was incomplete and didn't know it. I pity her.'

Bells Brightley, parenting blogger (MommaKnowsBest) and bestselling author of *Reason for Being: Blessed to Be a Mom!*

'What have I lost to motherhood? Sleep, perkier tits, bottomless brunches, international travel whenever I feel like it, sleep, champagne breakfasts, all-nighters that were actually fun, sex in unusual places, sleep, a vintage two-seater car, being blissfully unaware what breast pads are, getting through a day without handling someone else's shit, that light, carefree feeling of only having to worry about myself and my needs . . . I could go on.'

Hazel Matthews, mother

26

Haze

We were an hour into drinks-nibbles-party-planning, and I was doing great. I had not offended anyone. I'd smiled in the right places, and had even succeeded in not rolling my eyes at Araminta's worry that the party did not have enough gluten-free dairy-free options. There were five of us here, our little ones all the leading stars of the play. I did feel a little smug. Little nods that my daughter was as spectacular as I thought she was always helped morale.

Frederica, resplendent in a flowered trouser suit, leaned towards me and started firing questions at me about my house. She kept going on about whether the garden was north-facing, and did it get morning sun, as those were the best gardens. I told her I didn't know, as I didn't own a compass, which she frowned at.

The two other women were called Devrika and Sasha, and they were huddled together mainlining Prosecco as one talked about how much she hated her husband. I was realising this wasn't so much about party planning as it was group therapy.

Women needed each other in a way that men didn't. They needed to share everything they were going through, to ask each other for advice on all the little things right up to the really big ones. I was still relatively new to the sisterhood, but I was a fully signed-up member now. After decades of being out on the fringes, I'd grown to realise how important female friendship was. I just didn't want any more of it. Jenny was enough for me.

'You're an artist,' Frederica announced.

'Yes.'

'I like your stuff. It's very angry. How is your husband's business going? It's still quite new, isn't it?'

'He's doing great.'

She seemed to know a lot about us. If we were getting to know each other, I could have free rein on questions too.

'Why do you put your life online?' I asked.

'Why wouldn't I? Curating images of how I'll always be remembered? I want the highlights reel at my funeral to make people jealous.'

Was this a friendship interview? Us circling each other, working out if we met each other's criteria? I mean, clearly she didn't meet mine. I wasn't about to choose to hang out with someone who used the hashtag '#handbagsaremypassion'. I liked pretty things too, but they were decorations, not a calling.

I sneaked a peek at my phone. Two missed calls from Fox. He was home with Bibi and Reggie. I tried to ignore my creeping heart rate. Had The Chameleon come for him? Or did he just want to know where the iPad was?

I walked away from the table, mobile clasped in hand, and rang him back.

He answered on the second ring. He was talking fast. 'You need to come meet me. Right now. Problem. Big problem.'

'Where are you?'

'I'll send you a pin.'

'Are Bibi and Reggie with you?'

'Jenny's at work. Frank is babysitting them.'

'Why did you have to go out?'

'I'll explain when you're here.'

'What is going—'

'Not on the phone, honey.'

He only ever used 'honey' when something bad was going down and he was overdoing the 'I'm a totally normal husband' part.

I hung up and looked at my phone. I had three missed calls from Jenny earlier in the evening, and then one text, saying:

Ignore my calls, babe. Enjoy your evening!!

She only ever used 'babe' when something bad was going down and she was overdoing the 'I'm a totally normal bestie' part.

And a second text.

Don't worry, Fox is sorting it!

Clearly, Fox had *not* sorted whatever it was.

I went back to the table.

Sasha was in mid-flow. '. . . and they never listen and just never get it right.'

Frederica nodded. 'Doesn't matter how many times you tell them.'

I chimed in. 'I know, toddlers are the worst.'

Devrika looked up at me. 'We're talking about our husbands.'

'Oh. Yes. Of course. I'm afraid I need to go. The baby isn't well.'

'And your husband can't handle it?' huffed Sasha.

'Exactly.'

'So typical. Why is it always down to us? Why can't we ever just enjoy one evening out?' Devrika downed her glass of Prosecco. 'I bet you'd never have to ring asking him to come home if a kid was ill. Men are useless.'

Sasha snorted. 'God, do you remember that time Andy couldn't even remember what uniform the kids had to wear, so he rang me in the middle of my big presentation?'

'Dick,' said Devrika.

'Such a dick.' Araminta nodded. 'And what about when Sean couldn't find the ballet stuff, so just sent her in a track-suit? And when he—'

I turned to Frederica, as it seemed Araminta's rant wasn't going to end any time soon. 'Very sorry to leave early.'

'Let's plan a spa day! We're all members at River Court. It's essential. I have so much upper back tension that needs working out.'

Fluffy robes and faces masks with Frederica. God no. I needed to scare her off. 'I only make plans involving alcohol.'

Frederica didn't flinch. 'Perfect. I was going to say we should do dinner one night. With our husbands. We can really get to know each other.'

'Fun!' That was all I could think to say.

I got into the car and clicked on Fox's pin. He was twenty minutes away, out by the recycling plant. What the hell was he doing there? There was no point calling him again. Whatever was going down was something that he didn't want evidence of over the phone. That meant anything to do with our little sideline.

I had to keep stopping myself from slamming my foot down on the accelerator. The roads got quieter and quieter until I turned into what looked like a dead end. I was metres away from Fox's pin. I reduced my speed to a crawl. Just up ahead, I saw the back of his car in front of a large oak tree. He was standing alongside it. I parked up behind him and got out.

He held out his hands. 'I know you're going to find this hard to believe. But it was an accident.'

I looked around. It was so dark, I could barely make out anything except a few trees.

'You hit a deer? What? Just tell me!'

Fox sighed and popped open the boot. Inside was a body. A male body. He was half wrapped up in the black tarpaulin we usually kept folded up along with the spare tyre.

I got closer and pulled back the tarpaulin. The crinkle as it unwrapped. A bad present.

I looked down at the dead man.

Danny.

Somehow, in the middle of nowhere, Fox had killed my ex.

'What the fuck did you do?

'Can we start by acknowledging how great it is that even though I killed someone, and knew it would look bad, I didn't try and cover it up? I rang you straight away and told you to come here. Open and honest communication about wrongdoings is—'

'Do not therapy-speak me!'

Fox went silent. He was choosing now to remind me of my previous indiscretion? It'd been nearly two years! You think someone is over a betrayal, only for them to fling it back at you first chance they get.

I tried to think about this calmly. My ex was dead, in my husband's boot.

'How exactly did this happen?'

'Jenny rang me. She had a lead on The Chameleon. She told me to come out here and check it out.'

'And what? Danny just ran in front of your car? It was suicide?'

'I was driving, and I spotted a man behind that tree. He was wearing a cap. But he was holding a gun. I ducked, accelerated and hit him.'

I looked more closely at Danny's body.

'You mean hit him and then ran over him?'

'I didn't stop, as I didn't know I'd hit him. I was ducked down, remember. Not wanting to get shot. I just slammed my foot down, heard the clunk and realised . . .'

'This is ridiculous.' I put my hands to my head. 'What the fuck? Danny is dead. Actually dead.'

'Why are you so upset?' Fox chewed on his bottom lip. 'I thought you said you didn't care about him.'

You have to be kidding me. He was still jealous. My wounded Fox was so off-kilter we were arguing over my squashed ex, and he was worrying I still had feelings for the guy?

'I'm not upset about him being dead! I'm upset that you killed him behind my back!'

'No! I did not!' Fox took a step towards me. 'We've learned from all that, remember? I would never do that to you. We're a team. We do it together or not at all. This was not planned.'

'You're saying he was waiting for you out here, ready to kill you, and it was self-defence?'

Fox nodded vigorously. 'Yes.'

'So, where's the gun?'

27

Fox

It was a fair question.

Was now the moment to admit that I was starting to have doubts that there even was a gun? No – that would definitely make things worse.

'I . . . I haven't been able to find it. But, you know, it's dark!'

Haze was staring at me with her arms folded.

Why did I feel like she didn't believe me? I tried to ignore my mounting anxiety. I needed her to know that I would never go behind her back, that I wouldn't ever risk losing her, not now, not ever. Judging from her outburst earlier tonight, she had clearly been stewing over me being dead weight – and that was before I ran over her ex-boyfriend.

'I swear, there was definitely a gun!'

'You're trying to tell me that it's just a coincidence that right after I reference your recent inability to kill, you go out and kill my ex?'

'It was self-defence!'

Haze stared at me. 'You didn't see that it was him? Before your foot hit the accelerator?'

'No!' He'd been wearing a cap – hadn't he? But then, where

was the cap? The same place as the gun? I walked away from Haze. I didn't want her to see my face.

I couldn't admit to her that it had all happened so fast I didn't really make a conscious decision. There was no cool, calm, controlled decision-making. I'd panicked. Like an amateur. Like I hadn't ever faced down a threat before. What was wrong with me? I'd trained for moments like this! And then I'd just ducked and slammed my foot down. No control. Sloppy. Desperate. God, I was a total mess.

Haze was looking down at Danny. 'We've got enough going on as it is, and now we've got to go dump his body and get Jenny on the case to make sure we're covered.' She looked around. 'Why the hell would Danny be out here, anyway?'

'Isn't it obvious?'

Haze frowned. 'None of this is obvious.'

'Danny must've been working for The Chameleon. His company is organising the Balgray party. The Chameleon has been linked to the party. The dodgy name from guest list was renting an Airbnb at the end of this dead end.'

'You think The Chameleon had Danny working for him? As what? Danny was a party planner! He's not in the criminal world.'

'How do you know? What else would he be doing out here? You hadn't seen Danny in years and he appears back in your life the same time The Chameleon comes to the UK? Of course it's linked!'

'You could've waited to find out before you killed him.'

'Forgive me for being too busy trying to stay alive to think to ask him nicely how the hell he was involved. He was aiming a gun at my head!'

'A gun you haven't found.'

'It happened like I said, Haze. You have to believe me.'

Haze ran a hand through her hair. 'Jenny sent you out here because of a lead on The Chameleon, and you happened to come across Danny, who happened to be trying to kill you?'

'Yes!'

'And it's not that you discovered he'd groped me the other day, so you followed him out here and ran him over?'

'He did *what*?' I resisted the urge to drag him out of the boot and run him over a few times more.

'It's not a big deal. I handled it.'

'You didn't tell me, though!'

'Because I was worried you'd do something like this.' Haze gestured at the dead Danny.

'God, Haze. You can't trust me?'

'Look at how you've been behaving! You're all over the place! I wasn't about to upset you with information I wasn't sure how you'd react to.'

'I'm sorry. I know I've been . . . off my game. It's been hard. I'm trying.' I risked putting a hand on her shoulder. 'Please, let's find the gun. I don't want you doubting me. It has to be here somewhere.'

I didn't want to tell her it was more for my own peace of mind than hers. She was right. I *was* all over the place. I kept seeing danger where there wasn't any. What if that was what had happened here?

Haze huffed and slammed the boot closed. 'Where was he when you saw him?'

I motioned towards the large oak tree. 'He was standing halfway behind there. He came out just as I approached.' I turned on my torch. 'I'll take this side. You go over there.'

Haze walked over to the other side of the road. 'Have you told Jenny?'

'Not yet. Didn't think it was a good idea to even insinuate something was wrong when she was sitting at work, in an actual police station.'

Haze turned on the torch on her phone. We started sweeping the ground.

I didn't want to think about what I'd do if I found anything other than a gun. In our line of work, I had to be able to rely on my instincts. What if mine were broken? I chewed the inside of my cheek as I stared at the ground. We worked silently for ten minutes or so. And then I saw it. A black object in the long grass. I held my breath as I reached down towards it and picked it up. A gun. It was an actual gun. A Glock 45. I recognised it right away. I might now be an honorary Brit, but I'd grown up American.

'Found it!' I called out to Haze as I examined it. The safety was off. My shoulders loosened a little. It had been a righteous kill. I had got him before he'd got me. I clicked the safety back on.

Haze came up to me and took the gun from me. She turned it round and round in her hands.

'You believe me now?'

'I didn't ever doubt you. Not really. It's just . . . you can see how it looked.'

Now that I was redeemed in my wife's eyes, I felt a little calmer. But my head was hurting with trying to piece it all together.

'Danny had a gun. He was pointing it at me. Who the hell was he? What was he into?'

Haze shrugged. 'Back when I knew him, he was just a party boy with a six-pack. We didn't talk much.'

I gritted my teeth.

'He had a fancy car,' she continued. 'A nice flat. Didn't

seem to work much, as he was always hanging out in clubs. I just presumed he had rich parents.'

'He was out here pointing a gun at me. I'm thinking it wasn't rich parents, but . . .'

'He was a criminal! And I didn't even notice.' Haze's eyes widened. 'Ohhh, he was a drug-dealer! Out at the clubs, he was always saying hello to random people. Carried a lot of cash. And he did always have a weird amount of energy. He was always wanting to keep going, never wanted to stop, really—'

'Haze! Come on.'

'Dancing! I'm talking about dancing!'

I paced around in front of the car. 'He was working with The Chameleon. Running this event at Balgray. Whatever they're planning, it's big.'

'What did you find at the Airbnb?'

'I . . . I haven't been to it.' God. I had forgotten all about it. What was happening to me?

Haze stared at me. 'Wasn't that the whole reason Jenny sent you out here?'

'I got a little distracted! What was I meant to do? Drive the body down to a house to discover who-knows-what waiting for me there? The Chameleon could be in residence with a whole host of—'

'Okay, okay.' Haze gripped me by the shoulders. 'I'll go check it out.'

'You shouldn't. What if—'

'I've got this.' Haze waved Danny's gun at me. 'And my phone. I'll just creep down the road and see if anyone's even there. You need to stay here with the cars and work out where we're going next.'

Before I could reply, she'd jogged off down the road. I ignored my racing heartbeat as I scrolled through our shared Google Drive spreadsheet titled 'Picnic Sites!'. Jenny had created this document – it was a handy guide for potential body-disposal locations, and each entry had a notes section as well as a star rating.

I'd just decided on where to go when my phone beeped. A message notification. Mike Martin asking 'Harriet' if she had any food allergies. Haze's secret dad was texting me, just as I was working out where to dump Haze's ex. Sometimes, just sometimes, I wished we were a normal family.

I looked up to see the light blue of Haze's jumpsuit returning. I silenced my phone and put it back in my pocket.

'There's no one there. No cars, and no lights on. Let's just get out of here.' Haze scraped her hair up into a ponytail. 'Where are we going to dump him?'

28

Haze

The first time I dumped Danny, it was with a hastily typed text message. This time would be a little more final.

Life was funny like that. One year, you're spending a lot of time naked with someone. And, another, you're standing over their dead body, debating the best way to get rid of it. You never knew how someone was going to come into your life, or how they were going to leave it. Maybe I should get that on a bumper sticker.

I'd never suffered through an acrimonious break-up, as I'd never been invested enough in a relationship to care. I'd never had to experience the trauma of having someone who knew every square inch of me, who had once held me at night and heard all my secrets, being downgraded to someone I crossed the street to avoid. Or, worse, had to exchange pleasant annual small-talk messages with. Danny was just someone I'd had repeated carnal knowledge of without ever noticing he was a drug-dealing criminal. Maybe this was why people said you should think carefully about who you sleep with. Or at least get to know them a little first.

Together, we shifted Danny from Fox's boot to mine.

Driving Fox's car with its dented bonnet was too risky. Having checked it over for any tell-tale blood splatter we determined it was safe to leave it there overnight.

Fox had suggested a dump site that might work that was less than eight miles from our current location.

It was not a peaceful drive as we debated how best to proceed.

I parked up opposite the abandoned house that had become a popular place to chuck unwanted rubbish. It was far enough from any neighbouring houses that kids wouldn't come playing around here. There had been talk of developing the plot, but due to its proximity to a sewage plant it seemed unlikely it would ever be touched. Fox's plan was that we'd dump Danny here. Thanks to the emergency items we always had in the car, we could make him indistinguishable enough that it would take a long time for him to be found, and even longer for him to be identified.

We just needed to get him across a country lane and through twenty feet of undergrowth surrounding the house before carrying him another twenty feet to the old septic tank. It was a workout I was not looking forward to.

I opened the boot and took a deep breath. I tightened the tarpaulin that was securely wrapped round him. Fox picked him up by the shoulder, I got the feet and together we yanked him out of the car.

'God, he's heavy.' I groaned. 'He's so tall.'

Fox mumbled something.

'What was that?'

'He's not *that* tall.'

'Seriously? Will you stop?' The fragile male ego couldn't even stop feeling competitive with an actual dead man.

Fox grimaced at me. 'Let's get him across this road, and we can take a break once we hit the undergrowth.'

We set off. I was struggling.

'Hurry up!'

'You try doing this in heels!' I hissed back.

We were halfway across the road when we both stopped. We were lit up. I turned my head and squinted straight into the lights of a Tesla.

Fucking electric cars.

They were so quiet. Creeping up on you without any warning.

We both blinked in the beam of the headlights: killers caught in their glare. A spotlight on body disposal.

We were holding separate ends of a long, rolled-up tarpaulin. At 11pm at night. On a deserted country road.

'Fuuuuck,' I let out quietly.

The driver's car door opened as the lights were dimmed. And out stepped an elderly man. 'Now I know what you two are up to!'

I remained silent.

'Good evening, sir,' Fox stammered out.

Yeah, as if manners were going to help us.

'Fly-tippers!' the man exclaimed.

'What?' Fox and I looked at each other.

'Don't worry, I'm not going to dob you in. This is my perfect spot to do it too!' He leaned on the car door as he grinned at us. 'What do these councils expect if they make it so bloody difficult to get rid of anything?'

'Yes!' Fox smiled. 'Those pencil-pushers are ruining everything.'

'Quite right. Fuckin' bureaucracy!' I chipped in.

The man chuckled away. Fox and I joined in laughing. My arms were about to go. Danny was bloody heavy.

'Well, we'd better get on.' Fox cleared his throat. 'In case someone who isn't an ally comes across us!'

'Hah! Too bloody right. Keep it up!' Still chuckling, the man got back into his car. We quickly got out of the road and carried on towards the undergrowth. We both dropped Danny as soon as the Tesla drove off.

'Now what?' I stretched out my throbbing arms.

'Well, we can't dump him here now, can we?'

We took a minute's rest, then hoisted Danny back up and walked as fast as we could across the road before dropping him back into my boot.

We got into the car. I let out a long breath. 'That was too fucking close.'

We sat quietly for a moment.

Fox shook his head. 'Of all the things that could've ended us, I did not have running over your ex-boyfriend on the shortlist.'

'You sure that old man won't be a problem?'

'Only if a body is found too near to here. Then he might put two and two together.'

We both took this in. It meant another car journey. We'd need to head further afield and choose somewhere even more discreet.

Fox looked down at his phone. 'We're twenty-two miles from the graveyard, and a funeral is booked in there for tomorrow.' Jenny had hacked the calendar of a local church's booking system. She had discovered that the gravediggers usually prepared the holes the day before a funeral. The best place to bury a body was underneath one. No one checked an empty grave before placing a coffin inside it.

'I can't dig in this!' I motioned at my outfit. 'It's Stella McCartney.'

'We've just established we cannot let Danny be found. It's the safest solution.'

I chewed on my lip. *Fine.* 'There must be something in the car I can change into.'

It was nearing 3.30am when we finally got home, tired, grumpy and covered in dirt. Jenny grimaced at the sight of us. She'd taken over babysitting duty from Frank as soon as she'd finished work.

I was wearing nothing but a large black waterproof poncho I'd kept in my car for emergency downpours. My legs were streaked with dirt. We'd spent hours in the grave, digging far enough down that Danny's final resting place wouldn't be discovered. Thankfully, no one had discovered *us*. I doubted anyone would've bought our prepared cover story of being a couple who got off on doing it in grave sites.

I turned to Fox as we entered the kitchen. 'For fuck's sake, you didn't even tidy the house before you left?'

'I got Jenny's call just as I was about to start!'

I slumped into a chair at the kitchen table. Jenny put down three glasses. She poured whisky into mine and Fox's, and into hers a slosh of Bailey's.

'Seriously?' I motioned at her glass.

'I don't want to feel left out of the post-kill alcohol debrief, but I hate whisky.' Jenny took out a notepad. 'Begin.'

Fox downed his whisky in one. The new health-conscious, fitness-obsessed Fox had come up with the rule of only ever drinking after a body dump. Considering this rule, I was surprised he wasn't pushing for more kills.

Fox once again recounted the story of Danny coming at him

with a gun, and the way he'd panicked and run him over without ever seeing who he was. He kept pointedly looking at me as he said this.

Jenny stopped him after he got to the part where we'd left the crash site in my car.

'And there was definitely no one at the Airbnb?'

I nodded. 'No cars. No lights on. Shutters on windows. Didn't look like anyone was staying there.'

Jenny tapped her pen against her mouth. 'Maybe The Chameleon is one step ahead of us, and knew we'd clock the fake name on that guest list.'

Fox gripped his empty glass. 'You think it was a trap? The Chameleon wanted to lure us out there?'

Jenny shrugged. 'It's something to consider. This fake name rents a house in a remote area, at the end of a dead end. And Danny comes at you with a gun.'

Fox poured himself more whisky as Jenny scrawled in her notepad. 'I'll be doing a deep dive soon as I'm back in the office.' She looked up at Fox. 'And give me the exact route you took from here to where you hit him. I'll do a check for any CCTV that might've picked up anything.'

Fox tapped his phone and showed her the highlighted route on Google Maps. 'I'll send it to you.'

'Where is your car now?'

'Halfway down the road from the Airbnb. We'll go back to it tomorrow and call a garage. We can use the "swerved to miss a deer" line.'

I took a gulp of whisky. 'I'll say I was driving. Bit of eyelash-fluttering, silly me, shit woman driver. And we won't get any questions.'

Jenny looked at her notepad. 'Okay, and the body is in our favourite graveyard. I'll check and make sure that funeral tomorrow goes ahead with no hiccups. I'll also double-check no cameras have been installed since my last sweep.'

I stretched. My forearms were aching from all the Danny-lugging and grave-digging. 'Can we go to bed now?'

A loud Reggie cry erupted from the monitor. Jenny and Fox turned to look at me.

I downed my whisky. 'I guess not.'

29

Haze

'You need quicker reflexes, love!' The mechanic with the baseball cap had scoffed at my dramatic re-enaction of a deer hopping out in front of me. As predicted, he had not questioned my story, merely patted my shoulder, understanding that it wasn't my fault my womanhood limited my reaction speed and spatial awareness.

Jenny had driven me back to the scene of the crime, as Fox needed to be in the office. His assistant, Richard, had insisted he come in early to prepare for their meeting with a potential new client.

We waited until the garage pick-up truck had removed Fox's dented car from the country lane, then walked down to the Airbnb.

'This house is rented until the day after the Balgray Hall party. I'm thinking Joe Jones is The Chameleon, and they've been using it as a base to plot whatever the hell they're going to do at the party.'

'And Danny?'

'He was standing guard. Maybe they'd positioned a camera

at the top of the lane? Or Fox's car triggered an alarm, and he was going to see who was coming?'

We stood outside the house. It was two storeys and red brick with a glass extension. It had looked eerie in the darkness last night; now it just looked ugly. Ugly and clearly empty. No cars in the drive. No lights on. No response to the doorbell we'd rung repeatedly.

Once Jenny had established there were no cameras anywhere in the vicinity, she'd used a rock to smash the ground-floor bathroom window and we'd climbed in.

The large wooden table in the centre of the open-plan kitchen-dining room had several glossy eight-by-ten photographs laid out on it.

I walked up to it and took it all in.

Jenny joined me. 'What the hell is all this? Pretty bloody random.'

I stared down at the photos. A skillet pan. A broken bottle of Cristal. A long green scarf. A police badge. A pair of pliers. A nightclub paper napkin. A chocolate-bar wrapper.

I'd seen it instantly. 'These are all linked to us. To our kills.' I touched each of the photographs, one by one. 'A skillet pan was what I used to kill one of my first men . . . A bottle of Cristal is what we used to knock out a man in Capri . . . Our third victim had been wearing a scarf just like this one . . .'

Jenny had picked up the police badge photo and stared at the number engraved on it. 'That's . . . that's Bill's! How the hell did they get that?'

Bill Grundy, Jenny's ex, had 'disgraced police officer' as well as 'deadbeat dad' on his résumé.

'The Chameleon knows everything! What the hell does he have planned for you at Balgray?'

'Maybe it's a killers' convention. We get to unionise. Compare notes on dump sites.' Fox's therapist might suggest I was guilty of frequently using humour to mask emotion – and I'd say, 'Well, yes, loser. It's better to laugh than to moan.'

I stared at the table. I picked up the photo of the chocolate-bar wrapper. It was from a Twix bar. I frowned at it for a moment before it hit me with a chill. 'We were eating these on our way to dump Clark Dixon.'

We looked at each other as we took in what this meant.

'He's never stopped watching you.' Jenny chewed on her thumbnail. 'I'm betting he started that fire at the dump site.'

He was the reason we'd missed Bibi's ballet show? I would kill him even more slowly than I'd originally planned.

My phone pinged. The Chameleon himself.

Do you like my surprise? I didn't like yours.
Don't think you can outmanoeuvre me, Haze.

I tapped back.

Danny was a friend of yours?

Danny was a loose end.
You saved me the trouble.

Was that true? Or bravado?

Seems like you know all the men in my past.
Lovers and victims.

A pause. Then:

I know everything about you, Haze.
I could send the authorities all the evidence
I have on your crimes. But I'm choosing
to let you be free.

I walked to the window and looked out.

> *I got your invitation to Balgray Hall.*
> *I'm guessing RSVPing 'no' isn't a good idea?*

Attendance is mandatory for you and your husband.
Or the police get a little care package of some
of your past highlights. We need to talk. In person.

I showed my phone to Jenny and nodded at the front door.

> *Just talk?*

Jenny gently opened the door and slipped outside.

If I wanted you dead, you'd be dead.

> *Why Balgray?*

I watched Jenny walking up and down outside the house. She was looking up at the trees.

It's a secure location. You can't try anything.

He was right about that. We couldn't risk ruining our cover as a nice, normal couple by going in there with our weapons raised.

*Is it your retirement party? You fucking
off for good is something to celebrate.*

His reply was instant.

It will be a memorable goodbye.

Jenny shook her head at me and motioned for me to come outside.

We got back into Jenny's car. 'There could be a hidden camera. Or maybe he had someone follow us here.'

I chewed on my lip. 'He's been keeping tabs on us this whole time.'

Jenny started the engine and turned to me. 'How do you think he's been kept in the loop? How is he so up to date on what you've been doing?'

'He must have had people watching us.' I felt a creeping dread as I realised it wasn't a case of *if* we'd been under surveillance, but more for how long.

The only solace was that we knew the house was clear. Jenny had been militant with her frequent bug-detecting sweeps. No one could've planted any listening devices within our home without us realising.

'You can't trust anyone you've met in the last year. He's a well-connected criminal with unlimited means. Anyone could've been recruited and parachuted in to report to him on your lives.' Jenny started the engine. 'Start thinking of anyone who could be working for him. Anyone who's now a part of your life. Who maybe doesn't quite fit.'

'Jen, you know how shit our social life is, right?'

'What about the gym? School? The neighbourhood?'

Something clicked. Someone who didn't seem right. 'Mr McCabe! Bibi's hot new class teacher.' I took out my phone. 'Here! Look.' I googled and clicked on the school's website, zooming in on his grinning photo. 'He's an ex-army twenty-six-year-old who looks like a male model and is now teaching kids their times tables. He started as a temp last month when Bibi's teacher had a car accident.'

Jenny stared at his photo and nearly swerved the car. '*He's* a primary-school teacher?'

'You should've seen parents' evening. I've never seen so much make-up and hair flicking for discussions on the phonetic alphabet.'

'Okay, I'll check him out. Any other red flags? Anyone who's appeared in your life? Or been trying to insert themselves into it?'

I tried to think over the last few months. 'I guess Frederica, the leather-trousered mum I've told you about. She seems weirdly keen to hang out. But maybe it's just because our kids are both very talented at acting.'

Jenny shook her head. 'She's a school mum; she's probably interested in you for more basic reasons, like she's really bored, or wants to nose around your house, or thinks you might be actual friends.'

I tried to imagine Frederica in sunglasses, staking out our house. 'I can't imagine someone who's an Instagram influencer being a good choice for covert spying.'

Or maybe that was the whole trick? Someone whose life you thought was open, someone you thought had everything on display, could actually be hiding the most of all.

We'd thought we were home free when it came to our past crimes. A closed chapter. The past was happily behind us.

And now The Chameleon was here to remind us we weren't as safe as we thought we were. *You're only not in prison right now because I'm choosing to let you be free.*

I wasn't one for looking back. I felt the same about my victims as I did about my exes. Once you were done with them, you really didn't want to ever think of them again. Dispatched and done for. Dead. Dead to me. Same thing.

Danny had dared to turn up back in my life, and look how that had ended. And now someone was taunting me with past receipts on past kills.

This jaunt down memory lane was going to mean a lot more bodies.

30

Fox

I was a strong, independent man.

I had to keep reminding myself of that fact. Back in Ivrea, being saved by my wife and her best friend had knocked me. Why couldn't I have saved myself? Yes, those men had outnumbered me four to one. Yes, I was injured. But still. I was a trained elite killing machine. That's what I had convinced myself of over all those years of feeling invincible. And look what had happened: they'd found me, taken me and nearly killed me.

I knew I was broken. What I didn't know was how to get fixed. I wanted to come back stronger. To learn from this. To be better.

This morning, I'd woken up in front of the television. I knew people did that all the time. But normally that was because they passed out there. They didn't go to bed, kiss their wife goodnight, fall asleep and then, in the middle of the night, go back downstairs – before waking up with no recollection of doing it.

I knew I should probably talk about this with someone. Haze. Sally. But I couldn't face the sad eyes. The panic at the fact I was quite clearly going crazy. Doctor Google had reassured me that sleepwalking was down to stress. That was all it was. Another manifestation of stress. And it wasn't anything to worry anyone about, as I was just wandering around the house. Maybe I was even catching up on chores. Enjoying the quiet time when no one else was around.

I wasn't even sure how much therapy was helping my current situation, but I had to feel like I was doing something. Taking control of my problems. Which was why, rather than going straight to the office, I was here yet again, trying to give Sally my edited version of 'running over my wife's ex-boyfriend'. It was not easy.

Sally peered at me over her glasses. 'You're not being very clear, Nathaniel.'

'Sorry. I just . . .' I cracked my knuckles. 'Last night, I was walking down a dark street, and a man looked like he was going for my phone. I reacted instinctively, to protect myself. But for a moment I wasn't sure if I had imagined him going for my phone. You know, maybe I was just expecting the worst from him, but he wasn't really a threat?'

'You hit the man?'

Thunk.

'Yes.'

'And how did you know if you were right or not?'

I found the gun!

'He had several phones on him, which made me realise I was right. He must've been planning to take my phone too.'

'What did the police say?'

'I ran off, in case the man had other friends with him.'

'Right.' Sally went to write something on her notepad and then stopped. 'So what you're saying is your fear of being mugged again nearly came true – but you were able to save yourself?'

I nodded as I took this in. 'Yes, I guess so.'

'And how does that make you feel?'

'Good? I think? That my instincts were right. That I didn't get hurt again.'

'This is wonderful progress. What did Haze have to say?'

'She was . . . initially confused. Thinking I'd hit the man for the wrong reasons. But she understands now. That I was right.'

'I'm so glad she is supporting you, finally.'

I frowned a little. 'Haze has always supported me.'

Sally tilted her head. 'Do you think so?'

'Yes! I mean . . .'

'Look at you, and all you've achieved. Does your wife ever tell you that she's proud of you?'

'Well . . . no. But then she's not big on emotions. She had a complicated—'

'It's something that's inherently important in marriage. To be able to express feelings. Have you ever asked her to come here?'

I laughed.

Sally's eyebrows raised.

'Sorry, it's just – Haze would never. Ever. It's not her thing. Therapy.'

How to explain that Haze didn't rate talking about feelings, only ever acting on them?

Sally nodded. 'Do you think the fact she doesn't really talk about these things means you might sometimes try and take on Haze's emotions as well as your own?'

Was I subconsciously absorbing Haze's unresolved issues? Was she bringing me down without even realising it?

'You don't need to be the big tough man for her. You show me how vulnerable you can be. You show me your true self. Why can't you do that with her?'

'It's hard to talk about Haze when she's not here. We had some problems last year.' I flashed back to us brandishing our knives at each other. 'But we got through them, and we've come out stronger.'

'Really? Have you? Or do you just think you have?'

I stared at her. 'What do you mean?'

'You're keeping things from her. That makes me wonder if she is hiding things too?'

I gritted my teeth. Seeing Sally was meant to help me with my problems, not make me think of new ones. Were Haze's suspicions about Sally being no good correct? Were Sally's suspicions about Haze keeping things from me correct? Were my beliefs I was a total ridiculous mess correct? I only had the answer to one of these questions.

31

Haze

I drove straight from the Airbnb to Bibi's school. I'd phoned and requested a meeting with Mr McCabe to discuss Bibi's recent violent outburst, and more importantly to assess whether he had been planted to keep tabs on us. He was in a position of authority and was with my daughter every weekday. I had to know if there was any risk that he could be involved in whatever The Chameleon had planned.

'I'm sure you will agree, hurting that boy was very out of character for Bibi.'

We were back facing each other in little plastic chairs.

'Absolutely.' He nodded. 'I think it was just a miscommunication.'

'I know she's been having trouble with that particular boy, and maybe that's why she lashed out.'

'Mrs Baring takes a very strong line on any type of physical altercation. I have encouraged her to see the context of certain incidents.'

Was that teacher-talk for him agreeing that Bibi was right to hit that thug Ted? We'd looked into Backhouse Dunne.

It was one of the top law firms in the country, and Ted's mother Diana had a formidable reputation.

'If you could please keep an eye on him, that'd be much appreciated. If his actions are properly managed, then I don't think Bibi will feel the need to take matters into her own hands again.'

Mr McCabe nodded. 'She has a very strong sense of right and wrong. Don't worry – I'll be keeping a close eye on things.' His shirt sleeves were rolled up. He had very toned arms. Of course, teachers could work out and not be part of a criminal gang. But when you added his physique to how he was a last-minute temp parachuted in after Bibi's teacher had her freak car accident, it made him a little more suspicious.

Jenny was already doing a deep dive into his background. Maybe I could get something from him myself. I just needed to get him talking.

'I guess at least you're used to such displays of violence – rumour has it you used to be in the army?'

He frowned. 'I don't really think you can compare soldiers in the battlefield to kids in the playground.'

I laughed, but it came out a little too high-pitched. 'Of course not! I was just making a joke. It's just quite the career change you've had.'

Mr McCabe brushed a lock of hair away from his eyes. 'When you realise how fragile life is, you understand it's important to chase your dreams.'

I tilted my head. 'And your dream is being a primary-school teacher. In Berkshire.'

'The buzz I get from teaching a kid to read – it's just priceless.' He beamed at me.

My worst nightmare would be spending my days surrounded by twenty-three children and their twenty-three different demands for attention. I was struggling with two, and, having given birth to them, I was naturally disposed to like them more.

I nodded in all the right places as Mr McCabe proceeded to talk me through the phonics programme he was using. Either he was an incredible actor or he really did just love teaching.

'And how has Bibi seemed otherwise?'

'There have been no more drawings of blood. Glad we cleared that one up!' He gave a little chuckle. 'She can have her serious moments, but, on the whole, she seems happy and well-adjusted. A lovely little girl.'

I smiled to myself. It felt good to hear someone confirm we were doing okay with her.

He shuffled the papers on his desk and checked his watch. 'We've got a couple of talks about the importance of respecting your peers coming up. I'm sure that will help the children understand personal boundaries.'

He was getting ready to dismiss me.

'I used to have this imaginary friend.' Enough flirting around the issue; it was time to make a move. 'I called him The Chameleon. I'd see him everywhere.'

'How charming! Impressive to even know what a chameleon is at that age. It's so—'

'And then one day, I just stopped seeing him everywhere. Because he was dead. I killed him.'

'You . . . you *killed* him?'

I stared into his eyes and saw nothing but confusion.

'I killed him off, as I didn't need him any more.'

'Oh. Of course.' He let out a breath. 'That makes sense.'

'So, really, I know that children go through phases. And then one day they wake up and it's over.'

Mr McCabe was nodding vigorously. 'Hopefully for Bibi it's not even a phase. Just a one-off incident. I will keep a close eye on things, so, really, there's nothing to worry about.'

I stood up. 'Sorry to take up your time.'

'Not at all! I seem to be meeting with mothers here very regularly – it's so heartening to see how involved you all are in your children's education.'

I tried to suppress the smirk. Hot and oblivious to it. No wonder he was such a hit.

32

Fox

Mike was constantly texting 'Harriet' with little updates and random questions.

Any musical talent? I have a good ear, apparently.

There is a recessive red hair gene on my mother's side – have your children got it?

I could understand his excitement. This was a man who'd got to his seventies thinking he'd never had children. And now he'd discovered he had a daughter. I'd answered everything truthfully. Then, just as I got to the office he texted again.

Next week I'm going to be in Berkshire for a friend's wedding. It would be wonderful to meet you while I'm here. I'll be on my own as Sarah's back is playing up and she sadly can't really face the flight.

I shouldn't have told him the truth about what county we lived in. Then I wouldn't be facing this latest predicament.

He was going to be in the area next week. Without her even knowing, Haze was tantalisingly close to finally meeting her father. *Wasn't this the reason I started all this? To get to this big moment? I'd talk to her tonight. Maybe I could break my no-drinking-unless-I'd-just-killed-someone rule.*

Richard had set up the boardroom for the imminent arrival of Benjamin Norwood, a potential big client. Richard had been corresponding with his financial manager for the last couple of weeks, and this had culminated in today's meeting. He'd bought croissants and cookies from the ridiculously expensive bakery round the corner and arranged them artfully on a large blue platter. I didn't want to upset Richard by letting him know that the platter was actually Lalique, and had been an incredibly generous Christmas present from a grateful client.

Richard placed the platter in the centre of the meeting room's mahogany table.

'Benjamin Norwood is the eldest son of the Duke of Drysdale. He was born with a silver monogrammed spoon in his mouth. The family have a huge stately pile in Northumberland.' He handed me a bio on Norwood. 'I haven't been able to find much on him online. Only photographs of him at big splashy parties, usually hanging out with minor royalty, someone with a triple-barrelled surname or a glamorous blonde.'

I flicked through it. Templeton Estate was very impressive. Beautiful Georgian architecture, and so huge it must have at least thirty bedrooms – and no doubt a ballroom or two.

'He's never had a proper job, just been involved in running the family estate. Whatever that means.'

I had a pretty good idea. It sounded like Norwood had had a very nice life.

'How did he hear of us?'

'He said he was recommended by friends. Declined to mention who. Norwood's father, the duke, is on his last legs. He transferred the family home over to Norwood several years ago. Rumours are rife that Norwood has decreed five generations is long enough for his family to have owned it, and that it's time to let someone else take it on. I'm guessing it's why he's looking for help with what do with the eight-digit payday he'll be getting as soon as it's sold.'

'Did he mention how much he wanted to invest?'

'He said a substantial percentage of his portfolio.' Richard rubbed his hands together. 'I'm excited. Are you excited?'

I scanned down the bullet points on Norwood. Two words shouted out at me. ' "Restore Glory" – what's this about?'

'It's a foundation Norwood set up to help restore houses of national importance to their former glory. They do fundraisers – posh parties at stately homes.'

'Who donates to places like that?'

'History buffs. National-pride-filled rich people.' Richard paused. 'Flag shaggers, really.'

Restore Glory was the charity that the event at Balgray Hall was in aid of. Was this just a coincidence, or was every aspect of my life currently being invaded by The Chameleon?

The buzzer went. Richard jumped to attention. 'I'll let him in and get the coffee organised. He mentioned in an interview that he loves this particular Turkish blend, so I've had it ordered in.'

I sat down at the head of the small boardroom table. We couldn't compete with the larger firms, so our whole selling point was a discreet and very personal service. That and our usually outstanding numbers.

I heard Richard in the reception room. 'I'll show you in to meet Mr Cabot, then I'll bring in that coffee.'

Norwood was tall and dishevelled with dark hair. He was better-looking than the photos of him Richard had located online indicated. According to his bio, he was forty-nine. He looked in pretty good shape. I supposed not having the inconvenience of work meant he could focus on himself. I tried not to think about how much he could bench-press. Four years older than me, but could he still outdo me in a fight?

Get a grip, Cabot.

I stood up, holding out a hand. 'Nathaniel. Good to meet you, my lord.' Norwood's title was Viscount Norwood. In his bio, Richard had included information on how to address him correctly. He didn't want his American boss letting him down.

Norwood had a strong handshake. 'Now, now, call me Benjamin. I don't worry about any of that.' Norwood was wearing a blue shirt, red chinos and a navy blazer. The blazer did look like it had seen better days. He had recently gone through a messy divorce – his ex was a striking Russian model fifteen years younger than him. I wondered if this crappy dress sense had been caused by the divorce, or if it was part of the reason for it.

'I'm delighted you wanted to meet. Your family home is really very famous. We've even heard of it back in the States.'

'How lovely! Yes, the old pile isn't too shabby. Can you believe my ex tried to lay claim to it? The very cheek of it!' Norwood chuckled as he sat down in the chair next to me.

'I was just reading about your foundation, Restore Glory. You set up that charity to help other houses like yours?'

Norwood reached for a cookie and took a bite. He spoke with his mouth full. 'Yes! Thought it would be good to do a little something to give back, not just because a tax man highlighted the benefits. And if I was going to do charity, why not one that helped houses like ours?' Cookie crumbs sprayed from his lips.

'It must be a lot of work, organising all that.'

'Oh, I outsource it.' Norwood chuckled to himself as he ineffectively brushed crumbs off his shirt. 'An events company does it for me. They know which rich people to target for tables. It's all about who can stump up the cash.' Norwood tapped his finger against his chin. 'My finance man says I need to ask you all kinds of clever questions, but I can't seem to think of any.'

'I know Richard has already sent a pack giving our figure highlights. Is there anything else you want to know?'

'Why don't you give me a little sales pitch, and I'll see if I like the sound of it all?' Norwood grinned at me as he reached for another cookie.

Richard brought in two cups of the special coffee. After one sip, Norwood recognised it, and decreed that we clearly had excellent taste.

I talked for fifteen minutes straight. Norwood seemed to be listening, but it was hard to be sure – he was very interested in the Lalique platter.

When I finished up my spiel, I asked him if he had any questions.

'I'll say something I do know. Your early position on Boltons' stock did very well for you.'

I nodded. Clark Dixon had been Finance Director of Boltons. It seemed Norwood had at least read the highlights of the pack Richard had sent.

'What's your process?'

'I read up on companies, the market, and go with my gut.

There's no great art to it. Mostly luck, really.' Dixon had been very easy to get talking. His information on an upcoming sale had practically tripped off the bloodied tongue.

The first line of a *Barbie* song rang out. Norwood quickly reached into his jacket pocket and took out his phone. He answered it and spoke gently about being there soon before hanging up.

I stared down at the papers in front of me. Norwood had a five-year-old daughter with his ex-wife Cecilia.

'Duty calls.' Norwood stood up. 'I like you, Cabot. Let's do this. My finance guy will be in touch.' He reached out and shook my hand.

'Wonderful. We'll do our best to make sure you don't regret it.'

'I never regret. We all must own what we do.' Norwood smiled and ambled out of the meeting room.

Thirty seconds later, a grinning Richard popped his head round the door. 'Did you see his jacket? It's like a badge of pride with the poshos. I bet he drives a crap car as well.'

'What do you mean?'

'It's a class thing. They think it's crass if everything looks too flash. Everything is old and they're always making do, despite their vast wealth.'

I shook my head. It was not a concept Americans would ever understand. 'You're sure he's got money?'

'The valuations on that family pile of his hit thirty million, minimum. And that's before you factor in the family money. They've been living off the interest alone for the last generation.'

Norwood was also exactly the type of incredibly rich new client we needed right now. With The Chameleon breathing down our necks, the distraction of throwing myself into my nine-to-five job was going to be a blessed relief. I could choose to be at one with numbers on my laptop rather than out in the field with my knives.

Maybe this was how the people I'd always looked down on got stuck in their dead-end jobs. They were scared to make the leap and live their dreams. Go for a promotion! Aim big! What's the worst that could happen?

Kidnap and torture.

33

Haze

I drove to Jenny's parents' house to pick up Reggie. Sandy had been looking after him all morning, and opened the door bouncing him on her hip. Hearing the doorbell, Jenny appeared from their living room, holding her laptop.

Sandy beamed at us both. 'He's so precious. I just can't wait for our family to have a new addition.' She nudged Jenny.

'Mum!' Jenny shook her head. 'I told you it could be a long wait.'

Jenny wanted to adopt. She'd been through all the checks, training and assessment, and was now hoping for news that a child had been potentially matched to her. The process had been so thorough, and Jenny had done so much to prove she was a good parent, it made me realise how horribly unlucky I'd been with the foster families I was placed with.

'You enjoyed your girl time this morning?' Sandy believed we had gone out for breakfast and a massage.

'It was bliss. Very relaxing. Thank you for taking Reg again.'

I picked up Reggie's nappy bag and listened as Sandy lectured Jenny on her reading of a recent *Daily Mail* article that warned about the importance of washing vegetables in lemon juice.

Jenny was in the middle of nodding along when Frank shouted down from upstairs. 'You all right, love? That door still sticking, or is it okay?'

'He slept badly last night, so he's just getting up now.' Sandy patted Jenny's shoulder.

'Should I go see him?' Jenny looked up the stairs.

'No need. He's probably not decent.'

'It's good thanks, Dad!' Jenny shouted up. 'You did a grand job. Runs smoothly now.'

Jenny had been renovating her house for the last year. She'd been working non-stop on many different DIY projects to make it a more functional and aesthetically pleasing family home, while also wiping out any trace of its previous owner – her ex Bill. Jenny gave Sandy a hug and shouted again. 'See you later!'

Sandy held her ear. 'You're going to make me deaf.'

'No, the old age will.'

Sandy gave her a tut and a shove as we left.

We got into Jenny's car. 'Why are you smiling to yourself?'

'Am I?' I hadn't realised. 'I guess it's just because you're all so cute. They're so old and still worrying about you. And helping you out. It's so handy.'

Jenny laughed. 'It's called family, Haze.'

Family.

Of course.

I was still learning.

I pictured Bibi and Reggie all grown up. Of course, we would be there for them and help wherever we could. The worrying didn't end just when they were old enough not to face-plant in the bath. Jenny was forty-two, and she still got lectured like a child.

I felt a stab of realisation. I thought I already knew about everything that I'd missed out on by not having parents. Now I could see the loss was about more than just that crappy childhood I'd grown up from too fast. I might've aged out of foster care, but you didn't just age out of needing parents. I might be an adult now, but I still wanted to be a daughter. I was still two loved ones down. I was still missing having a couple of people with whom I could be completely myself, as they knew everything about me and were obliged to love me, no matter how horrifying parts of me were.

I had my Fox. And he had me. And we had our babies. It was more than I'd ever thought I'd have. But, somehow, the gaps were still noticeable.

I couldn't say if we'd adopted Jenny and her family, or if they'd adopted us. Either way, it was what we needed. More people to rely on. More people who cared about us. It was too much pressure with it being just the two of us. I'd been feeling this more than ever since Fox started struggling to be himself.

I turned to Jenny. 'Let me guess, you've turned up nothing on McCabe.'

She nodded. 'Squeaky clean.'

'He was impressively vanilla.'

Jenny stretched. 'Lunch? Carluccio's?'

'Oh yes, I can have that salmon thing you had last time.'

'No, that was at Redford's.'

'Are you sure? I thought that's what you were eating when we saw that blonde you had a thing with. You know, the—'

Jenny frowned. 'Greta?'

'No, the smoker you hid from behind the menu! Remember?'

'Oh, god. Polly. Yep. She ghosted me after one date. Let's not go back there in case she's there again.' Jenny shuddered.

A few months ago, Jenny had decided she was ready to start dating. She'd asked me to help her fill out her profile, and had held her breath while she waited for me to notice she'd ticked 'women' under 'looking for'. I told her there was a huge mistake with what she'd written – she'd described herself as a fitness enthusiast, and we both knew that was a massive fucking lie. We'd cackled for a good few minutes, and then I'd got to work with swiping right for her, just in case her taste in women was as terrible as her taste in men.

'Don't be ridiculous. I want the salmon thing. And, besides, I make you look good. You need ex-dates to see you out with smoking-hot competition.'

'Lactating smoking-hot competition.' Jenny let out a giggle.

'Thinking about it, you really should add to your profile that you have a best friend who will kill anyone who fucks you over.'

'You set the friendship bar really high.'

I held up my hand, and Jenny high-fived it.

34

Fox

That morning, I'd made the mistake of announcing to Haze that I'd unloaded and loaded the dishwasher and wiped down the kitchen surfaces.

'*Do you want a fucking medal? For doing the bare minimum? Imagine being me. Do you have any idea what it's like to have a human baby gnawing at you? Do you realise how exhausting it is? Why couldn't you have the babies? Why does nature hate women? It's our bodies that bear the children, and then we have to sodding feed them! Why should we then also be loaded up with the domestic shit you avoid by being lucky enough to leave the house! You cleaning this house is the least you could do after all I've been through bearing YOUR children.*'

I'd tried offering to hire a cleaner, and she'd shouted that with everything else we had going on, we didn't even have the time to find one – and if I wasn't such a selfish pig I would already know that.

Then she threw a dog toy at my head. But it was one of the soft ones, so I knew she wasn't really trying to hurt me.

I'd backed out of the house shouting that I loved her, that I appreciated her and that I'd bring her back treats. All I could think about was how if this was the reaction she had to me being insensitive about housework, what kind of hell would be unleashed when I broke it to her I'd been secretly talking to her father?

I was in a taxi five minutes away from my office when I saw Jenny. She was holding a takeaway coffee and walking down Park Lane. Was she coming to see me? I rang her mobile.

She answered on the second ring.

'Where are you going?' I asked.

'Fox? I'm with my mum. I just got to theirs, as they need help with getting some things down from the loft.'

'I see.' I frowned as I kept staring at her departing back.

'I can't come meet you guys anywhere right now.'

'Right. Okay. Don't worry – I was just checking if Haze had filled you in on my meeting.' I outlined the Norwood and Restore Glory link.

'She told me last night. I'll look into Norwood in case there's any reason he's come to you as a client.'

I hung up and watched as she turned the corner. It was definitely Jenny. She was even wearing the same blue-and-white spotted raincoat that Haze was always ribbing her about, saying she dressed like a 'fucking toddler'.

Why had she just lied to me?

'You must've got her confused with someone else,' said Haze. 'Jenny wouldn't lie about where she was.'

I'd told her about seeing Jenny as soon as I got home. Despite my repeated assurances that it really was Jenny, she had brushed it off, saying I'd been mistaken. She was so certain it made me unsure of myself. Maybe it was just a woman wearing the same ugly coat, and my mind had presumed it had to be Jenny?

Haze was more interested in the Tupperware box of leftover cookies and croissants from yesterday's Norwood meeting than she was in wondering if her best friend had lied to me. Richard had insisted I take them all home, explaining that his four kids were 'mental enough without all that sugar'. Haze ate three of the cookies as I kept staring at the box, imagining how good they tasted.

Haze shrugged. 'None of it makes sense. Jenny thinks we need to work out who in our lives could be in a position to report on what we've been doing.'

I considered this. 'I can't think of anyone who would know everything about us. It's not like we go around telling people our business.'

Haze was reaching for a fourth biscuit, but she stopped. 'What about someone you started seeing in the last few months? Someone you've opened up to?'

I frowned. 'I don't get who—'

And then I did.

Haze folded her arms as she stared at me.

I gulped. 'Sally? Don't be ridiculous. She's a licensed therapist!'

'How did you find her?'

'I . . . Her business card came through our office door. I think it was a kind of advertising mailout.'

'You chose a therapist from junk mail?' It didn't sound great when she put it like that.

'I was having a dark moment. And then, bam-clatter, the letterbox went. I got up and went to pick it up, and there it was. I thought it was a sign.'

'A sign from fucking who? The God you don't even believe in? Or the devil watching us?' Haze stood up from the table.

'I wasn't thinking straight! I mean, you're right. I didn't look into her like maybe I should have. I just rang the number and booked an appointment, and that was it.' I ran a hand through my hair. Was Haze right? Had I been opening up to our biggest enemy? 'Her office was a five-minute walk from mine. I went and met her once, and she seemed nice, and it kind of clicked. So I kept going back.'

'What does she know about us?'

'Nothing!' I mentally scanned back over my sessions with her. 'Okay, well, everything except the whole killing thing.' I tried to think how bad a breach it would be if Sally was part of this big bad plot against us. I'd opened up to her about all my insecurities. She'd tried to make me question Haze. She'd made me feel that I was underappreciated. Had she weaponised my feelings?

'Did you tell her about Jenny?'

'Of course I told her about Jenny. I mean, just that she's your best friend. I only spoke about how that made me feel. Never about her being police. Never about working together.'

'Are you—' Haze stopped. 'And how does Jenny being my best friend make you feel?'

Be open. Be honest. Sally's voice was in my head.

But was that good-therapist advice, or was that potential-evil-therapist advice?

I went for it. 'It makes me feel left out sometimes.'

Haze scoffed. 'Fox, come on. Really? You feel threatened by her? After everything we've been through?'

I put my head in my hands. 'It was always you, me and the bad men. That was our thing. What bonded us even further together. I guess . . . Having her share in that too, it feels like she's entered sacred territory.'

'We needed her! Remember? And she's been so helpful. We have—'

'I know all that! Practically, I know all that. I love Jenny. She's been amazing – for everything she's done for us as a family, for how she supports you. I know all that. But I can still sometimes find it tough.' I took a breath. *My feelings are valid. My feelings are valid.* I wasn't totally sure whether I'd said that out loud. 'And really, if we're talking about someone involved in our lives who could give away everything on us, have you considered the fact that she's a top candidate?'

Haze laughed. 'Jenny? You really think Jenny is betraying us?'

I didn't know what I was saying, but it could make sense. 'She lied about being in London today. I saw her. I know it was her. Why would she do that?'

'She told you she was with her parents, so she must've been. You're the one who's been all over the place, so sorry if I don't believe you.'

My wife wasn't taking my word for it. Had I really lost her trust when it came to my mental state? She was choosing to believe Jenny over me.

'Think about it! Who better to be reporting on us? She knows everything! Not the watered-down, censored version of events I give Sally.' I tried to talk myself into it. 'She's had a taste of criminal life, and now she wants more!'

Haze was still looking at me blankly.

'Don't you see? She only gets a small percentage of what we make,' I continued.

Whenever we killed a man who had useful stocks and shares information, like Clark Dixon, Jenny got a percentage of the profit. We were a team, and it was her payment for everything she did to help us take out the target.

'Maybe she's got greedy! She'll soon have two kids to support, and that's not cheap!'

'Jenny would never give us up. Besides, she couldn't – not without reporting on herself. I trust her. With everything.'

'What if she was offered a deal? With the police? Or one of the gangs? She could've set us up in Ivrea for them.'

I knew I was grasping. But I couldn't bear the idea that I had brought more trouble to our door. That my weakness at needing to seek out professional help could've flung us further into the deep.

'The other night, with Danny – Jenny was the one who told me to head out there. It was her lead, remember?'

Haze kept staring at me. 'And exactly why would she be doing all this?'

'Maybe she's scared of going to prison, of getting caught, and so she's sacrificing us for her own safety.'

'You're being ridiculous. Jenny is family. She's in this with us. She has just as much to lose if we get exposed.'

'No, we lose more! We're the killers; she's just the help. They'd let her off to betray us!' I jabbed my finger at her.

'You really believe all this?' Haze took a sip of her tea.

'I . . . I . . .' I took a breath. 'Okay, no. Not really. I'm just saying it *could* be a theory.'

I didn't know what I was trying to achieve here. All I knew was that now was definitely not the time to mention that I'd tracked down her father – and that he wanted to meet her next week.

35

Haze

What a fucking mess.

We couldn't trust anyone in our lives, and it seemed like we couldn't trust each other. He was really coming after Jenny? I knew he didn't like the idea of Sally being a plant, but to try and accuse *Jenny*?

We didn't have time to thrash it out properly as Bibi needed picking up from school and Reggie was waking up from his nap. A temporary truce. Our arguments needed to be scheduled.

I let Fox deal with a cranky Reggie and headed out to pick up Bibi, as at least that got me out of the house. The painting I'd started after Clark Dixon's death was nearly finished. I was pretty confident it was one of my best yet. I was excited to share it with Hamish at the gallery and hear the flood of praise I needed to feel good about myself. The large cheque when he eventually sold it would help too.

I was ten minutes early to pick-up. I stood a little further away from the gates than the clusters that were already beginning to form. I looked up from my phone when I sensed someone standing next to me. A little too close.

I turned to see Diana Morgan staring at me. 'Hello, Hazel.'

'Hello, Diana.'

We stood in silence as we watched the other groups of mothers laughing and talking.

I just needed to keep quiet.

Keep quiet.

Fuck it.

'Ted pulled any hair recently?'

She was straight back. 'Bibi punched any faces recently?'

'My daughter only attacks threats.'

'Maybe she'll grow up to be a lawyer.'

'Oooh yeah, lawyers are scary.' I scoffed.

Diana looked at me with a small smile. 'You'll see.' The gates opened, and she strode purposefully towards them.

What the hell did that mean? It struck me how Diana was someone who had recently come into our lives, a ripple effect from her child attacking ours. Maybe little Ted was tasked with singling out Bibi? Could Diana also be working with The Chameleon? Or she was just a pissed-off mum, out for merely metaphorical blood? God, this was getting exhausting.

I walked towards the school gates as my phone pinged. It was Jenny announcing to our group chat that she'd got us tickets to a conference at Balgray Hall in a few days. It was being held in the ballroom, the same location as the Restore Glory party. It was the chance to try and get to know our battleground ahead of our confrontation with The Chameleon.

Bibi bounced into my arms, her pigtails swinging. 'I did no hitting today!'

She said it loudly enough that a couple of the other mothers turned to look at us.

'Great, baby, that's great.' I hugged her close and added, in her ear, 'No need to tell me, okay? I'll just presume you haven't.' It wasn't a great idea to celebrate each day she didn't whack someone.

We got home to find Fox pacing the kitchen and talking on the phone. 'I don't understand this! It's just ridiculous. Okay . . . Right . . . Bye.' He hung up and turned to me. 'That was our lawyer. The council are coming after us saying the kitchen extension didn't have the correct permission. Apparently a law firm representing a couple of concerned locals are kicking up a fuss over the fact it's three metres bigger than what was put in the original application.'

'That's insane! We bought the house with this already here. How is it our—' I stopped as something clicked. 'Which law firm?'

Fox tapped at his phone as he scrolled through his emails. He looked up at me. 'Backhouse Dunne. Isn't that . . .?' He trailed off when he saw the rage I was struggling to control.

Backhouse Dunne. The law firm where Diana Morgan was a managing partner. That crazy bitch!

'I *just* saw her!'

Fox said, 'And did you antagonise her further?'

'No.' I paused. 'I mean, it wasn't friendly on either side. But *she* was the one talking about lawyers being a threat. And now it's clear why!'

Fox shook his head. 'This is going to be messy and expensive to sort out.'

'She's bloody counting on it.' Diana had taken time out of her undoubtedly immensely busy schedule to find a way to fuck with us. In case it wasn't enough that we had to worry about a criminal organisation and an assassin being after us, we also had to deal with a well-connected and pissed-off mother. I really needed to get better at playing well with others.

36

Fox

The Chameleon and Mike were still on rotation in my head the next morning. It was too early to drown out my worries through the power of music. I got onto my motorbike and headed to the gym to pound them out instead. Revving the engine. Beating the punchbag. I was perhaps overdoing being over-manly.

I couldn't get into the zone. I lost track of how many reps I was doing. My back started to hurt. I must've slept funny. Was that all it took these days?

I hit the showers and went to change. Standing opposite me was a short man in his twenties. He had the most incredible six-pack. Was that really all through working out? Not steroids? Just youth and hard work? He caught me staring at him and smiled. I nearly smiled back, but then realised that staring at a topless man in the gym locker room might be misinterpreted. How could I explain I wasn't lusting after him, but my own lost youth? I finished changing quickly, grabbed my stuff off the bench and rushed out.

I was just through the gym's double doors when I heard an, 'Excuse me!'

I turned round to see the man standing there, still smiling. Oh god, he'd definitely got the wrong idea.

'I'm straight!' That was all I could think to say.

The man nodded. 'Good for you, Daddy. You picked up my gym pass.'

Ah.

Awkward.

Of course.

How could I think a young guy like him would even want to ask me out?

'I'm so sorry. I didn't realise. My mind's all over the place.' I rifled in my gym bag where I had flung my workout clothes, and handed him back his gym pass. I rushed out to the car park without a backwards glance.

Getting into the car, I sat and checked myself in the rear-view mirror.

He'd called me 'Daddy'.

How did he know I was a father? It wasn't like I wore a badge or anything. A creeping dread hit me. Was he saying I was old enough to be his father? He was only twenty years younger than me! I mean, it was possible – but really? I had to find another gym. My ego couldn't take this.

By the time I got home, Haze had already taken Bibi to school.

I'd promised her I'd work with our lawyer to try and solve the planning permission nightmare. I hoped this would show her that I was stepping up for us as a family and pulling my weight.

The next issue to combat was who in our lives could potentially be reporting on us to The Chameleon. Haze had asked Jenny to do a deep-dive background check into Sally, something to which I had wholeheartedly agreed. And I had now made the decision to follow Jenny – something to which Haze would have wholeheartedly, and with numerous expletives, disagreed.

I didn't believe Jenny was working for The Chameleon, but I did believe she had lied to us the other day about where she was. And, considering how we were on high alert, it had to be worth checking out why our business partner, our closest confidante, our extended family member, was lying about where she'd been.

I had snuck an AirTag into her car last night.

It was not my proudest moment, but I needed answers.

Jenny had told us she was going to be busy at the station all morning. And now I had a way of checking if that was true.

It was a waiting game, and I had the house to myself. I took the opportunity to try and lose myself in the music, but it's hard when you can only play four chords. A phrase concerning 'old dogs' and 'new tricks' kept coming to mind.

I plugged in the amp and tried another strum. The amp squealed with feedback.I gave it another few goes. I felt I was slowly making progress when I was interrupted by a banging on the garage door. I pressed the remote and watched it open. Standing there, arms folded, was Barry Fenton from next door. Barry was the official head of the Neighbourhood Watch – and the unofficial headache of the neighbourhood. A widowed pensioner with nothing to do but spend his days curtain-twitching and complaining. He'd left us alone at first. An unsmiling nod was the most significant interaction we'd had. Then one day it started. We took a few days to bring in our bin after bin day. Barry called it sloppy and said we were inviting burglars to the neighbourhood.

'Barry! How are you on this fine day?'

'That noise is unacceptable.'

I held up my guitar. 'This? You don't like music?'

He shook his head. 'That is not music. Keep it down!'

My phone pinged. The AirTag was on the move. I let Barry rant about how the noise was several decibels over legal requirements as I checked Jenny's location. She was leaving the station. She'd lied again.

I half-heartedly fought back with Barry that playing music at a reasonable level on my own property at 10am was definitely permissible, keeping one eye on my phone.

Jenny was heading towards Slough High Street. I zoomed in. Barry was still talking. I zoned back in to hear him saying, 'It's so rude that you can't even give me your full attention!' He turned on his heel and stomped the few feet back to his pristine lawn.

'Bye, Barry!' I shouted after him.

Jenny's car was now parked off a side street.

I needed to go check she hadn't just nipped out for a sandwich. I needed to find out where she was that warranted lying to us. Again.

Before I could rethink my choices, I got into the car.

It wasn't going to be easy following a police detective. Especially one who knew me and the disguises I could use. She was, after all, the one who'd bought me my favourite wig. It was a very nice brunette shade with a side parting that actually really worked for me.

I parked up on the street next to the one where she'd parked. I had no plan other than to hover nearby and hope to see where she was coming from. Considering where she'd parked, she must be on the high street. Perhaps she was meeting someone in one of the cafés there – or innocently hitting Boots or another shop, and proving me to be a total idiot for doubting her.

I put on a baseball cap and tucked a copy of the *Berkshire Bulletin* newspaper under my arm. I took it out and stood on the street corner, and tried to scan the street.

Ten minutes went by and nothing.

My stomach was starting to rumble. The chia smoothie I'd had for breakfast was clearly not enough. I was looking at the shops up and down the high street, debating which had the best (and least-processed) snacks on offer, when I got a flash of her blue-and-white spotted coat.

The building on the other side of the road had floor-to-ceiling glass windows and doors. She was inside, shaking hands with a man in a suit. They spoke for a few minutes and then she came outside. I hovered behind the newspaper. She walked back towards her car, moving quickly. I looked up at the building she'd been in. NatWest Bank. Was she having financial trouble? Or the opposite? Had she recently come into a lot of money because she was selling us out?

I got out my phone and texted our group chat.

Busy day at the office? Any gossip?

I was just checking in, in my usual paranoid way, to see if there'd been any update on The Chameleon.

Going to be a late night.
No gossip apart from Neil daring to
use my favourite coffee mug in front of me

Neil sat opposite Jenny at her office, and was a constant source of irritation for her.

Have you confronted the little shit?

That was Haze.

*No, I'm right now giving him an evil
stare until he gets the hint.*

I watched as Jenny's car pulled out of the side street. She
wanted us to think she was in the office. She didn't want us
to know she'd had a meeting at the bank.

Was that enough to take to Haze to make her realise her
best friend might not be as loyal as she thought?

37

9th *March*

Female subject is approached by Barry Fenton as she walks to her car. Microphone picked up below exchange:

BF: There's been a lot of unusual activity around here recently.

Female: Barry, we've been over this. If people are smiling and laughing, it's called having fun.

BF: All these cars and bikes hovering around near your house.

Female: When? What type of cars? You get any registration numbers? Footage?

BF: People coming and going in the middle of the night. Don't think I haven't heard about swinging parties.

Female: Barry, most of us are married with young kids. We barely have the time and energy to shag our own husbands, let alone anyone else's.

BF: I know funny business when I see it. I'm watching you!

Female gets into car and drives off.

12ᵗʰ *March*

Female subject is with Detective Jenny Needham at Carluccio's for lunch. Microphone picked up the following:

Female: . . . Yeah, but then what?
    JN: It has to go with military precision. You overrun by even ten seconds, and that's it.
    Female: What about the other—
    JN: Ruthless. They see weakness, and it's over. You look nervous? You're never nervous.
    Female: It's my first ever parents' evening. I don't want to mess it up!
    JN: Have your questions ready. No small talk. And as soon as that bell goes, you vacate your chair.

(Continued conversation about parent–teacher relations. Absolutely nothing of interest.)

38

Haze

Reggie had only been asleep for twenty minutes when the doorbell started ringing. Sausage did her duty of furiously barking at the intrusion. I shushed her and picked her up before she could wake Reggie and ruin the quiet hour I had planned for myself.

I opened the door to find Alain Drake staring at me. The man from Interpol was here. In England. On my doorstep. I ignored my creeping heart rate and smiled back at him.

'We've met before, haven't we? In Ivrea?'

Drake was wearing another well-cut suit. This time in charcoal grey. 'Correct, Mrs Cabot. Can I come in?'

'Of course!' I opened the door wide and ushered him in. 'It's been a long time! I've had a baby. A whole new baby since we last saw each other.'

'Congratulations,' he said flatly.

'You're French, right? But I heard you speaking Italian at the hospital?'

'I'm French and Belgian. And I speak five languages.'

My bet had been seven.

I led him through to the kitchen.

I knew the house was clean. Not actually clean, but clean of evidence. There was nothing here that would give us away. No wall with pinned-up photos of targets. No cabinet displaying our extensive knife collection. No trophy cabinet of mementos from victims. Nothing that gave us away as anything other than a normal suburban family with two kids and a dog.

Yet everything in me was screaming that him being here was a threat.

'Is your daughter here?'

'No, she's at school. And the baby's asleep upstairs.' I motioned to the baby monitor on the kitchen table. 'Would you like a tea or coffee?'

Drake ignored the question. He wrinkled his nose as he lifted a damp baby toy from a chair and sat down at the table. 'We've had intelligence that suggests the man who was behind your kidnapping is in England.'

I gasped. Perhaps a little over the top. 'That's terrible! Do we need to be worried?' I sat down opposite him and leaned forward. 'Do you think he'll come after us again?'

'We have no evidence that he's after you or your husband, but I thought it was only fair to let you know to be vigilant.'

'We always are. We take our safety very seriously.'

'You'd think this was a safe area.' Drake looked around our marble-topped kitchen. 'But it doesn't seem to be.'

'It is safe! Nothing ever—'

Drake cut me off. 'The Backpacking Butcher.'

'Ah.' Remain calm. Of course Drake knew about him. The Butcher had put this area on the map. International true-crime podcasts had all done special episodes on his killing spree – the highlight being hosts pronouncing Slough, Berkshire, with varying degrees of success. I wasn't worried about him linking the Butcher to us. We had tied up everything ever so neatly. 'It was your car that he died in. Correct?'

So maybe not that neatly.

'Yes. That was very . . . unfortunate. I'm friends with his ex, and she'd borrowed my car to—'

Drake held up a hand. 'I've read the police reports. Interpol were investigating the Butcher for many years.'

The Backpacking Butcher had killed men all over Europe. The occasional clue of a rail ticket or hostel stub had led Interpol to believe that he was backpacking around Europe, killing rich men he happened to come across. We were quite proud of how good we were at hiding our crimes – and even prouder of having pinned them on a dead Bill Grundy.

'It was a very upsetting experience.' I had loved that Range Rover.

'It never felt quite right to me. That man, Bill. He was too sloppy for me. I'd pictured the Butcher as someone with more sophistication.'

I shrugged. 'Killers are killers. A mysterious breed.'

'They're human. Just a little more flawed than the average person.' Drake took a silver cigarette case out of his jacket pocket. 'What's interesting is that the Butcher's victims were all of questionable moral fibre.'

'Really?'

'Yes. Nothing proven, but they'd all had allegations of various sorts made against them.' Drake plucked a cigarette out of the case.

'Maybe Bill, being a former police officer, would've known about that and thought he was doing good by killing them.'

'A violent killer with morals? A ridiculous notion, don't you think?'

I chewed on the inside of my cheek. I had plenty to say on that subject. 'It's not really my area of expertise.'

Drake tapped his unlit cigarette on the table and stood up. 'It's funny that you're this nice couple living in the suburbs, never been in trouble with the law. Yet you have this brush with a serial killer last year, and then this year you're kidnapped by men with ties to violent European gangs.'

'We've certainly had bad luck!'

Drake kept staring at me.

'I just count our blessings. Two beautiful, healthy children. This lovely house.'

Drake was staring at the laundry I had drying from the designer standing light by the sofa. Three Baby-gros, two of my bras and one of Fox's shirts were hanging from its black metal arms.

'We're doing okay,' I continued. 'Although my poor husband has been struggling. He's in therapy.' Finally, his therapist could be useful. 'It was quite an ordeal for him.'

'But not for you?' Drake tilted his head.

'I wasn't hurt like he was. And you know I had blackouts. Not remembering everything has made it much easier processing it all.'

'If you see anyone you recognise from Ivrea, if you notice anyone new hanging around either of you, then please call me.' He put his card on the table. 'Intelligence shows that the man behind the attack in Ivrea is leaving the business. Whatever he's here for is our last chance to bring him to justice. And I'm sure you want him caught so you can go back to your nice, normal life in peace.'

Drake clearly didn't believe we were a sweet, innocent couple caught up in something bigger than we understood. But our previous international crimes had been carefully pinned on a dead man. He'd have no reason to look into the past – would he?

I showed him out and closed the front door behind him, then slumped back against it.

The Chameleon. And the Interpol agent. Both far too interested in us.

Drake being here, sniffing around our family, was dangerous.

My phone pinged.

*Here's a poll to mark what dates
you can do for dinner at ours!*

For fuck's sake.

Not now, Frederica.

She'd given fourteen options. Was it believable that I'd be busy for all of them?

I ignored her message and texted my group chat with Fox and Jenny.

*That Interpol agent Drake came to see me.
That awful man behind Ivrea is in England!*

We always texted each other as if our phone records could one day be read out in court.

Fox pinged back right away.

*Oh honey. Are you okay?
Do you want me to come home?*

Then Jenny:

Babe, that's so scary. Let's all have dinner together tonight.

I took a deep breath. It was going to be fine. We had each other. We'd talk it through. We'd find our weaknesses and protect ourselves.

My phone rang as I was gripping it. Hamish from the gallery. I picked up.

'Darling, you're not going to like this. Not one bit.'

'That's not a good way to start a call, Hamish.'

'I've sent you a video of an interview with Kristoff Klein. He's a new up-and-coming Algerian artist who's getting a lot of buzz.'

'I'm not going to be jealous of every bright new thing making their way up. I'm a bigger person than that. I celebrate those—'

'Just watch the video.' Hamish hung up.

Ping. My phone went again.

Class 1RM, Caroline Wilfie Mum Class Rep:
Don't forget it's International Day tomorrow.
As always, homemade costumes preferred!

I gritted my teeth, and forwarded the message to Fox with a series of expletives and question marks. Let him deal with how to fashion an American flag out of coloured felt and a glue gun.

Then I clicked on the video link Hamish had sent. Kristoff had spiky blue hair, blue eyeshadow, blue lipstick and thickset glasses. He couldn't have been more than twenty-three. He was talking about his process as he walked the interviewer round his loft studio. God, he was so pretentious.

'*I am the voice of my generation, chronicling our loves, our hates, our passions. We are messy and unafraid.*'

The camera moved past his face to linger on two of his canvases hanging on the back wall. I zoomed in on them and frowned. They looked near identical to two of my canvases. My *Beat It* (2014) and *Bite Me* (2018) were not as well-known as some of my other works, but were still lauded and both had sold for large sums. Kristoff had used the same colour palettes for each, and had mimicked my painting style. There was even a screwed-up rag in the centre of the larger canvas.

It was painstakingly clear to me that the four-eyed Smurf had ripped off my work.

I rang Hamish back. 'What the actual fuck? What can we do? Kill him? Sue him?'

I was cut off from Hamish's response by the high-pitched wail of the baby monitor. A hurried goodbye, and I went to get Reggie.

I channelled my rage at the copycat by spending the afternoon finishing my new painting, while imagining the different ways in which I could inflict pain on him. I rocked Reggie's bouncy chair with my foot and alternated making silly faces at him with each ferocious brushstroke.

My art. My baby. I knew what I needed to feel better. Couldn't Fox work out the same? To help yourself you needed to know yourself. A serial killer wasn't ever going to find peace in downward dog and the broken chords of U2's 'With or Without You'. Why couldn't he see that?

39

Fox

I'd come home from work to find Haze and Jenny in the kitchen. The kids were already in bed and a Thai takeaway was laid out, with the table set for three. They had at least waited for me before digging into the spring rolls and divulging the latest on Drake.

I hadn't yet told Haze about Jenny lying to us about being at the bank. With Haze being so dismissive last time I'd caught Jenny in a lie, I wanted to go to her with more evidence. Not a story she could rebuff by saying perhaps Jenny was too embarrassed to tell us she had money issues.

'Drake has been at the station,' announced Jenny. 'He's been asking for everything we have on Bill. He mentioned to my boss something about Interpol wanting to finally close their file on the Butcher.'

'Haven't they already closed it?' I asked.

'Not according to Drake.'

'Fuck.'

Jenny shrugged. 'He won't find anything. I've checked everything a hundred times. We tied everything up.'

Who should we fear more? The shadowy Chameleon who

was hoping to kill us, or the tenacious Interpol agent who was trying to catch us?

I felt that the younger me might have relished this challenge. Coming up against two sparring opponents and getting the better of them both. What a thrill! Adrenalin burning. The race to win. But old me was just too tired by it all. It was too much to handle. I felt like I needed to get away from it all. But how to take a holiday from anxiety?

'What about the bodies?' I asked. Drake was sniffing around, and we'd disposed of two corpses in the last two weeks.

'Both dump sites are clear, and neither Clark nor Danny have been reported missing yet. But even when they are, there's nothing linking us to them.'

'The party is in nine days.' I shook my head. 'We don't have long to work out what exactly we're walking into.'

Jenny flipped open her notebook. 'Benjamin Norwood said he lets an events company run Restore Glory events for him. Unique Events is the company Danny said he was working for, right?'

Haze nodded. 'I met him at their offices.'

'Unique Events is registered in the Cayman Islands. I looked through all the paperwork, and there's no individual named in any of the documentation. It was all done through their lawyers, Backhouse Dunne.'

Haze got to her feet. 'What the fuck?'

Jenny looked between us. 'What?'

We filled her in on the drama with Bibi and Ted and the icy Diana Morgan.

Jenny chewed on the end of her pen. 'Backhouse Dunne is a massive law firm. It's got a reputation for representing all manner of dodgy clients. I don't think a woman is engineering your downfall because of a four-year-old's playground dispute.'

'You haven't met her!' Haze snorted. 'And don't underestimate what a mother would do for her child. She's already coming after us through planning permissions.'

'The timing doesn't fit,' I reminded her. 'The Chameleon was already in the country and coming after us to go to Balgray before Punchgate.'

Haze sat back down. 'Okay, but I say we destroy her too, for getting us on the council's radar.'

Jenny patted her hand. 'Let's just get through this Chameleon threat first. Unique Events don't have a website, and they don't seem to have put on any events other than ones for Restore Glory.'

'Norwood said they approached him and don't charge anything for their services, as it's for charity.' Something in my muddled brain sparked. Something that seemed to fit. 'They're a shadowy company who organise events for rich criminals to attend. The Corporation is a shadowy organisation who work with criminals.'

Jenny looked up at me. 'They're one and the same?'

'And that's why The Chameleon wants us to meet there,' said Haze. 'He knows it's a secure location, as it's an event that's been organised by his bosses.'

We were finally getting closer to understanding what lay ahead for us.

Jenny was flicking through her notebook. 'The only thing we really know about The Corporation is that they are discreet. They kill people, but quietly. They're not going to have some big gun fight waiting for you at Balgray.'

'You really think they're using an events company in London as a cover?' Haze frowned. 'There were lots of people at their office. They didn't look old enough to be part of an international gang.'

Jenny shook her head. 'They could be using freelancers to do their bidding without them having any idea of the bigger picture. The staff there are just organising parties at stately homes. They wouldn't know who they're really working for, or how the company is being used.'

Jenny had mentioned previously that The Corporation has been so hard to pin down and track because there was no money trail to follow. Unique Events put on the parties and organised ticket sales. Something clicked. 'It's a perfect front for money laundering.'

Jenny nodded. 'There are lots of different ways they can do it if they're using a charity and criminals are the ones making big donations.'

David and Goliath. That's what it was starting to feel like. Our little kitchen-table trio up against the might of an international gang.

Jenny looked at her notebook. 'Did you see that it's a masquerade ball? Convenient, considering the clientele.'

I shook my head. 'We're turning up to a party where we can't see who anyone is; we just know that they're likely to be linked to a gang that want us dead.'

Haze frowned.

It was good she was taking it seriously.

'What am I going to wear?' she murmured.

Or not.

I was feeling a little light-headed. I started stabbing at the pad Thai as they compared ideas on outfits that 'shouted slay' and were also 'comfortable enough to slay in'.

I chewed on the noodles. I hadn't had one of my funny blackouts in days. Maybe they were finally over?

Haze and Jenny were huddled together, cackling and looking at photos on Jenny's phone. Why did *I* sometimes feel like the third wheel? Had Haze told Jenny about Clark Dixon? About how I hadn't been able to finish him? Had they been laughing together over my impotence? Was my new weakness something they bonded over, mocking the big man who was now a big flop?

Haze put two spring rolls onto my plate without pausing her conversation with Jenny. She moved the sweet chilli sauce towards me, knowing I couldn't eat them without it.

No, she wouldn't mock me behind my back. My weakness was her weakness. We were one. If I looked bad, she looked bad.

I might be constantly questioning myself, but I didn't need to question my wife's loyalty.

I woke up in the middle of the night in a panic about where I was. It took a moment, but then I realised – it was okay. I was in bed. I lay back on my pillow before bolting upright again. Tomorrow was bin day. After coming home to the horrors of hearing that Drake had been here, in our home, I'd been more than a little distracted.

I headed down to the kitchen in my dressing gown and slipped on my loafers by the door. I wheeled out the trash can from the side of our house and on to our drive. It was still dark. Streetlights on. The road quiet and empty. I heard a noise down by the Campbells' house. Was someone there? I stood, staring into the darkness.

What would I do? Give chase in my dressing gown?

It was 1.05am. A teenager could be creeping back to bed. I didn't have to see everything as a threat. But I *felt* it. Someone was out there, watching us. Watching the house.

This was what our life choices had resulted in.

We'd tried to have it all, and look what we'd brought to our door.

I couldn't entertain the thought of giving it all up. It hadn't gone so well last time we'd tried. And we were making a difference. We were doing good things. I wanted to leave a legacy for my children. Make my mark on the world by making it a better place. Yes, it was one I couldn't ever shout about. But maybe after Haze and I were dead we could let them know. A sealed letter, explaining the good we'd done. Haze would roll her eyes at me for being 'so fucking dramatic', but I wanted our children to know us, to truly know us. I just didn't want that to happen until after we were already gone, in case they felt horror, not pride, at our bloodthirsty past.

It was difficult getting back to sleep.

Drake. Was he on to us?

The Chameleon. Was he coming for us?

Bibi. Had she inherited our violent streak?

Jenny. Was she betraying us?

Clark. Why hadn't I been able to finish him?

Mike. When was I going to tell Haze?

I lay staring at the ceiling trying to calm my mind. Deep breaths as I started to drift off. I'd made a decision. I might not be able to get answers to all the questions I had racing around my head, but I could at least get a handle on one.

Tomorrow, I would tell her about Mike. She would understand that what I'd done had come from a place of love. It was going to be okay. And if it wasn't? Well, she'd have to forgive me, as we were about to come head to head with the biggest threat we'd ever faced.

40

Haze

Today we were heading to Balgray Hall for a conference and a chance to snoop around the building. 'No time lost in reconnaissance,' old Fox would say. Current Fox was giving himself a pep talk in the bathroom mirror. He was running the taps to try and drown out the sound of one of his ridiculous recordings.

I was spooning porridge into Reggie while Bibi was feeding toast to Pinga, her fluffy penguin. Around its neck was a silver pendant. Why did her soft toy have jewellery? I frowned at it, until I remembered it was Bibi's lucky charm. She'd found it when we were at the hospital in Ivrea.

'You remember getting this?' I tapped it.

'Yes. When Dada was in hospital.' Bibi looked at her penguin's necklace. 'The fairies gave it to me.'

I smiled to myself. Last month she'd had a twenty-minute conversation with her imaginary friend Princess Snufflepot where they bonded over their hatred of cooked carrots. I hoped she kept believing in fairies, and magical things, and anything brighter than the reality of the sad, grey world we lived in.

Once we'd dropped Bibi at school, we headed straight to Balgray, Reggie gurgling away in the back seat. Jenny had assured me he would be welcome too.

Sorry I can't make it. School cake sale.

Jenny had texted that an hour ago. I wanted to believe that Fox niggling away at me with his ridiculous suspicions about her was just the jealousy talking. But this was unlike Jenny. She was, what? Volunteering at a cake sale rather than helping us plan our potential escape routes from The Chameleon? Maybe Felix had got into trouble. Maybe he'd guilt-tripped her into being there for him for something. But if that was true, why wouldn't she have just said that? I would've understood. We were in this together, weren't we? And there was nothing more important than protecting us from the person who had us in their crosshairs.

I tried not to think about how Jenny knew all our history. Last year, we'd given her a list of every man we'd eliminated on foreign soil. The details of how and where. It was for our own protection. We'd armed her with information on our every kill in case she had any insight into what could give us away.

She knew everything – but she would never betray us.

If there was someone in our life reporting our every move to The Chameleon, we hadn't found them yet.

My phone pinged. I looked down at it. Frederica, confirming plans for our double date tomorrow night. I'd only agreed as she was so persistent. I had no way of getting out of it, short of admitting we would rather watch Netflix than hang out with them. And upsetting the queen bee of the school mums could have repercussions for Bibi – I didn't want her to be blacklisted from parties for having an antisocial mother. Especially as Diana Morgan was clearly determined to make my life hell. How long until she tried to turn the other mothers against me? Although, in fairness, I wouldn't notice – Frederica was the only one who seemed determined to get to know me.

Frederica. Wanting to be friends. Someone who had recently inserted themselves into our lives. We'd always said The Chameleon could be a woman. There was every chance the criminal mastermind, a subcontractor of services for the most dangerous European gangs, could be female. And Frederica was steely. She was a formidable new arrival at the school gates. Almost as if she had experience of navigating complicated groups and how best to rise within them. Jenny had written her off as being just another mum, but she hadn't met her.

I comforted myself with the thought that this dinner had now gone from being a boring duty to another reconnaissance mission.

We arrived at Balgray Hall to find it busy. Very busy. It was mostly women. A surprising number of them had brought babies and toddlers with them. I walked up to the sign by the front door of the Hall.

Parenting top tips with US bestselling author and mindful parenting coach Bells Brightley.

It became clear why Jenny had failed to tell me exactly what kind of 'conference' we were attending. I turned to Fox. 'Bells is one of those nutters who loves everything to do with kids.'

'What's wrong with—'

'You know what I mean. She embraces every shit stain.'

I put on an American accent. 'You are a mama now. Be grateful. Be present. Meditate.' I shuddered. 'What even is mindfulness? I'm mindful of how fucking tired I am.'

We walked into the ballroom. A small stage had been set up at the back with a large screen behind it. Rows of chairs were laid out, nearly all of which were already full. Every row had at least one person with a baby or toddler on their lap. It looked like Fox was one of only four men here.

I was wearing a baby carrier with Reggie snuggled inside. It felt like I'd strapped him to me to announce to the world my eligibility for being inside a room of simpering parents.

Fox looked around. 'Wow. She's popular. There must be more than two hundred people here.'

'She has three million Instagram followers. She lives on a farm in the Midwest, and it's all homemade, everything. No help. Being with the kids twenty-four/seven. Still managing to look perfect. Still managing to run her reassuringly expensive homewares shop. Sitting at a pottery wheel making perfect vases while breastfeeding. Never raises her voice. Never shows any sign of being a normal human being who regularly loses her shit. I hate her.'

'If you hate her, why do you know so much about her?'

My husband really was clueless. 'Come on! Everyone knows we love watching people we hate.'

Bells walked on to the stage to enthusiastic applause. She was a blonde wisp of a woman in a flowered dress and cowboy boots. She always looked tiny in her photos when standing next to her hulking six-foot-five former-American-football-player husband and their children (all born naturally at over ten pounds without even a helpful Panadol).

'Hello, darlings! It means so much that you're here, and I love that so many of you have brought your precious little ones.' Bells clasped her hands to her chest. 'We don't trust our children to anyone outside our family. My mother has been a huge support. Blood looks after blood.'

There was a cheer from the crowd. I rolled my eyes.

'I love that my children need me so much. Hearing them call to me, at all hours, no matter the time, I can't help but think how blessed I am.'

I leaned over to Fox. 'She must be on drugs. No one enjoys being woken up all night.'

Fox scanned the ballroom. 'This is where the main dinner will be. If The Chameleon is going to try anything, surely it won't be in here?' He shook his head. 'The fact everyone will be wearing masks means he wouldn't necessarily even be able to find us.'

I was annoyed that Fox wasn't engaging with my commentary on the rubbish Bells was spouting, but in fairness I couldn't complain. He was focusing on the job at hand. I tried to do the same.

'The auction is happening in the library.' I remembered the evening's programme from the booklet I'd stolen. 'We should check it out.'

We slipped out of the ballroom as Bells was saying, 'My husband is the head of the family, and I am the heart.' I dug my fingernails into my palms and took deep breaths. Reggie could feel me tensing and looked up at me. I gave his little head a kiss. I loved my kids my way. I hated being told how best to raise them. It was, though, hard to argue that Bells should keep her stupid opinions to herself, given that so many people seemed to want to hear them.

The library was closed off for today's events, with a red rope blocking access. Not quite enough to scare us off. We slipped behind it and into the library.

Reggie was gurgling. I jigged him up and down as we walked past the mahogany bookcase-lined walls.

I looked around. 'If things go to shit in the ballroom, this is our easiest route out. There's a back room leading to an outside door.' Jenny had found an old floorplan online, which we were now well versed in.

At the very back of the library was a heavy oak door. 'Let's give this a try.' I turned the handle and it loudly swung open to reveal a small snug filled with a few ratty old armchairs.

'What are you doing here?' A woman in her fifties was staring at us. On the floor were two toddler boys plugged into iPads.

'We're looking for the changing facilities.' I tilted Reggie slightly towards them to prove we had a real live baby with us.

'It's right by the ballroom.' The woman saw me looking at the children and moved to stand in front of them. 'You'd better head back so you don't miss any more of Bells's talk.'

The bigger kid was wearing a Spiderman T-shirt. He had ruffled blond hair and a couple of moles on his right cheek. I stared at him. '*We don't call them moles, we call them beauty spots, as they just add to his gorgeous good looks.*'

I knew this boy!

The smaller kid had luscious golden locks, which were half up in a man bun. Or, I guess, boy bun. '*Our homemade goat's-milk hair mask is what gives his hair this beautiful shine.*' They were brothers!

I hadn't recognised them straight away as I'd only ever seen them with wooden toys or chasing after chickens while dressed in matching checked shirts.

Bells's middle two boys.

On devices.

This was just great.

'These are Bells's children?

I pointed at them.

'They're actually on a mindfulness app,' she said just as the unmistakable sounds of the Spiderman theme tune rang out. She winced.

'And you work for Bells as . . .?'

'I'm Bells's . . . helper.'

'You mean nanny?'

'No, that's not a word we'd use.'

'But you help her with the children.'

'Among other things.'

I shook my head. 'You're telling me that she's out there implying she's winning at parenting through mindfulness and dedication and not missing a second of her children's lives, but really she's cheating? She has a *nanny*?'

The door to the outside swung open.

'Have you seen the steriliser?' Another woman walked in, clutching a baby. Bells's baby.

I laughed. 'Oh, wow – two nannies! And not a helpful granny in sight!'

'Please, you can't tell anyone about this,' said Nanny Number One. 'Bells's mother moved to Barbados a while ago.'

'Probably to avoid the grandchildren,' muttered Nanny Number Two.

'She should be ashamed of herself,' I said. 'Making other women feel inadequate for not doing enough. You should write an exposé.'

The two women glanced at each other.

'We've signed NDAs,' said the first nanny.

'The amount of money you'd make from whatever you have to say would be enough to fight any lawyers she sets on you! Think of the women you could help!'

Nanny Number One was nodding. 'That's a good—'

Fox cut her off. 'How did you guys get in here without anyone seeing you?'

'There's an underground passage that leads to that little forest at the back of the house,' said Nanny Number Two.

Fox looked between them both. 'Show us where, and we will promise to keep your secret.'

41

Fox

We were driving back from Balgray. Finding a hidden exit had made us both feel better about the approaching showdown – although Haze seemed to get even more joy from discovering that an Instagram stranger was living a lie. She was singing along to a Gracie Abrams song. What she lacked in tune, she made up for in sass. Reggie was fast asleep in his car seat.

Mike had asked me to meet him tomorrow.

It was now or never.

'I'm driving the car, so if you hit me it will be dangerous.' I kept staring at the motorway. 'And our baby son is in the back of the car.'

'What are you talking about?' Haze spun round to look at me. 'What have you done?'

I needed to say it fast. Like ripping off a band-aid. 'I sent one of your hairs to Find My Heritage, and it matched you with your father. I've been talking to him. He never knew about you. He's called Mike Martin. Seventy-four. Lives in Scotland. Married. No children.' I stumbled. 'No other children. Seems a very nice man. He's in Berkshire tomorrow and wants to meet you.' I clenched the steering wheel and risked a look at her.

Her face had paled. 'You found my father.'

'Because I love you! It's about love. I just wanted to help.' She kept staring straight ahead. A beat of silence. Then another. It was worse than shouting. 'Please understand, I–'

'What does he do?' Her voice was quiet and level.

'He's a retired accountant.'

She frowned. 'That sounds ridiculous.'

'It's quite a normal career path, I think.'

'How can *I* have an accountant's genes?'

This was going better than I'd expected. 'So, do you want to meet him?'

She remained silent.

'I know we've got a lot on at the moment, but he lives on this Scottish island that's a real pain to get to, and he's not sure when he'll next be over this way.'

I handed her my phone and let her look through my messages with Mike.

'Harriet? Harriet Smith? Really?' She scrolled down and came across a conversation about hobbies. 'I like cooking and long walks in the park? Jesus. Couldn't you do a better job of being me?' She zoomed in on the photos of him. 'What about the timing? Don't you think—'

'I logged you on the system a while ago. Mike only joined a few months back.'

'You kept it from me for this long?' Her eyes flashed as she turned to me.

'I wanted to make sure he was worth knowing!' I kept talking. Listing everything I knew about Mike, the research I'd done online, the Facebook account that showed charming photos of him visiting nice gardens with his wife, a ruddy-faced woman with a warm smile. A large fish he'd caught on a fishing trip with some other grey-haired men. How he steered away from politics and always posted links to his friends' Just Giving fundraisers for marathons or fun runs they were doing.

Haze listened to all of this silently.

I stopped to draw breath.

'He doesn't sound anything like me!'

'Little one, no one is like you!'

Haze was staring ahead now, chewing on her lip. 'What did we say about secrets? We shouldn't have any!'

'I know! I agree. Absolutely. But this was only a temporary secret until I knew he was worth knowing.' I took our turning off the motorway and looked over at her. 'Are you telling me you don't have a single secret from me?'

Haze was silent.

'Haze?'

She sighed. 'Bibi saw me covered in blood in the utility room after I'd killed Clark.'

My mouth dropped open.

'And she was drawing pictures of me covered in blood at school. Her teacher was worried. But I've sorted it. Told him it was about my period. I've talked to Bibi, and she's not traumatised – and she's not drawing any more pictures. Everything is fine.'

I was struggling to hold it together. Our precious Bibi had seen Haze post-kill? How much therapy was she going to need?

'Don't you think—'

Haze cut me off. 'Isn't stealing someone's DNA a crime?'

I felt we were going to call a truce on the being upfront with each other issue.

We drove the rest of the way home in silence.

* * *

The next morning, Haze seemed calm. I wasn't sure she wasn't in shock. She'd texted Mike when we'd got home yesterday, and had arranged to meet him at 10am on the high street. We'd decided she would go alone, but that Jenny and I would be at home waiting for her to get back, ready to jump in the car for moral support if needed.

I sent her off with two coffees and a hug. She looked a bit of a mess, for her. Perhaps she hadn't slept well.

Jenny arrived just as she was leaving. Another hug and more wishes of good luck, and Haze was on her way.

'This is a big moment!' Jenny said, turning to me. 'I can't believe you found him! And that she actually wanted to meet him.'

I was feeling good. It was like I knew what Haze needed better than she did. She never would've tried to find her father. She hadn't wanted to even think about him. But I'd done it for her. I'd taken the decision away from her.

Jenny took a sip of tea as we settled down to wait for Haze. 'What checks did you do on him?'

'Online ones. Enough to confirm he was who he said he was.'

'Great. Always good to be careful. What kind of things?'

'His Facebook profile. Google searches. And then there's the emails and texts. He gave me a lot of detail on his life. I verified it with company websites.'

'Reverse image search?'

'Yes! I did that. Didn't turn up anything I hadn't found already.'

'And the fake photo doctor?'

'The what?'

'You know, that software that checks if an image has been manipulated using AI or by distorting existing images to show what you want?'

'I . . . I hadn't heard of that.'

Jenny chewed on her lip. 'Bad people have you on their radar. There's no telling what they'd do to mess with you.'

'Right.' I stared at my coffee mug. The good feeling was fast evaporating. 'As we're waiting, you might as well, you know, run the images through that photo doctor thing?'

Jenny was already opening her laptop. She tapped a few buttons. 'Is this his Facebook profile?' She showed me the screen.

'That's it.'

'It'll just take a few minutes.'

I was starting to feel a little sick.

42

Haze

Bibi's childhood had imaginary friends. Mine had an imaginary dad. Today, for the first time, he'd be real. Flesh and bone. I thought I'd get through life never even knowing his name but today I'd be sitting down opposite him. It was long overdue and yet too soon.

It felt weird to dress up for this occasion, so I'd dressed down. Minimal make-up, and tracksuit bottoms and a hoodie. I was meeting Mike at Bridget's Books. There was a downstairs café I'd been to a few times before where the tables were spaced quite far apart and it was always busy enough that no one could overhear neighbouring conversations.

A private meeting in a public place. A blind date with my father.

I'd seen enough photos of him by now that I knew I could recognise him. Fuzzy grey hair and a beard. Looked nothing like me. I didn't know what I really expected, but it wasn't him.

It took a while to find a parking space. I was going to be a little late, but what did a few more minutes matter at this point?

I tried to think about what I was going to ask him as I put

my phone on flight mode. Whatever he had to say, I was going to listen. I wasn't going to get distracted by an Instagram notification.

Growing up, I'd hated him. My mother had never told me anything about him, but somehow in my head I'd created him. He was a cold, unfeeling monster with a black moustache that he'd twirl. I could never remember which film baddie it was that I'd based him on. I'd picture my mother, her belly swollen with me, going to see him to tell him their happy news. He'd spit in her face, tell her he didn't care and laugh as she ran away, crying.

When life wasn't going your way, you tried to understand why. Blaming a person was easier – misfortunes happened due to someone else's unpleasantness and poor character. Somehow, that was easier to accept than something as random and nonsensical as 'bad luck'. You couldn't lash out at 'bad luck'. You couldn't make 'bad luck' pay.

Mike had said that he never knew about me. My mother had never told him. If that was true, then he wasn't the bad guy that chose to abandon me. He was just a normal guy who was living his life, oblivious to everything I'd been going through. I couldn't go barrelling in there furious. We were both in the same position. We'd both been deprived of each other's company. This was a meeting of equals, and of strangers. We would each be assessing the other.

I chewed on the inside of my cheek. What if he didn't like me? Normally, parents met their kid when they were born and instinctively loved them. A parental bond arrived at birth. It was against the natural order to wait until the baby was a fully grown adult, then meet for a cappuccino and a croissant. I was finally meeting my dad, and the first five minutes would be small talk about how hard it was to find a parking space.

I knew from the Facebook photos that he liked fishing. Maybe I could google some fishing facts to drop in.

Fuck.

This was going to be awkward.

Hopefully, I'd find out he did know about me after all.

I was better at being angry.

I looked up at the 'Bridget's Books' sign.

I was here.

No backing out now.

A car was speeding down the road towards me, its horn beeping repeatedly. Fox's car. He screeched to a halt alongside me. 'Get in!'

I didn't have time to think. I just did what he said. I jumped into the passenger seat, and he was setting off again before the door was even closed.

'What the hell is happening?' My heart was hammering.

'I messed up.' Fox's voice was shaking as his hands gripped the wheel. 'I wasn't thorough enough. I let you down. I let myself down!' He shook his head and kept talking at high speed. 'I was so caught up in all the rubbish I've had going on. I should've asked Jenny! But I was trying to prove we didn't always need Jenny!'

He explained to me something about a fake photo doctor, about a back-to-front image, about extensive software to check for manipulated images. He said all kinds of technical things that neither of us understood. But the message was simple.

Mike Martin did not exist.

And that was it.

I was back to having an imaginary father.

I'd barely had time to adjust to the gain before he was once again lost to me.

Fox was so angry at himself, I couldn't be angry at him too.

I listened as he went on about Jenny checking the surrounding streets' CCTV.

Fifteen minutes ago, a black van had arrived at the back of the
bookshop. Right by the café's fire exit. She couldn't get a visual
on the driver, and the numberplate was half obscured by mud.

'This is it, Haze! I can't carry on like this. I'm never going
to let you down again. I promise!'

I looked at him. Was this the breakthrough I'd been waiting for?

'Don't blame yourself. There's only one person to blame.'
I pulled out my phone.

> *Making up a fake dad? You sick fuck!*
> *If you want to take me,*
> *come get me. Let's end this!!*

The reply was instant.

You should be more careful.

> *You're giving me advice? Are you fucking*
> *kidding me? I can't wait to kill you.*

Patience is a virtue.

I threw my phone down.

My hands were now shaking. I let it all hit me. The antici-
pation, the slight adrenalin kick, the nerves. Everything that
had been stirred up at the thought I was going to come face
to face with the man whose genes I shared.

I was angry.
So fucking angry.

But what else?

Disappointed?

No.

I'd left the house thinking I was going to meet my father, but it was all a mind game from The Chameleon.

I should be feeling crushed. Robbed. I was back to 'father unknown'.

But right now I was safe. Driving home with my husband, back to the house we lived in with our children. My real family.

From everything Fox had told me about 'Mike', I had felt no connection, no understanding of the man he was. I wouldn't have to sit through strained chit-chat with a man whose life sounded so vanilla I felt zero affinity to him. I wouldn't have to sit there trying to understand how I could've been fathered by such a steady, balanced man.

And I'd been worrying about what he was going to think of *me*. I'd been worrying what this made-up, AI-generated fake dad was going to think of *me*. Ridiculous.

I laughed and shook my head.

Fox looked at me, his brow furrowed. He thought I'd lost it. That I'd gone mad.

'Of course my father wasn't some angelic man living in a converted lighthouse! I mean, come on! How did we ever believe that?'

Fox reached over and squeezed my hand.

I might have my father's genes, but who I was – who I really was – had happened without his input. My father was as irrelevant today as he had been last week.

When Fox had first mentioned Mike, I'd realised I hadn't thought of my father since childhood. I didn't want to dwell on the idea of a man fathering me and then not wanting to know me. I didn't want to think about how frustrating it was to know nothing about him, not even his name. Today, I'd been forced to confront the idea of him. I'd had to go through all that – and I was fine. Better than fine.

I didn't care.

The Chameleon saw me as a threat. He was trying to spook me. It wasn't going to work. I wasn't going to let my mind get fucked by some sociopathic assassin intent on talking in riddles. I was going to get him at the Balgray party.

I could vanquish my childhood demons by vanquishing this devil in my sights.

43

Fox

Haze had been surprisingly upbeat all day.

It was almost as if she was relieved.

We were in our bedroom getting ready for dinner out. Haze was at her dressing table, applying eyeliner. 'I don't know what I was thinking. I've got this far without a father, why the fuck would I need one now?'

'I'm sorry. Getting taken in by Mike was all my fault.'

Haze looked up at me in the mirror. 'If you go behind my back again, I will cut you.'

I nodded. 'Totally fair enough.'

I was going to do better.

I could see it now. I'd been self-pitying and self-indulgent. Worrying about letting my family down had nearly made me let my family down.

Stop looking inside. Start looking out.

Had I heard that on one of my inspirational recordings, or did I just come up with it myself?

Balgray Hall. We had one week to go. We might still be walking into a trap when we turned up masked and ready to party, but at least we'd now located a hidden exit. If things went bad, we had a way out.

My mood had been helped by the fact that Jenny had undertaken an extensive background search on Sally. She'd checked her bank accounts and gone through her mobile phone records, and had even spent a day following her. According to Jenny, she was clean – except for a couple of reports on questionable conduct, which Jenny couldn't fully access without a warrant. The reports may have been a mild concern, but the main takeaway was that she was a bona fide therapist who did not appear to be involved with any European gangs.

The relief for me was huge.

The doorbell rang, and I went down to let in Jessica, who was going to be babysitting for us. She was the niece of one of our neighbours and charged three times the going rate as she was training to be a Norland Nanny. I was pretty sure their supposedly elite training didn't extend to what to do if an international assassin tried to break in, but we were confident she could hold the fort for the hour and a half we were out at a neighbourhood dinner.

By the time we were standing on the doorstep of a large detached new build on a quiet street, all jagged lines and a glass extension, I realised Haze hadn't fully explained exactly who we were having dinner with.

'Who are these people again?'

'Best-case scenario, they're just school parents who want to be friends. Worst-case, they're working for The Chameleon to bring about our untimely death and destruction.'

The door flung open. 'Welcome!' Frederica was in a tight black dress with a low-cut neckline. 'Come on in.' We followed her into the dining room, and a flurry of hellos were exchanged with her husband Roger, a short man who introduced himself as a 'property magnate'.

The table was only set for four.

'An intimate dinner.' Frederica smiled. 'We don't have staff tonight; we're all alone.'

Frederica kept flicking her hair as Roger droned on about a big property deal he was undertaking with a Russian billionaire. He was a little sketchy on what part he had to play in it all, or what his job actually entailed.

We ate a truffle risotto and made strained small talk, mostly focused on school. I clocked that Haze drank a large gulp of wine every time Frederica mentioned how advanced for their age her children were.

Roger was wearing a patterned shirt that had one too many buttons undone. I had nothing against hairy chests – I just preferred to not be staring at one while I ate.

Frederica leaned towards Haze. 'And how are you doing? I mean, really doing?'

Haze shrugged. 'Same shit, different day.'

Frederica nodded. 'It's so dull, isn't it? This just surviving, not really living.'

Roger took a sip of wine. 'You can understand why people need to shake things up. To try and live a more exciting life. To feel like you're really making the most of this one chance on this earth.'

'Especially when you're hot,' Frederica purred at me as she touched my arm, letting her hand linger there.

I dropped my fork. 'I . . . Yes, it's important to feel you're getting the most you can from life.'

Luckily for Frederica, she removed her hand before Haze's fork stabbed it.

Roger smiled at Fox. 'I knew you'd understand how vital it

is to have certain excitements to help you feel alive. To stray from the status quo.'

Frederica played with a lock of her hair, curling a tendril around her finger. 'We've been looking for a couple like you. We feel that you're more like us than you probably realise.'

Roger nodded. 'We all have a dangerous side. Some of us lean into it more than others.'

'We know certain things about you. We have a similar hobby in common.' Frederica smiled.

Haze and I looked at each other. They couldn't be – could they?

What were the chances of two serial-killing couples living in the same neighbourhood? I'd say slim to none. But I guess not impossible.

'We don't want to be competition for each other,' Frederica said.

'That would not end well for you.' Roger put his arm around his wife.

Were they outing themselves as worthy opponents? Or wanting to get their freak on?

They were giving very mixed messages.

Frederica and Roger both stood. 'We'll leave you for a moment. We need to get dessert.'

We watched them go through to the kitchen and speak quietly to each other as the door swung back behind them.

Haze turned to me and whispered, 'Do they want to fuck us or kill us?'

I shrugged. 'It's not clear, is it?'

Haze yawned. 'I'm really not up for either.'

I could understand if they'd got wind of the killer part to our personalities. From the sound of Roger's dodgy business, it wasn't a stretch to believe he'd had brushes with The

Corporation. But what about us made it seem like we'd be into swinging? Unless they always invited over couples they didn't know and hoped for the best.

Haze stared at the closed kitchen door. 'Frederica and Roger could be working for The Chameleon. They could be the ones watching us and messing in our lives.'

I nodded. 'Jenny needs to look into him. He could have all kinds of dark contacts who may have got wind of what we've been up to.'

'Whatever they're after, let's not stick around to find out.'

The door opened and they both walked back in, now holding a can of whipped cream and a bowl of strawberries. I couldn't be sure, but it looked as if Roger had undone another button on his shirt.

Haze stood up. 'We're so sorry, but the babysitter can't get the baby to settle. We need to leave.'

'That's such a shame! We were just getting comfortable,' said Frederica, as she followed us into the hallway.

We said our goodbyes fast, without using eye contact, and were out of their front door before we'd even put our coats on. As I helped Haze into hers, I noticed a white moped parked up opposite the house. The helmeted rider sat atop it, staring at us. The numberplate was indistinguishable thanks to the artfully placed thick smear of mud across it.

I took a step towards him. He started the engine and drove off with a backward glance. Was he a henchman who was bad at covert surveillance, or did The Chameleon want us to know we were being watched?

44

Haze

I woke up to a text from Frederica gushing about how wonderful last night's dinner had been and how we must get another date in the diary. Despite further debating it when we got home, we were still no clearer to understanding if their interest in us was down to lust or bloodlust. But it had to be one of them as there was no way anyone could sit through an evening of inane small talk and want to do it all over again soon.

Tonight we were going to my gallery for a drinks reception. Hamish had messaged repeatedly saying I needed to come as he'd forgotten what I looked like, and we had things to discuss.

I'd slipped into a green minidress and made an effort with my make-up. It had taken longer than expected, and I'd had to rush to pick-up. At the last minute, I'd taken Danny's gun from its hiding place in Fox's office and put it in my tote bag. People often kept mementos from an ex. A gun was more useful than sentimental. People were watching us, and they might need some encouragement to stop.

'I really respect how you wear whatever you want.' This

was offered up by the thin-faced blonde mother standing next to me at the school gates.

I shrugged. 'Well, obviously.'

'Some women your age would freak out, thinking it was too young for them. But you just do what you want and that's so brave.'

This crazy woman was congratulating me for wearing a minidress? Then I saw it. The triumph in her eyes. Oh, she was trying to shame me? Really? She was dissing me, and I had a gun in my bag?

The gates opened and children streamed out before I could retaliate.

And then I felt it.

The first tickle of self-doubt.

Fuck her.

This was new. I did what I wanted, I wore what I wanted and I didn't care what people thought. How was she piercing my confident armour of not giving a flying fuck? I wasn't proud of much, but I was proud of being unapologetically me. Maybe I was tired. Feeling rundown. More vulnerable. Goddammit. To do everything I needed to do, I needed to believe in myself. That had always got me through everything.

My age was not going to be something to get insecure about.

I remembered an Instagram reel I'd watched the other day where a woman in her forties had compared trying to put eyeshadow on her eyelids to colouring in a ball sack.

Is that what I had to look forward to? Ball-sack eyes?

No.

Absolutely not.

If I ever stopped liking what I saw in the mirror, I'd stop looking. Focus on my art. My children. Looks fade. Big fucking deal. I had plenty more awesome to enjoy. Unlike that miserable cow at the school gates trying to do others down.

I was still cursing that blonde bitch by the time I got back home. Jessica was arriving just as I pulled in. She never really smiled and didn't even seem to like kids, but Bibi didn't complain at seeing her, which was a positive sign. We couldn't rely on Jenny and her parents for everything, and at least Jessica was a professional – she was being officially taught how to look after kids, while I was just winging it. I opened the door for us all and waved goodbye to Bibi and Reggie.

Fox was waiting for me outside the gallery. He didn't see me approaching from the opposite side of the street, so I got to watch him looking for me. Handsome in his suit. He never felt the need to stare at his phone, to fidget. He smiled when he finally saw me. I kissed him long and hard.

'Good to see you too.' Fox tapped my nose.

Last night, I'd only had to wake up for Reggie once, and good sleep was really helping me like my husband more. Without meaning to, The Chameleon and Mike Martin had helped us. Killer Fox was coming back to me. I could see it in his eyes. They were clearer, more focused; there was less staring off into the distance. His fuck-up had unfucked him. Hah. I should be the one trying to write poetry.

We held hands and walked into the bustling gallery.

I took a glass of champagne from the waiter by the door and looked for Hamish. He spotted us from the other side of the room and rushed over, air-kissing us both.

'I have an update on Kristoff.'

I clenched my glass a little harder. 'I hate that fucking waste-of-space copycat fraud. He's a fucking disgrace. He should—'

'He's dead.'

'Oh.'

'He was on acid and having drinks on the roof garden of his apartment building. Got asked by a friend if he could fly, and . . . well, he couldn't fly.'

It was quite something wishing someone dead and then finding out they were actually dead. I mean, obviously, this had happened to me quite a lot. But this was the first time without my involvement. And now I had to pretend I felt something other than creeping glee.

'Terrible,' I managed to muster. 'Drugs are very dangerous.'

'It's a big shock for everyone, but . . .' Hamish stopped as he debated whether it was too soon, and then decided to go with it. 'I suppose at least, you know, that drama is all behind us.'

'That is true.' The three of us all nodded.

I wasn't about to mourn a guy I'd never met, especially one who'd so clearly ripped off my work. But what were the chances of someone who'd so recently pissed me off professionally happening to die in a drug-induced accident? Judging by Fox's frown, it was niggling him too.

'On to brighter news: there's a big art collector who seems to have fallen in love with your work. They bought one of your paintings last month and are now wanting to buy up anything else still available. They've even asked if I can ask the owners of sold pieces if they'd be willing to sell them!'

I waited to feel it. That glow of knowing someone loved your work. That they understood your vision, your passion, what you wanted to scream to the world. But it did not come.

It was because I knew the timing sucked. Someone was after us. And now someone wanted to buy as much of my art as they could? My paintings held our secrets. I had to presume Interpol didn't have the resources to buy them. My work was not cheap, and spending hundreds of thousands on art was a tricky purchase to expense. That left The Chameleon. If he was buying them all up, what was he planning?

'Amazing news!' Fox remained straight-faced as he patted Hamish on the back. 'I'm not surprised, of course. She's one hell of a talent!' He caught my eye as I took a glug of champagne.

'This is great to hear, Hamish,' I said. 'Do you know the name of my biggest fan?'

'No idea. All the negotiating is being done through some company to protect the buyer's privacy. Maybe he's a huge celebrity!'

'What company?' asked Fox.

'I can't remember; it was something Eastern European-sounding.' Hamish smiled at us. 'Probably some tax thing.'

Neither of us reacted, but inside I was screaming. The sharks were circling. This was definitely The Chameleon and The Corporation. The more proof they had on our past kills, the more they could use blackmail to control us.

We lasted less than an hour before we left the gallery, our cheeks aching from fake-smiling at the acquaintances who accosted us as we headed for the exit. Outside the gallery, with a squeeze of my hand and the slightest nod of his head, Fox drew my attention to the white moped parked just a few cars down.

'What now?' I tried to work out how big the guy sitting astride it was.

'We start by getting hold of our newest shadow and finding out what the hell he knows.'

'Shall we take him to the office?'

The converted townhouse that served as the offices for Cabot Matthews Investments had an expansive wine cellar that we had taken the liberty of soundproofing. This helped keep the temperature level, and also ensured that if we ever needed a quiet chat with someone we didn't have to worry about the neighbours.

We got an Uber to our office, our shadow diligently following us on his white moped. He could at least have used a more discreet form of transport. How was he so bad at his job?

Fox let us into the front door of the office. I went downstairs to prepare the wine cellar for our guest while he nipped out of the back door to get him. It only took him six minutes. The guy must've parked nice and close to the house.

I heard the front door slam and the muffled shouts of a man who had Fox's scarf over his mouth.

There were some stumbling sounds as they came down the stairs, and then Fox and the man were in the wine cellar with me.

Fox closed the door behind him, and together we shoved the man into the waiting chair and tied him to it.

'That was quick,' I said.

'The idiot was staring at his phone. Didn't even hear me approach.'

'Anyone see you?'

'There was a couple entering the street, but from that distance it would've looked like I was helping a drunk friend to the door.'

I tried calling Jenny. No answer. We needed her to work her magic on the CCTV outside our office. I texted her.

Hun where are you? Need you!

I took Danny's gun out of my handbag and aimed it at our prisoner. He might have been easy to take, but you could never underestimate an enemy. And, god, it was so much faster than having to threaten someone with a knife and be a little bit stabby to show you meant it. People saw a gun and just talked.

Fox pulled his scarf off the tied-up man.

'Man' might have been pushing it. He looked like he was barely old enough to start shaving.

'Jesus, how old are you?' A flash of panic from Fox that he'd abducted a child.

'Fuck off, I'm twenty. Just look young.' His voice was deep enough to confirm he had, in fact, gone through puberty.

'Why the fuck have you been following us?' I waved the gun at him.

'I was paid to!'

Fox crouched down in front of him. 'We just want to know who you're working for.'

The man-child continued staring at me.

'Don't look at her, look at me.'

The man-child's eyes flicked over me. Over my body.

'Did you just give me the once-over? Seriously? I'm holding you hostage, and you're perving on me? Where's the respect? The terror?' I took another step towards him, the gun pointed right at him.

'I'm sorry, okay? I'm sorry! You just look good.'

I paused. 'You don't think the dress is too young for me?'

'Nahhhh. With those legs, you can totally pull it off.'

'You're not just saying that because, you know?' I gestured, trying to signify the whole him-being-tied-to-a-chair-and-me-holding-a-gun thing.

'No! I mean, I probably would still say it even if it wasn't true, because, you know, I don't want to die. But I really do mean it. Total fire fit on you.'

Fox looked up at me. 'If you've finished getting fashion advice from the prisoner, can we . . .?'

'Oh, yes. Right. Who are you working for?'

'I don't know! I mean, like, I know who hired me, but he said it was a job *he'd* been hired to do by someone else. He doesn't actually want to be up in your business himself.'

'What's his name, and where do we find him?' I waved the gun at him.

He talked fast. 'Dave Milligan. He's not just a drug-dealer, he's a fixer too. He gets involved in all sorts. He's doing really well, actually. He's the one who's paying me, and I can give you his address. No problem. Whatever you want. But you'll need to ask him who hired him, and actually *they* were probably hired by someone else. And on and on.'

The idea of working our way through a line of low-level criminals sounded both time-consuming and boring.

'Dave is big on this whole set-up where it's hard to trace it back to the original customer. It's pretty clever, actually. It's to protect all of us. You can see why I left school to get involved, as—'

'You left school? You didn't finish your education?' Fox sat down in the chair opposite him and leaned forward. 'You really think this is a great career path for you?'

I understood Fox's concerns. 'Do you think your failings are down to your parents, or do you feel like you would've kind of ended up this way anyway?'

'Oh god, just shoot me now.' He closed his eyes.

Fox didn't get the hint. 'We're just trying to understand how a young man like you ends up doing this. Was it drugs? You got addicted? They actually ruin lives, you know. It's not just a slogan.'

'I've told you everything I know! You can take my

phone – he's saved under Uncle Dave. I can give you his address as well. Just, please, quit with the questions.'

'We're just trying to learn from your mistakes,' said Fox. 'Do you think you were born into a life of crime, or was it down to the lack of positive role models in your life?'

'Let me go! I've told you everything. You can take what's in my wallet too!' He nodded towards his pocket.

'You came on a job with your wallet?' Fox reached into the guy's pocket and pulled out a battered black canvas wallet. He pulled open the Velcro and plucked out his driving licence. 'Rob Dexter. A real ID with your home address on?' He turned to me. 'It's okay, he really is twenty.'

'I didn't expect to get caught!'

Fox shook his head. 'You really have a lot to learn, Rob. Always prepare as if you could be taken. You need to—'

'I don't think we should be giving him tips,' I said.

'Right. Of course.' Fox shook his head. 'It's just hard when you see someone messing it up so badly.' He turned back to Rob. 'Find a real job. Anything. You're not cut out for this.'

Rob puffed up his chest. 'Are you going to kill me?'

We looked at each other and laughed. 'God, no. Give us some credit.'

Fox pulled him to his feet. 'Just get out of here – and make better choices.'

'And no warning Dave.' I tucked the gun back into my tote bag. 'We've got your home address, remember.'

Rob nodded repeatedly. 'Please don't go there. My mum'll kill me.'

45

Fox

The address Rob gave us was in Slough. The neighbourhood was blessed with a local park, but it was one that had made headlines for being considered such a hotspot for crime that locals refused to venture into it.

'Has Jenny run a check on the address?' I was pulling into a parking space several streets away from Dave's house.

'She's not replying to texts.'

'Right.' I looked at Haze. She was staring straight ahead, doing her very best impression of someone who felt it wasn't a big deal that our teammate was not jumping to help us in our time of need.

Nothing about the semi-detached house on a quiet street stuck out – except the state-of-the-art security system.

Dave opened the door to us on the second ring of the doorbell. He was in his early fifties. He had dark hair in a side parting, and was wearing a shirt and sleeveless sweater. He looked like an accountant. 'New customers?'

I nodded.

'If someone has given you this address, you've been vouched for. So come on in.'

He opened the door wide and ushered us into his living room.

I didn't want to rush to any judgement on how someone of a certain profession should live. But a beige carpet, a mauve three-piece sofa set in a floral pattern and ceramic ducks on the wall was not what I pictured as the décor of choice for a drug-dealer. The only items that didn't make it look like an ancient grandma's home were the sixty-inch flatscreen television over the fireplace and the high-spec home computer set up on a desk in the corner. There were even coasters on the coffee table. *Coasters.*

Dave motioned towards the sofa. 'Please, do sit.'

We sat down slowly on the edge of the sofa. Haze gripped her handbag on her lap with both hands.

'So.' Dave rubbed his hands together and grinned. 'Let me guess. Viagra and cocaine?'

Haze leaned forward and hissed, 'Did you just accuse my husband of having a limp dick?'

Dave's smile disappeared. He had good instincts.

I touched her knee. 'It's okay, honey. He sees a nice, well-dressed couple and presumes that's what we are here for.'

Dave shrugged. 'Your man has it right. So no need to get out whatever weapon you've got hidden inside your Louis Vuitton.' Very good instincts.

Haze loosened her grip on her handbag and continued to stare at Dave steadily.

'We just want information.' I adjusted my tie. 'An associate of yours has been following us. You paid him to.'

Dave tensed.

'But we know it was a pass-on,' I continued. 'You were hired by someone else. We had the full rundown of the pyramid scheme.'

'Rob is fucking useless.' Dave shook his head. 'He's my wife's nephew. Wants to have a go at learning the family business.'

'I sympathise.' Nepotism was clearly the only way Rob had got the work. 'We just need to know who hired you and we'll be on our way.'

Dave bridged his hands together. 'I don't want any trouble.'

I smiled. 'And we will not give any if you tell us what we want to know.' I looked around the living room. 'Rob was so kind in giving us this address, but he's made you a little vulnerable. I don't think you want the police sniffing around here. Or looking into your finances.'

Haze brushed a bit of imaginary fluff off my shoulder. 'The authorities really tend to listen to a well-dressed upstanding member of the community when they have concerns about an individual.' She leaned forward. '*He's* all about the chat. *I'm* a little more physical when it comes to being persuasive.' She tapped her handbag.

Dave's eyes darted towards the door. Was there someone out there?

He cleared his throat. 'I don't think anyone would be too upset if I told you that a fake name made the booking, but that the payment was made through an Eastern European bank account in the name of some shell company.'

Exactly how The Corporation operated.

'You can take heart in the fact that if they wanted harm done to you, they would've gone for a different package. This was low-level surveillance – as you can tell by the calibre of man I sent to do it.'

I had reached the same conclusion. The Chameleon didn't want us dead; he just wanted to know what we were up to.

I stood up. 'Thank you for your time.'

Haze followed suit.

Dave stayed seated. 'You won't come back.'

Haze pretended it had been a question. 'Don't take on any other jobs that involve us, and no – we won't come back.'

Dave tilted his head. 'Do you two ever freelance? I'm always looking to expand my database. Should I get your details in case—'

I cut him off. 'We work to our own agenda. Our skills are not for sale.'

Dave stood up. 'Then I wish you well.' He led us out to the hallway and opened the front door. Haze walked out on to the street.

Dave touched my arm. 'Is my wife going to be angry at the state in which you left her beloved nephew?'

'He's fine. We strongly advised him to find a new job.'

Dave sighed. 'Last week he posted a photo of a knife and a bag of coke with the caption "hashtag slayingandsnorting". I kinda wish you had killed him.'

There was a noise from the floor above. I stiffened and looked towards the stairs.

'My mother,' said Dave.

It seemed such an unlikely lie that it must be the truth. And it explained the house.

Dave called up the stairs. 'I'm coming, Ma!' He looked back to me. 'She has dementia.'

'That must be difficult.'

'Least it means she doesn't ask any awkward questions about my job.' He smiled.

'It's a good set-up you've got here.'

Dave shrugged. 'Don't think you're special.' He waved a hand over my suit. 'The veneer of respectability distracting from your true self. We're all doing the best we can.'

We shook hands, and I closed the door behind me.

46

Haze

It was a ten-minute walk back to the car. Fox was walking fast. 'What would you do if our kids dropped out of school?'

I thought about it. 'If it was to do something they loved, something they were good at, I'd be okay with it.'

Fox nodded. 'Yes. Exactly.'

We'd done this dance before. Every now and again, we'd test each other's opinion on a parenting situation. It hadn't taken us long to realise we needed to be in sync. Present a united front. We could not show weakness. Children could sniff it out, and then you were done for.

'And if what they wanted to do was illegal?' Fox looked at me.

Killing was not going to be a family business. Like all parents, we wanted our children to be better than us. And the risk of death or life imprisonment meant this was not a life-style we wanted to pass on.

'It's not ideal, but if they could show us it was a good business model and that they had talent for whatever it was they were doing, I think we'd have to be okay with it.'

Fox stopped walking. 'I don't want them to ever get hurt, and in our world it's a bigger risk.'

'We can't always protect them from everything. Just like we can't force them to do a job we want them to.'

A childhood was preparation for adulthood. We needed to load them up with a starter pack of strength and skills to get them into the next stage. They were going to get hurt. Who ever got to go through life without experiencing pain?

I knew all this, but maybe Fox wasn't ready to hear it. He had the type of love where he wanted to wrap them up in cotton wool so no one could hurt them. Whereas I wanted a barbed-wire fence to cut the people who tried to.

'Let's just keep them safe and fed. We can work out the rest later.' I touched his shoulder.

'Tonight felt good.'

I knew what he meant. We were back in sync. Working together. 'We're a good team,' I said.

He smiled. 'We are.'

I felt a stirring of something. Muscle memory. I pushed Fox up against the wall and kissed him. He kissed me back and, in a flash, we were back to what we once were. Young. Powerful. Alive.

Laughter made us break away from each other to check who had dared interrupt us.

A few teenage boys were standing on the opposite side of the road. Looking at us – and giggling. What was so funny?

'Move on!' Fox shouted over at them. The laughter died, and they straightened and ran off.

A creeping dread hit me. 'Do you think they were laughing because we're old?'

'Perhaps.' Fox smirked.

'Can we kill them?'

'For what? Being young?'

'And not appreciating it? Definitely.'

Fox slung an arm round my shoulder. 'Let's go home.'

Just then, Jenny pinged me a message.

Sorry so late to reply. Was at a briefing and
we weren't allowed our phones. Let's talk tomorrow.

I trusted Jenny with my life. I loved her. She was family to me. But she was hiding something from me, and I couldn't think what that could possibly be. We told each other everything. I'd been the first person she phoned after she'd kissed a woman for the first time. I'd held her when her self-image plummeted after a bad haircut – and I'd threatened actual bodily harm to the hairdresser. I knew both her mother's maiden name and the name of her first pet. I knew that she never cried at sad films, but always cried at happy love stories. I knew what size tampons she bought. I knew that she only ever wore tops with long sleeves, as she had a weird thing about her arms. I knew that about once a month she had a freakout at 3am about her having some awful terminal illness that she didn't yet know about, and then couldn't get back to sleep.

What could be happening in her life that she couldn't tell me about?

I had to talk to her. I had to understand what was going on. There would be a reasonable explanation. There had to be.

I didn't want to let Fox know I was having any doubts about her loyalty to us.

Last year, I'd nearly lost faith in my husband. I wasn't going to let that happen with my best friend.

Part 3
Negotiation

'We are all equals in our family. Our children have a right to their opinions. If they're wanting to make a poor choice, we help them to help themselves with calm reasoning, collaboration and caffeine-free chai tea. Together we make better decisions.'

**Bells Brightley, parenting blogger (MommaKnowsBest)
and bestselling author of *Reason for Being:
Blessed to Be a Mom!***

'You don't negotiate with terrorists. You don't negotiate with toddlers. You just bribe them – with sugar, saturated fat and screen time.'

Hazel Matthews, mother

47

Jenny

Haze and Fox.

Fox and Haze.

How long had it been since I'd got through a day without uttering their names? Without thinking of them? They had become as ingrained in my life as my son, as my parents, as breathing.

It would be difficult to try and explain us to anyone else. We weren't just friends, we weren't just colleagues: we were family.

Haze, Fox and Jenny.

Jenny, Haze and Fox.

It might not be as catchy, it might sound a little crowded, but that was what we were. A team.

Before Haze came into my life, I was a single mother living at my parents' house, on the brink of being made redundant. My job as a detective, the one I'd worked so hard for, the one place where I'd started to shine, was about to be taken from me for good.

Felix was my one bright spot. He was my reason for getting up every day. Loving him made everything feel better, yet also worse. He deserved the world, and what could I give him? The poor sod, to be lumbered with me for a mother.

And then I met Haze, and everything changed.

Spotting her across the room at some god-awful kiddie music class, I was immediately drawn to her. In a world of women who all second-guessed themselves, who'd been sub-liminally brainwashed into thinking they weren't ever enough, she held her head as high as one of her eyebrows as she assessed everyone around her.

Maybe I wanted to be friends with her just so I could see her up close. Haze had the type of beauty where she just fell out of bed, and her bone structure and perfect skin gave her the glow of a woman who'd spent hours perfecting a no-make-up look with ten different products. She might have faced much hardship in her early life, but she'd never once had to face down the indignity of looking in the mirror and not liking what she saw. Haze ate without thinking and never had to cope with the pinch of jeans that were too tight. She didn't know what it was like to see creases, lines and bulges, and still try putting your best foot forward to get out there and seize the day.

Maybe I wanted to be friends with her because I loved to self-hate, and being so close to perfection fuelled that daily. Don't get me wrong, I could feel good about myself. I wasn't totally beyond hope. It just took the magic combination of seven hours' sleep, a crate of make-up, a trip to the hairdresser, support pants, a new outfit and soft lighting.

Haze had no clue that people treated her differently because of how she looked. She never noticed the eager-to-please atti-tude of those happy to be talking to her, the constant double-takes in the street, the grumpy shopkeepers who always managed to have a smile for her. I understood part of why she always had the balls to ask for whatever she wanted, as in her experience people would say yes.

Neither of us obsessed over our appearances. But it was for different reasons. For Haze, it was because she never had to give it a second thought. For me, it was because it was a lost cause – an irrelevancy to my everyday life. All that mattered was a quick glance in the mirror to check I didn't have breakfast on my face before I left the house.

Her commendable inherent confidence was helped by both her beauty and the peace of having found her soulmate, her life partner, her other half.

Haze and Fox had the kind of love immortalised in poetry, songs and Hollywood movies. Their passion, the deep, all-encompassing love they had for each other, their meet-cute in Paris over the gut of a bleeding-out bad man, the joining together of two beautiful beings with a serious purpose, united by their mission to rid the world of evil – who could not be charmed in the presence of such intense perfection?

And what did I get?

Bill, my dead ex, was a gaslighting, abusive, deadbeat dad who couldn't have given a shit about me. I often thought about how one night coming home from dinner with friends, I'd fretted over how quiet and distracted I'd been, worrying that our friends must be thinking I was boring. Bill's reply of, 'Yes, probably,' had crushed me.

If Haze had said that to Fox, I knew, I just knew, that he would've exclaimed it was impossible that anyone might feel that about her, the most exciting person he'd ever met. To him, she was *it*. Everything. The peak. No question we were all lucky to breathe the same air as her. That's how much he believed in her, how much he enjoyed her and worshipped her.

The fact was, though, Haze would never have questioned

or cared what other people thought in the first place. She believed in herself in a way I'd never seen before. Certainly not in another woman. We were more guilty of getting bogged down with insecurities, second-guessing, self-hate. And that was all before the perimenopause party of things really going to shit.

Haze might hide her darkest side, but otherwise she was unapologetically her, from her resting bitch face to her deep frown at anyone talking shit. She was easy to read because she didn't bother hiding what she was thinking.

It had taken me time to realise that I wanted to channel Haze's confidence more than anything else.

I didn't want someone to love me like Fox loved Haze. I wanted to love myself like Haze loved herself.

Believing in myself would make life far better than just relying on someone else to make me feel good.

Haze had helped me realise I needed to be true to myself. I had never really thought about what I wanted. My disastrous love life was a perfect example. I had gone out with men because it was what was expected. I'd never felt that spark, that overwhelming desire the movies and the books all talked about. Then last year, one night out in a bar after work, a woman with red hair and a dirty laugh had bought me drinks and kissed me. Then it clicked. This was how it was meant to feel! How had it taken me decades to realise *this* was who I was? I'd been so suppressed I hadn't let myself realise what I actually wanted. I'd rung Haze and told her about the redhead, pretending it was a funny random story. 'Well, did you like it?' was all she'd responded with. It took months until I was able to tell her yes.

It might have taken me too long to put my own needs first, but not any more. I wanted another child. I had enough love to give, especially to someone who had not been blessed with the loving parents I'd had. The old me may have tied herself in knots chasing the traditional nuclear family. But the new me, the real me, knew that family was what you made it.

I might have accepted who I was and what I had, but it was hard not to be envious of Haze and Fox. Their looks, their love, their money. This perfect, glamorous package. They glided while others walked.

I'd never been a greedy person. All I'd ever wanted was enough to give Felix everything he needed. But seeing Haze and Fox and their lifestyle had made me realise how truly life-changing money – *proper* money – was. It allowed them to live however they wanted to live. It cushioned everything.

Our first summer trip abroad together had been to Corfu with a three-year-old Felix and Bibi. Haze and Fox had insisted my parents come with us (*'They're grandparents to our kid too!'*). It was the best week of my life. Out in the sunshine with the people I loved most in the world.

Once we'd successfully dispatched the target, we'd followed out there, it had become a real holiday. Haze and Fox had rented a fully staffed superyacht for a few days. I think Mum took at least two hundred photos. Sitting on the deck, sunning ourselves, we'd passed a small boat. An overweight man with a beer in hand was splayed out at the back, asleep. A sunburnt woman my age in a flowery swimsuit was gripping the steering wheel, her mouth set in a thin line. I looked down at their open cool box, the wilted sandwiches, a plastic bottle of Pepsi. I had never felt surer – *that* was more the type of holiday I was meant to be on. That's what staying in my lane would've looked like.

Ice-cold vintage champagne, a butler offering lobster rolls, silk sheets and jacuzzi baths – this was a type of living I'd never been destined for. This was Haze and Fox's life. I'd made the leap. I'd broken through the gold ceiling – even though it was only because they had issued me a guest pass, given me a taste of the high life with their money.

Haze and Fox had shown me you didn't have to stick to the path you were given. You didn't have to accept your lot in life. You could go out there and change it.

We worked together, making the world a better place.

I wasn't quite one of them, but I was *with* them. They were the strutting peacocks. I was the pigeon basking in their reflected glow.

I didn't need the glory of being out there on the front line. I knew my place: in the back office, making sure everything was ticking over smoothly. I was the paperwork queen, the one worrying over the details and the CCTV traces.

They went out and spilled blood, and I was the one making sure our hands were clean of it.

I had chosen this life to give my son a better one. The ten per cent I made from Fox's investments, off the back of a bad man's dying intel, helped pay my mortgage and finance the endless expensive DIY projects I had going on. Haze killing Bill had got me the house, and now working with them was helping me turn it into a proper home. I could pretend that risking my life, my freedom, for Haze and Fox's enterprise was all for Felix, for the money, but, really, it was for me. I finally felt like I was living, not just watching everyone else.

I'd become a police officer because I wanted the high of the chase, of being the person who got to cross behind lines. But I'd never got the buzz I'd thought I would. The long hours, the endless paperwork, the average pay. Then, just when I'd hit rock bottom, humiliated, chased out of work, Haze came into my life. She killed my bastard ex, got me my job back, even set me on path to a promotion. When everything kicked off, when I discovered the truth about them, I could've ended them. Got them locked up for good. But I chose to join them.

The buzz I had always been chasing was found, not in interview rooms at police station, not onsite at crime scenes, but being out in the field with Haze and Fox. Knowing that we weren't just going to catch the bad man, but punish him too.

What kind of person would I be if I was resentful – jealous, even – of everything they had? They had made my life infinitely better. I was nothing without them.

I felt good seeing how far I'd come. How much they'd improved not just my life but me. I had a faith in myself, in my abilities, that I hadn't had before. I watched them now and realised they weren't so different from me. I might never have their natural beauty, their charm and grace, but I knew what was needed to get the job done.

If I'd been a different person, I might have started thinking that I could be like them, maybe even better than them. I'd had a taste of their life, of how things could be, and it was difficult to not want more. Wasn't it human nature to keep aspiring? I knew I should just enjoy all I had, but who ever really stopped wanting more?

If I had their kind of money, imagine the life I could have? The good work I could do, the people I could help.

I was brought up to always be grateful, to appreciate the little things. I'd been blessed with wonderful parents. Love. Support. Guidance. All in abundance. Full marks. But all that attentiveness had also made me feel a certain pressure that Haze and Fox, with their terrible parents, had never experienced.

Haze and Fox were trying to lead good lives *despite* their parents. I had to lead a good life *because* of mine. I didn't want to let them down. I couldn't. Not after everything they'd done for me. Making them proud was the very least I could do. Even at my absolute lowest points, they'd never made me feel any less for the literal car crash of my life. Instead, they'd loved me extra hard. Come round even more. Done even more. There was never any tut-tutting, never any judgement. I needed to reward them for this by being everything they had wanted for me and more. Seeing me happy made them happy.

Sometimes, it felt too much. Smiling despite the cracks. Always being the one everyone else could rely on. Trying to be a good mother, a good daughter, a good friend, a good worker bee. Sometimes I wanted to blow it all up. Let loose.

But, of course, I'm not that type. I'm good old dependable Jenny. The back-office pigeon. Flying high in their tailwind.

48

Haze

I woke up with a start. The bedside clock said 3.11am. No sound of a baby crying. No sound of anything. Had I woken up because it was too quiet? Jesus, was I ever destined to sleep properly again?

And then I heard it. A thump. From downstairs.

I shook Fox's shoulder. 'I think there's someone down there.'

'What? No? What?' Fox's head remained on the pillow. 'Shhh.'

I hit him on the arm. 'I'll go check it out. You stay with the kids.'

''S nothing. Sleep.'

I turned the light on as Fox groaned.

The light flickered as another thump came from downstairs. Now Fox sat up.

'See?'

'I'll go.' He pulled a knife out from under the mattress.

'What the fuck?'

'It helps me sleep.'

'What about Bibi?'

'She's never going to go hunting under the mattress, and she knows that sharp knives hurt her, and—'

'I just think it's really irresponsible. We really—'

Another thump from downstairs.

'Not now.' Fox stalked out of our bedroom, dressed only in his boxers, knife in hand. I pulled on a dressing gown and went to check on Reggie. He was fast asleep, arms out over his head. If this intruder woke him up, I would absolutely fucking kill him.

I went to Bibi's room. She was also zonked out. The penguins from her nightlight were dancing around the room.

'Haze!' Fox was hush-shouting me.

I peered over the top of the banisters. 'What?'

'You need to come down here.' He was just out of sight, standing at the top of the stairs to the garage.

'I shouldn't leave the kids,' I hush-shouted back.

'You can. I've checked everywhere. But you need to come here.'

I tiptoed down the stairs and followed him into the garage, where I saw exactly what was making that thumping noise. Barry Fenton was splayed out on the floor. His lifeless body was jolting, his foot hitting the drum set next to him. Barry Fenton, head of the Neighbourhood Watch, was dead. On our property.

'What the fuck?'

Fox locked the garage door behind us and motioned towards the bolt-cutters on the floor by Barry's right hand. The guitar amp wire was tangled up round him. He had a deep cut on his forehead.

'He could've been cutting the wire . . .' Fox pointed at the slightly shorn wire resting on Barry's stomach '. . . and it . . .

well, electrocuted him. And then he hit his head on the way down?'

We both stood there for what felt like three minutes staring at fried Barry. How the hell had this happened?

I shook my head. 'This can't be an accident.'

'You think someone dragged Barry in here and forced him to cut the wire? Someone who just so happened to know how much he hated our family's musical talents?'

I did not think this was the right time to question exactly what musical talents he was referring to. His sporadic strumming of a guitar and Bibi's whacking of a drum were both as tone deaf as my singing.

'What are the statistics for getting electrocuted from a household accident? It can't happen that often. Or maybe he was already dead when he was dragged in here, and this was all staged?'

Fox picked up a broom from the other side of the garage and poked at the cut wire until it was off Barry's body. He stopped jerking.

I tried to process it all. Barry. Dead. In our garage. 'This doesn't make sense!'

'We need to forget about working out *how* this happened and focus on getting him out of here.'

'Do you think that's what The Chameleon wants? Do you think he's already called the police?'

'I don't think we should wait to find out.'

'For fuck's sake. You mean we've got to dump another body?'

We looked at each other. Our hearts really weren't in it.

Fox sighed. 'We could just cart him back to his house. Make it look like he electrocuted himself there.'

'This is literally shitting on our doorstep.' I poked at Barry with my foot. 'But we didn't do the shitting, so why are we clearing up the shit?'

'Trash can,' said Fox

'What?'

'We can put him in the trash can.' Fox motioned to our black wheelie bin, which stood in the corner. 'Wheel him over and then find a way into his house.'

That seemed blissfully simple compared to what we were used to.

Fox leaned down and patted down Barry's pockets. He pulled out a set of house keys. 'We don't even need to break in.'

I looked from the bin to the keys. 'Wow. Dead neighbours are so easy to dump.'

We yanked the wheelie bin on to its side and, working together, we half rolled, half shoved Barry into it.

'Lucky he's so short,' I huffed. I wanted him out of the house as soon as possible. This was not the type of bringing your work home I was ever up for.

49

Fox

It was ten feet to Barry's house. It was 3.44am. I was standing just past our front doorstep wearing a dressing gown and white tennis shoes, and gripping a wheelie bin filled with Barry. I looked back at our house. Haze was peering out through our living-room window, on the lookout for anyone who could be watching us.

I didn't like any of this. We'd been so distracted by everything we had going on, we hadn't clocked someone swooping in and killing a man not just on our home turf, but in our actual home.

I started pushing the bin. The street was so quiet the rattle of its wheels across the paving stones was painfully loud. I walked fast, head down, round to Barry's side door.

I reached for his keys and let myself in. No beeps of an alarm. Did this weaken or strengthen the case that Barry had not come to harm by himself?

I yanked the bin over the step and into the house.

For a man so meticulous when it came to the outsides of all our homes, inside, his was an absolute mess. The kitchen was overflowing with clutter. Piles of junk mail, empty cardboard boxes. The dining table was covered in ceramic vases, one with dead flowers in.

I walked past a pile of packages and saw one with Haze's name on. I picked it up. An Amazon delivery he must've signed for and then never bothered dropping off. I couldn't get too angry about that now.

I needed to work out the best location to leave him. I walked through his house, opening doors.

The study, which overlooked the street, had always seemed like he had the shutters closed. Standing there now, I realised he had just stuck darkened film on the glass. It might look closed up from outside, but he could see out, no problem. The perfect way for a busybody like Barry to spy on everyone. On his desk was a large A4 folder with a sticker on the front marked 'Observations'. I opened it up. Scrawled on each page were times and dates, along with a log of whatever infraction he had witnessed.

Our house number, twenty-nine, appeared several times throughout the folder. Most of the comments related to our bin habits. A fitting end.

The sections from the last month were missing.

Had Barry moved those entries to another folder?

Did whoever kill him take it?

What had Barry seen?

How long did I have until the police arrived?

I had to get moving.

I walked around the rest of the ground floor and determined that the living room was the best location. I wheeled him in, then jiggled him out on to the floor.

I checked over his body. No stab wounds. No visible head wounds apart from the cut on his forehead, which wouldn't have been enough to kill him. If it wasn't electricity, it could've been poison, but I wasn't exactly in a position to run a tox screen.

I could just leave him in an armchair and hope they'd presume it was heart attack. But it was better to hedge my bets: heart attack and a bit of being electrocuted. I dragged Barry over to the TV and began attempting to set the scene. By the time I'd finished, it was a bit of a mess. But I did, in theory, have a police detective on our side. Jenny's team would be the ones to investigate this, which gave us a little breathing space. No dog-eared, committed do-gooder would be out to make a name for themselves. Just a friendly face, quick to rule it an accident.

That was as long as Jenny wasn't betraying us.

50

Haze

I texted Jenny at 6am.

Hey hun, come over for breakfast.
Need to complain about how much I hate men.

She replied at 6.35am. Lucky her. A lie-in.

Course babe. I'll be over soon.

I worked out that getting Felix up and out the door to her parents wouldn't take more than half an hour.

Jenny walked through our front door at 7.01am. She was dressed for work. She insisted on only ever wearing these awful Next navy blue trousers suits that did nothing for her. She'd once laughed for a solid five minutes when I'd asked her what was wrong with a nice business-chic high-waisted trouser and a silk shirt. *'I'm dressing for a police station in Slough, not lunch in Sloane Street.'*

'How bad is it?'

Fox and I were sitting at the kitchen table, large coffees in front of us, still in our dressing gowns. Bibi and Reggie were, by some miracle, both still asleep upstairs.

Fox cleared his throat. 'We found our next-door neighbour Barry dead in our garage. Seemingly electrocuted from cutting the wire to my guitar amp.'

Jenny looked between us. 'Seemingly?'

'We're not totally sure that's what killed him,' I said.

Fox showed Jenny his laptop with the security camera footage. We had one camera positioned overlooking our garage. The garage door started opening at 2.46am. It opened right out and blocked the camera's view. 'Someone must've cloned our door opener,' he said.

Jenny shrugged. 'Pretty easy to do.'

The door stayed open for eight minutes and then closed. No one was visible on camera.

'No other angles?'

Fox shook his head.

'Eight minutes is both enough time to dump and stage a body, and enough time to manage to electrocute yourself.' Jenny stared at the screen. 'Why would The Chameleon want to leave a dead body in your house?'

Another day. Another dead man. This was busy, even for us. I felt a flicker of something. 'Danny. Kristoff. Barry. They've all died in the last couple of weeks.'

Jenny nodded. 'Maybe it's a warning shot to show how easily he can kill people in our lives?'

He could've set Danny up to die at Fox's hands. He could've been on the roof and pushed Kristoff. He could've been the one to break in with a dead Barry.

'But they were all people we didn't want in our lives – so why would he be doing us a favour?'

'We've had to dump two out of three of those bodies!

Maybe it's because he wants us to get caught?' Fox stood up. 'It's why we got Barry out of here fast, in case the killer had called the police on us.'

'Where is he now?'

'I took him back to his house in our wheelie bin and set the scene for him having died there.'

Jenny winced. 'How exactly did you set the scene?'

'I stuck him by an electrical socket, splashed some water around. You know . . . I've still got his house keys in case you want to . . .' Fox trailed off.

'I'll go check it out.' Jenny stood up, then paused. 'So, just to double-check – neither of you killed him?'

'We just found him here! Someone killed him and delivered him to our garage.' Fox pointed to the A4 folder on the table. 'He'd been logging everything he saw out of his window. I think he saw something – or someone – he shouldn't have.'

'I'll see what I can do.' Jenny took the house keys and left.

We went upstairs and got dressed. I plucked a hungry Reggie from his cot and went back down to the kitchen to feed him. I left Fox to deal with Bibi, who was having a breakdown over not being able to find her favourite hairband.

Jenny came back after half an hour. I was feeding Reggie on the sofa.

'Fox didn't do too bad a job.' She slumped down next to me. 'The bathroom is directly above the living room. I've run the bath. The water will overflow eventually, soak through to the living room, and that will help confuse the crime scene further. When we get called over, I'll lead with the theory that he was getting ready for a bath, and started fiddling with the TV. Electrocuted. Dead. Bath overflowed.' She checked her watch. 'I'd better get to work. Hopefully no one peers through the living-room window any time soon. The longer the water has to ruin everything, the better.' She got up from the sofa. 'What do you know about Barry? Partner? Friends? Family?'

'He lived alone, and I don't think he really saw many people.' I couldn't remember ever seeing anyone go in and out of his house.

'There were no photos of family inside the house. No pets, either. It's likely no one will miss him for a while.'

Barry had been a dick, but that was a depressing thought.

'It will help with making sure it's ruled an accident. If he's not found for a few days, things will be harder to work out.'

I watched her leave. I didn't want to think about how easy it would've been for someone with keys to our house, someone who knew where the security cameras were, to help someone else break in and kill Barry.

I shook it off. Jenny had come straight over and helped us fix everything. This was *Jenny*. Our Jenny. We were the ultimate trio. Every success, every high we'd had in the last couple of years, we'd shared with her. We were in this together. She wouldn't betray us.

51

19ᵗʰ March

Outside Cabot residence. Male subject is approached at his car by woman in her fifties (ID check confirms Edwina Marland, resides at number 23). Microphone picks up below exchange:

EM: *Morning, Nathaniel! We're having a little soiree next Saturday and we'd love you to—Wow, are you okay? You look very tired.*

Male: *Thanks, Edwina. Always a pleasure. The baby kept us up all night.*

EM: *You just need to give it antihistamine – it knocks kids right out. And before you get all moral, it's probably allergic to something.*

Male: *I . . . I hadn't heard that one.*

EM: *You've spilled something on your shoe. Is that—*
Male: *Ketchup! Cooked breakfasts are the best.*

EM: *Have you seen Barry this morning?*

Male: *No? Why? What do you want with him?*

EM: *He's normally done a patrol by now, and I've got a bottle of whisky for him. I don't want him to ruin the party by coming round with his sound decibel monitor.*

Male: I'll tell him if—

EM: Oh – maybe I could put antihistamine in the whisky.

Edwina Marland walks off. Male rubs at his shoe.

52

Fox

'Did *you* kill them all?'

We were in our kitchen, trying to make it not look like a family of racoons lived here. Haze was washing up. I was drying. I thought I'd misheard. Until she said it again. My wife. Staring at me. Holding a soapy coffee mug. Asking me if I'd killed behind her back.

She observed me for a quiet few seconds, then spoke again. 'Danny groped me. Kristoff ripped me off. And Barry was always fucking me off. And all three of them are dead.'

'You can't be serious?'

We stared at each other.

'I don't want to make a big thing of it. But you killed Danny, so I was just wondering if maybe . . . you killed the others too.'

'You don't trust me?'

'Of course I do. You've just got to admit it's weird, right?'

I did see her point. It seemed like an unlikely coincidence.

'I understand why you did it. You were helping me, protecting me . . .' She trailed off.

'I did not kill them! I mean, yes, I killed Danny. But it wasn't because of who he was, or what he did.'

'And that artist, Kristoff? We both know how easy it is to make it look like someone just fell off a roof.'

Barcelona in 2011. We'd done exactly that with a would-be rapist we'd come across.

'And when we talked about him, I looked him up remember? We read his stupid *At Home* feature about him living in his loft above that insufferably trendy coffee shop?'

I kept quiet. She was right. If I'd wanted to, I could've found him. Easily.

'And Barry being right next door would make it easy enough to get to him whenever you wanted!'

'Would you rather it be me betraying you? And not your precious Jenny? You wouldn't even entertain the thought of her working against us, but you're happy to accuse me!'

Was Haze turning on me because she couldn't believe her best friend would be the one doing this? Where was her loyalty? I still hadn't told her about Jenny's lie about being at the bank. It still sounded petty. I needed more.

Haze slammed the coffee mug on to the drying rack. 'I don't want it to be either of you! I just want to work out what the fuck is going on.'

I gripped her shoulders. 'I swear you can trust me. We're a team.' I paused. 'So, next time a man gropes you, you tell me.'

Haze observed me. 'As long as you promise you won't maim or kill him.'

'I can't totally promise that. But I'll do my best.'

A pause as we both debated our next move.

Haze relented. 'Okay, I believe you. Sorry I had to—'

I waved it off. 'I understand. I do.'

For other couples, accusing the other of murder would be a big event. For us, it was a quick kiss and back to the washing-up.

I might have reassured Haze, but now I needed to convince myself. Was I blacking out and killing people without realising? Could I be fitting that into one of my night-time escapades? I mean, didn't that happen to people? A psychotic break? Maybe I should check the medication I'd been taking. Sally had said it was for anxiety, but could blackouts be a side effect? Although I was pretty sure I'd remember killing someone. Wouldn't I? Or was it so natural to me, so much a part of who I was, that I could just do it without thinking?

Three men in our orbit were dead. Three men that Haze had issue with. I may have killed the first one, but wasn't I set up to? You wave a gun at a killer, of course I was going to react.

It came back to Jenny. Again. Maybe she had a hand in my blackouts. Was she trying to make me question myself? Was she doing this to get me sectioned? Was I being paranoid in thinking this way, or was I being smart?

Or was all this just The Chameleon messing with us? Sowing division, making us question each other so he could wreak even more havoc when we were fractured?

When I left the house, I got a glimpse of a tall man with dark hair on the opposite side of the road. He was talking into his phone with his back to me, sitting on a black moped. Rob's replacement?

By the time I got into London Paddington, I'd convinced myself he was an innocent bystander. That was right up until I saw him leaving the train ahead of me.

We were still being watched. I guessed Dave wasn't the only supplier of dodgy men to undertake surveillance jobs. I texted Haze and updated her that she might have a little shadow too.

I did my best to lose mine by taking a small detour to Fortnum and Mason. I last saw him by the chocolate section, and made it to Sally's office without seeing him again. Although really, if he'd done his research, he'd know it was likely I'd either be here or at the Cabot Matthews Investments office.

Sally wasted no time in launching in. 'Do you think your wife values you?'

'I . . . I presume so? I know she loves me.'

'And how does she show that? By the way she tells you all the time? By her actions? What's her love language?'

I was pretty sure I shouldn't have to convince my therapist that my wife cared about me. Maybe the whole illusion of them being quiet listeners was just something portrayed on TV. Of course, they were real human beings with opinions. It was just all a bit confusing.

I also didn't know how to explain that Haze's love language was simply not wanting to kill me. She allowed me to touch her. She allowed me to love her. She didn't show how she felt with love poems, hand-holding and presents. There was an implicit understanding that we belonged to each other. Through the death we brought and the lives we created, we were entwined together for eternity. When she looked at me, I knew she loved me. When she reached for me, I knew she loved me.

She didn't need to tell me because I already knew.

There was only one time I'd wondered, at a time when we were faltering. But that was pretty clear, because she'd come at me with a knife.

Sally tapped her pen on her notepad. 'What I find difficult, Nathaniel, is that you're clearly a man of exceptional intelligence, warmth and talent. For you to feel anything less than good about yourself, it makes me wonder where exactly you're getting these subversive messages from.' Sally leaned forward. 'No one could look in the mirror, see *that* reflection looking back at them and think they were not enough.'

I nodded to myself. It was true that, this last year, I had questioned myself. I hadn't been able to appreciate all that I had, as I'd been struggling to adjust to a post-Ivrea, post-Reggie life. I'd lost hours standing in the shower, staring blankly at our Italian marble tiles, wondering if I'd made the right life choices for myself and my family. There was no denying I'd been a mess, but that wasn't ever down to Haze. She had been there for me as best she could.

'I worry you're in a coercive-control situation, where this woman is undermining your confidence in yourself.'

What on earth? Haze coerced me all the time. But that was to take the bins out. To make sure I stored the breast milk correctly.

Haze had stuck with me through this rough year and helped me find my way back. My own ineptitude leading to her nearly getting kidnapped by the assassin chasing us had been the wake-up call I needed. I wasn't going to let her down again.

And I had faith in my relationship with my wife, even if my therapist didn't.

I stared at the diplomas that hung on the wall behind Sally. Jenny had confirmed they were real, but did what she was saying really have any merit? I thought of the two confidential reports Jenny had found questioning Sally's behaviour. If I was starting to lose faith in what she was saying, was there any point in continuing to see her?

53

Fox

We were lucky that Barry had been so deeply unpopular no one seemed to care that he was dead. It had taken three days before Rebecca Ukleja from number seven, irritated by Barry's refusal to answer her requests for the latest Neighbourhood Watch minutes, peered through the window and got a glimpse of a dead Barry.

We hovered, peering through our curtains at the coroner taking him away, and then unmuted the neighbourhood WhatsApp chat. It soon became clear that his death was officially regarded as a tragic accident. A blown fuse. There were a few 'how awful' messages, which, rather inappropriately soon, moved into which estate agent was going to list the house, as everyone seemed to have a friend keen to snap it up. Jenny confirmed the case had been all filed away as an accident with minimum interest or fuss.

The relief almost felt like we'd once again got away with murder, when for once we had not been the ones responsible for the dead body.

Tonight, Norwood had invited me to a backgammon night at his members' club. It was a men-only establishment on Pall

Mall. I'd thought Haze would be horrified at the concept, but she'd cackled about how funny it was that poor little men needed safe spaces.

Time spent with Norwood would further our efforts to find out more about Restore Glory, and was also a good way for me to solidify our working relationship. If he liked me, there was more chance he'd be forgiving if our numbers weren't as impressive as they previously had been.

Norwood escorted me through the club to the library, stopping for the odd back slap and hearty handshake along the way. Suit and tie were the strictly enforced dress code, and I clocked that half the men he greeted, all significantly older than us, had suits nearly as ratty as Norwood's. For the first time, my tailored Savile Row suit and silk Hermès tie made me feel out of place instead of quietly – and fashionably – superior.

Inside the library, several small tables were set up with backgammon boards. A few other men had already started playing.

Norwood tugged on his tie as he sat down at a table. 'I can't stand these things.'

I noticed the tie had an orange stain on it. I pictured him inside his grand dining room as a butler served him boiled egg and soldiers for breakfast.

'My ex hated me coming here,' he said. 'She thought we should only ever go out together to bright shiny places where she could show off whatever tiny dress I'd paid for.'

I looked around the library. Dark wood tables, leather chairs and musty curtains. I couldn't imagine his ex enjoying being here even if she had been allowed in.

'She didn't understand that it was good to occasionally spend time apart. And, sometimes, I had a craving for proper conversation, with like-minded people. Don't you find the same?'

I didn't feel Norwood would appreciate or understand hearing that I enjoyed talking to my wife.

'Shall we start?' I motioned towards the board, which was already laid out. 'I'll be black.'

We threw the dice as Norwood motioned at a hovering waiter for another drink. He had yet to finish his first gin and tonic.

We played for a few minutes and covered the usual small talk on the markets and the latest news, along with some further gripes about his ex.

Norwood's play was haphazard. He liked taking risks and made moves that rarely paid off. While he was crowing about having thrown a double six, I decided the time was right to launch in.

'Are you going to this party at Balgray Hall ? A friend has got us tickets.'

'Wonderful! Yes, I'll be there.' He moved a couple of his pieces. 'I'm hoping it all goes smoothly. The events company have been in a bit of a tizz since losing their non-exec director. He's missing, presumed dead. It's all a bit of a scandal.'

I felt a prickle. I threw my dice. A two and a one. 'That sounds terrible. Who is he? I haven't seen anything in the news.'

'Clark something. He was at Boltons, that company you did so well out of. Think he dabbled with the events company as a charitable thing. Always good to support small businesses. Boltons have been trying to keep it quiet, spinning stories of him running off with his mistress.'

I slowly moved one of my pieces three places.

Remain calm.

'That's terrible.'

Norwood threw his dice. 'Boltons should clearly check the books, as a finance guy going missing usually means he's run off with the money!'

I tried to focus on the board, on Norwood moving one of his pieces.

Clark Dixon.

Our low-hanging fruit. Our irrelevant little wife-beater and rapist. It turned out he had friends in very high places. If our theory that The Corporation was behind Unique Events was correct, that would mean we'd managed to kill a man linked to the very organisation we'd been trying to avoid.

How the hell had this happened?

Jenny had told us that a woman at her gym had told her about Clark. There was no way she'd just happened to come across a finance man with links to The Corporation by chance.

We'd killed Clark because Jenny told us to. She'd presented him as a perfect lowbrow victim. A nobody who would have useful financial tips for me. He'd ticked all the boxes – the most important one being that he did not have any gang connections.

Had she been setting us up all this time?

54

Haze

I tried to understand what Fox was saying. I was sitting up in bed, my eye mask on my head, after being rudely awakened by my husband telling me what he'd learned from Norwood.

Clark Dixon, the random bad man, was not so random.

The Chameleon's increased interest in us was beginning to make sense. Killing Clark could've been seen as a declaration of war. We'd thought we had been backing away, downing tools, showing The Corporation we weren't a threat. But to them it had looked as though we were coming for them.

Fox had killed Danny next.

Another member of their organisation.

One by one.

They must've thought we'd been escalating.

That Airbnb dining table covered with reminders of our previous kills. They had done their research on us. They knew who we were and what we had done.

This couldn't just be a series of unfortunate coincidences. Someone, somewhere, was pulling the strings.

Fox was trying to get me to come to the same conclusion he had.

Jenny.

But I couldn't get there. Fox had gone behind my back and followed her last week. She'd pretended to be at the office, when she was actually at the bank.

Another lie. Just like when she'd claimed to be at her parents' house, when he'd seen her walking down Park Lane.

I just couldn't believe she would betray us. She was family.

But she'd chosen Clark Dixon.

She'd got us to kill a man linked to The Corporation.

She had given flimsy excuses more than once for not being around to help.

She was the one who had told me that even tiny red flags were a problem when dealing with an unknown enemy and professional criminals.

She'd said we couldn't trust anyone.

Even though Fox was still not his usual self, I had to trust that he was right when he said he'd seen her in places she wasn't supposed to be.

Maybe she was being blackmailed? Had some sinister force threatened to hurt Felix unless she turned on us?

Fox thought she'd been recruited by The Corporation. That she was working with them to destroy us. Her head had been turned by money, he suggested. She had delusions of grandeur. She wanted to become us. She didn't care about us, we weren't her real family – she was chasing glory and riches for Felix.

No. Not my friend. She wouldn't do that to us.

There had to be a reasonable explanation. I couldn't think what the hell it could be, but that didn't mean there wasn't one.

I slept horribly and woke to Fox sitting beside me telling me he had to go in to our lawyers' office. The legal troubles

Diana Morgan had unleashed on us with the council were not going away. He needed to sign off on paperwork to help us form a case in our appeal.

We would discuss our next moves with Jenny when he got back. But I knew he wanted to start following her everywhere. To break into her house and go through her emails.

He didn't realise how much I had learned from the shitshow of last year, when we'd hidden things from each other, not spoken our minds, and let things fester into a near-bloody showdown.

Personal growth. No more sneaking around. No more secrets. If someone you loved seemed to be lying, then confront them. Get it all out there.

As soon as I heard him leave the house, I texted Jenny, asking her to come over.

I was going to talk to her. Woman to woman. I wanted to grab her and get her to look me in the eye when I asked her. 'What the fuck is going on?'

The doorbell rang, and a second later Jenny's key turned in the lock.

'In here!' I shouted. I was sitting upright at the kitchen table, trying to work out what to do with my hands. Clasping them before me on the table made me feel too formal. Having them by my sides seemed odd too. What did I normally do with my hands?

Jenny was shouting through to me from the hallway as she dropped her coat and bag. 'Some utter arsehole cut across me when I turned into your road.' She walked into the kitchen and looked at me. 'What's wrong? Why do you look so weird?'

'Sit down, please.'

Jenny half laughed as she sat down in the chair opposite me. 'Why does it feel like you're breaking up with me?'

'How did you find Clark Dixon?'

Jenny frowned. 'I told you. A woman at my gym. She knew I was police and started asking me if there was anything that could be done. I tried to get him through the normal routes, but you know the drill.'

I knew Jenny well enough to know that when she was nervous, she picked at her thumbnail. Now, she wasn't even looking at her hands. She was slumped back in her chair. Her hair was up in a messy bun, and she was wearing her grey hoodie. We'd bought matching ones on our holiday in Corfu; mine was upstairs.

'What is this? What's wrong?' Jenny stretched.

'Clark Dixon worked for The Corporation.'

Jenny's eyes widened. 'No! He was just the boring finance guy at Boltons. He had no gang links. No mention of him in any police records, even as a person of interest.'

'Norwood says he was a non-exec director at Unique Events.'

'This doesn't make sense.' Jenny pinched her nose.

'Of all the wife-beaters to pick, you gave us one that got us back on The Corporation's shit list!'

Jenny leaned forward. 'I promise you, Haze, I had no idea. How could I? Gretchen is a woman I met through the new gym I joined. Remember I did that taster session there? You were impressed I was trying to get fit. Gretchen got talking to me in the changing rooms, and . . .' Jenny stopped.

'What?'

She put a hand to her head. 'I only signed up for that taster session because I'd heard the gym had links to The Corporation. One of the owners used to be in an Albanian gang, and I thought they could be using him to run one of their shell companies. I couldn't find any evidence of ongoing criminal activity, but I liked the place, so kept going. Gretchen told me she'd joined as her husband got a discounted membership through his work. I just presumed Boltons had a deal with them.' She looked at me. 'I'm so sorry. I just didn't think . . . Clark was an English guy working at a finance company. His record was clean. There was no reason to think he had any dealings with that world.'

I took a breath. Was what she was saying making sense? Or was I just desperate for it to? Could it be just a horrible coincidence? Just bad luck? Really bad luck?

'You didn't actually think I did it on purpose? That I had some kind of death wish for us all?'

'But you've been lying to us!'

Jenny leaned back as if I'd struck her.

'You were in London when you told Fox you were at your parents' house. Last week you told us you were at the office when you were at the bank. You've skipped out on things we needed you for with lame excuses. Has someone got to you? Is someone threatening—'

'It's nothing like that.' Jenny closed her eyes. 'It's Dad. He's sick.'

I tried not to look too relieved. Jenny had been all over the place because poor Frank had been struck down with something. Why hadn't she just told us? She must've worried we'd get annoyed at her playing nurse when we needed her. But we wouldn't think less of her for being a good daughter.

'Is it that vomiting bug? Flu? Take as long as you need to look after him. Poor Frank. He's such a nice—'

'Cancer.'

'What?' I heard her, but I didn't want to hear her.

'He's got pancreatic cancer.' She couldn't meet my eyes.

'Right.' I nodded.

We were both quiet for a few beats.

'He'll get through it.' I finally said. 'It'll be fine'.

'No, Haze. It won't.'

I didn't know what to do. What to say.

We'd done all kinds of things together, hunted down bad men, scrubbed their blood off the floor, dirtied our hands burying them. But this was too dark.

'We'll get him the best doctors. Money is no object. We can—'

'I've already tried! I looked into all these different private specialists in London. I went to the bank to check if I could remortgage my house. But . . . He had consultations with two of the specialists I found, the top in their field, and they both said there was nothing to be done.'

'Nothing?'

Jenny shook her head as tears rolled silently down her cheeks.

'That's shit.' I wished I had it in me to be better than this. More eloquent. 'Really shit.'

'I'm sorry I lied.' Jenny pulled a tissue out of her sleeve. 'I didn't want to tell you guys, as you've got enough on. And I was worried you'd make me take a step back from all this. But I need it. I have to keep busy, or I'll go mad.'

I reached for her and held her in a tight hug. 'I'm sorry.'

'How am I meant to live my life without him in it?' she cried into my shoulder.

'I don't know, Jen. I don't know.'

I didn't need a father, but she did.

55

Fox

It had taken three hours with the lawyers to get to grips with planning rules and appeals that I had absolutely no interest in ever hearing about again. I'd signed whatever they'd asked me to sign. And I was seriously hoping that Diana Morgan would consider this little legal stunt to be suitable revenge, and would now leave us alone.

I had a little time to spare before my train. I'd made a decision.

I was going to cut Sally loose. It wasn't clear to me how much she was even helping, and her comments about Haze were making me feel uneasy.

I was going to stop seeing her, and I was going to stop taking the pills she'd given me. It was time to go it alone.

I might not be back to full fighting form, but I was heading in the right direction.

I walked into Sally's office to find her receptionist was not at her desk. Sally's door was ajar. I knocked.

'Sally?'

She flung the door open. Her hair was unkempt, her

glasses perched on top of her head. She looked like she'd been having a nap.

'Nathaniel? We didn't have an appointment scheduled.' She ran her fingers through her hair.

'We don't. I just wanted to let you know that I'm feeling much better. I wanted to tell you in person that I won't be coming in for a while.'

Sally stared at me, saying nothing.

A beat passed. And then another.

She finally spluttered. 'Really? How is that possible? It sounds like things are messier than ever. Haze isn't listening to you. You're still getting paranoia about people following you. We still have a lot of work to do!' She shook her head. 'I think you've been making such good progress. It would be terrible to stop now.'

'I'm not saying this is it. I'm just saying I think I can get by with less frequent sessions.'

'She put you up to this.' Sally leaned against the doorframe and folded her arms.

'I . . . You mean Haze? No. This is my decision.'

'I don't believe you. I know you realise how important our time together has been.' Sally put a hand on my shoulder. 'You need me, Fox.'

I took a step back, shrugging her hand off me, and stared at her. It wasn't just the intensity with which she was burning right now that troubled me. She'd just called me Fox. I'd never offered up that this was the name I went by. How would she know that? How? Had she been watching me too?

I was realising that Haze might have been right.

I'd trusted this woman. I'd told her things. I'd taken the pills she'd given me.

The pills.

Maybe the brain fog that kept hitting me wasn't from the trauma of what I'd been through. Maybe the blackouts were actually down to her poisoning me.

Was I being paranoid again? Or was I seeing clearly for the first time?

Sally might have passed Jenny's extensive background check. She might not be working for a criminal gang who had hired her to spy on me. But that didn't mean she was completely normal, either.

'I don't think this is working for me, Sally. You need to respect my decision.'

'*You* need to respect what I've done for you!'

This was insane. She was insane.

'Goodbye, Sally.' I walked to the door.

'Come back here! This can't be over! You cannot do this!' she shouted after me. She was still going as the front door slammed behind me.

Was breaking up with a therapist always as difficult as this? I knew it was meant to be an intense relationship, but this was extreme. She was acting like a spurned lover.

How was this my fault? I had done the right thing for my mental health and sought out help. It was just seriously bad luck I'd managed to end up with a therapist who was more in need of help than I was.

I couldn't tell Haze. She'd never let me hear the end of it.

I upped my pace towards the tube. I didn't have time to dwell on Sally being unstable and clearly overly into me. I needed to head home and get back to working out what the hell we were going to do about Jenny.

I took out my phone to check in with Haze. Six missed calls. All from her. I steadied my shaking hand to call her back.

'Where the fuck have you been?'
'What's happened? Are the kids—'
'Frank's got cancer.'
I stopped walking and listened as Haze rattled off everything Jenny had said.

56

Haze

Frank was sick, and there was nothing we could do about it. Reggie was asleep. Bibi didn't need picking up for four hours. I was too sad to paint, too angry to watch TV.

I'd given Fox a long list of special items to buy for a large hamper for Frank and Sandy, which would do absolutely nothing, except make me feel like we were doing something.

I got up to make a cup of tea and tripped over a toy car. I picked it up and flung it across the room.

I looked around the kitchen and the random piles of toys that we'd accepted as part of our lives now. I walked into the playroom and saw the overflowing cupboards, more toys, the corners of the room filled with treacherous piles of Lego. I might have no control over certain things in my life, but this total god-awful mess was something I could conquer. I pulled everything out. It was going to get worse before it got better.

I pressed play on a Beastie Boys album, ramped up the volume and got to work.

By the time pick-up was looming, I had filled five boxes with old toys, rejected toys and plastic crap I just didn't want to look at any more. Three I'd marked for the charity shop, and the rest for the tip.

I took a breath and looked around. I hadn't solved any of the big life problems I was facing, but somehow I felt a little better. Clearing out was therapeutic. I should tell Fox. Save money on talking to Stupid Sally and just clean the house.

I had just enough time before getting Bibi to drop everything off. I parked up outside the charity shop and started pulling things out the boot.

The bald man behind the counter spotted me and came to the door to help. 'You've got a lot here!' he said as he took two boxes off me.

'Finally had a big clear-out of the playroom.'

'Oh, thank god it's all kids' stuff.'

'Why?'

'We get a lot of women dropping off stuff belonging to their errant husbands, and then it all gets a bit awkward when said husbands come in demanding it back.'

'That happens a lot?'

'You have no idea. There's a lot of bad men out there.' He took a beat and looked at me.

What the fuck? Was he another of The Chameleon's plants?

I shook it off. How the hell was The Chameleon to know that I'd wake up one morning and decide to offload piles of stuff to a charity shop? This paranoia was getting too much.

'I'm Freddie.' He kept looking at me. 'You're local, aren't you? I've definitely seen you around.'

'Yes.' I checked my watch. 'I'd better get going.'

'Well, don't be a stranger!' Freddie whistled to himself as he put everything under the counter.

I left the shop, looking back over my shoulder once to see

him standing there, staring at me. I gave a little wave, to which he gave a thumbs-up. He was just a nice, slightly odd man who volunteered at a charity shop. He was a good person, and I was a killer who saw threats everywhere.

I picked up Bibi and got her to poke Reggie the whole drive back so he wouldn't fall asleep and ruin bedtime.

Fox was waiting for us when I walked into the kitchen. He'd had his black-tie outfit dry-cleaned in preparation for the party, and it was hanging up on one of the cupboard doors.

He gestured around the toy-free kitchen. 'It looks amazing down here. Thank you.'

'How were they?'

Fox had dropped off the hamper with Frank and Sandra. 'They were very touched. Frank said the cashmere socks and silk dressing gown were so ridiculously luxurious the nurses were going to think he was some kind of Mafia boss.'

Reggie was in my arms, and Fox pulled us both into a hug. He kissed the top of my head. 'I'm just starting on dinner. I tried calling before pick-up – where were you?'

'I took some stuff to the charity shop. I needed something to do.'

'What?'

I looked round to see Bibi staring up at me.

'What you take?' she demanded.

'Nothing of yours.' White lies save lives.

But she'd already run into the playroom. I handed Reggie to Fox and followed. She was wildly looking through all the neatly organised boxes.

'Do not make a mess!' The Zen-like calm I'd experienced earlier was fast disappearing.

Bibi cried, 'My one-legged doll with the chopped-off hair. I miss her!'

'You have not played with her in years. I took her to the charity shop so another little child could love her properly.' Another lie, but it sounded better than admitting I'd dropped her at the tip enroute to the charity shop

'That's not . . . She was mine. MINE!' Bibi pulled a soft bunny out of a box. 'What about my Playmobil vet?'

This was a plastic vet's office for which half the pieces and the roof were missing.

'And my Barbie caravan?'

The caravan had no wheels and was covered in permanent marker. It looked like it belonged outside a crack den.

'They might still be there. I'm not sure.' Lie.

'Not here!' Bibi threw the bunny down on to the floor. 'Charity shop, charity shop. My precious things are there!'

'Enough, Bibi! Sometimes bad stuff happens, and there's nothing you can do about it. You just need to accept it and focus on all the good stuff.'

'I'm too sad!'

'Then bloody distract yourself!' I kept thinking about Jenny. She was heartbroken, and I couldn't do anything to help. 'Sorry, I mean . . . I just . . .' My voice caught a little.

'You can go watch TV, Bibi.' Fox was behind me. He wrapped his arms around me as I leaned back into him.

Bibi stomped off.

'Let's get you a glass of wine.' Fox rested his head on top of mine. 'Two hours of watching *Octonauts*, and she'll have forgotten all about it.'

The doorbell rang.

Fox extracted himself from me. 'Another Amazon delivery, I'm presuming?' He squeezed my shoulder and went to the door.

57

Fox

I opened the door to a tall, debonair man in his sixties.

Something about him seemed familiar.

'Alain Drake.' He held out a hand, which I shook as my mind started shouting. 'Can I come in?'

'Of course! Mr Drake. Haze mentioned she'd met you.' I was speaking loudly. Why was I speaking so loudly? Haze would see who it was soon enough. And we didn't have anything to hide here. Did we?

'I heard your neighbour was found dead.' Drake did not believe in small talk. 'I wanted to check that he wasn't collateral damage in an attempt on either of you.' Drake walked through the hallway towards the kitchen.

'I don't think anyone could've mistaken him for either one of us.'

He turned. 'Obviously.' His look was withering. 'It just seems strangely close. To have another man turn up dead.'

'It's been ruled a tragic accident. Something about water and electrics.'

He entered the kitchen just ahead of me.

'Hello, Hazel.'

Haze was standing by the cooker with Reggie in her arms. She was stirring what I knew to be a saucepan of water. But it looked wonderfully domestic.

'You're asking about poor Barry?' Haze looked down. 'Such a tragedy. He was such a lovely man. Natural causes, and/or a household accident, apparently. That's what the neighbourhood WhatsApps are saying.'

Drake looked around the kitchen. 'It's looking much better in here.'

'Thank you!' Haze smiled. 'Just getting on top of things, finally.'

'Neither of you noticed anything unusual the night he died? No unknown people hanging around near your house?'

'Gosh, no!' said Haze. 'Things have been very quiet.'

'As quiet as they can be with a baby and a toddler!' I smiled.

Drake looked between us. 'There is a party at a place called Balgray Hall tomorrow.'

We both remained silent.

'I have confirmed intelligence that the man who arranged your abudction will be there, and that something bad will be happening, but my superiors are not realising the importance of this. I have no men to send there to control the situation.'

How much to give away? 'A business associate of mine did mention that party,' I said. 'It's meant to be quite a night out.'

Drake frowned. 'I implore you both to not attend. We don't know exactly what his plans are, but it will not be safe for you.'

'We like nights in,' said Haze. 'The baby's still not a great sleeper.'

Drake turned and looked at my black-tie suit hanging on the kitchen cupboard.

I cleared my throat. 'We will let you know if we see anyone suspicious around here. But, really, I'm sure Barry's death was just an accident. That's what the police are saying.'

Drake shook his head. 'The police here are no good. They do not have our attention to detail.'

I chuckled. 'I just don't think someone has followed us to England to kill our next-door neighbour.'

'I don't think you know much yet about what this man is capable of.' Drake held me in a stare. He turned to Haze. 'You still have my number?'

Haze nodded.

'I will be in touch again soon.'

I showed him to the door. He strode out into the night and then stopped. 'Be careful,' he said, then spun on his heel and walked down the street.

Did he mean, 'Be careful of The Chameleon'? Or, 'Be careful, I'm watching you'?

By the time I was back in our kitchen, Haze had topped up her wine glass. Reggie was in his bouncy chair on the table, watching her.

'What a fucking day.' She took another large gulp. 'What do we do about Drake and the party? We just told him we wouldn't go.'

'It's a masked ball. He won't see us. And, really, he might be useful. He seems to want to find The Chameleon as much as we do.'

'My enemy's enemy is my friend kind of vibe?'

I smiled. 'Exactly.'

I was calm. It was going to be fine. Despite the awful nature of her news, it was a comfort to know that Jenny was not betraying us. I'd cut out the psycho therapist and her dodgy drugs. I had my wife by my side. We'd go to this party, find the person who'd been making our lives hell and end him. Then I could go back to working on all the other simple stuff in my life that had been getting me down, like my advancing age and my own mortality.

Part 4
Confrontation

'Sticks and stones can break your bones, but words can cause everlasting damage and require years of therapy to heal from. We don't ever raise our voices. If a child has done something to displease us, we sing-song our pleas for calm.'

Bells Brightley, parenting blogger (MommaKnowsBest) and bestselling author of *Reason for Being: Blessed to Be a Mom!*

'No one ever sets out wanting to shout at a child. But when they're being little shits and not listening, screaming, "Get your finger out that plug socket!" is a fuck of a lot more effective at guaranteeing a non-frazzled kid than asking them to make better choices.'

Hazel Matthews, mother

58

8 September 2007
East London Police Report

Victim: James White. Died of three stab wounds to abdomen. Body discovered by Harry Hogg (bar security). All the cameras in the back office were not working. Bar was very busy that night. Andy Savage (customer) and Mike Tribe (customer), both reported seeing White wave at someone and point towards the back office. Neither saw who he was waving at – there were numerous people standing by the bar at the time. The bar staff claimed to not have seen anything. Unknown female DNA found on three hair strands on floor near body. The three hair strands have been misplaced from the evidence locker.

12 January 2008
East London Police Report

Victim: Julian Barrow. Head crushed by skillet pan. Body discovered 15:23 on 2 August by Andrew Winpenny (victim's landlord, responding to bad-smell complaints).

Estimated date of death 20/21 July. Neighbours interviewed. Reports from Chris Walker (tenant at 2B) that victim was seen on 20 July in the evening with a brunette woman in her 20s. No corroborating reports. Walker reinterviewed on 10 August and said 'he wasn't good with numbers' and he may have been mistaken on the date. No other current leads.

17 December 2008
Croydon Police Report

Victim: Will Callewaert. Died of one stab wound to the chest. His arm was burned four times with a cigarette. Body discovered by Laura Gracey (victim's foster daughter). The cigarette used was found inserted into his right nostril. The cigarette only had the victim's DNA on.

August 2012
Witness Statement
Cheryl Bell, Capri Grand Hotel guest

I definitely saw the two of them there. Her hair was different. But, god, I'd never forget those cheekbones. I'd die for them. She's so beautiful, right? Do you think she's all natural? I mean, the curve of her breasts look so perfect you'd nearly . . . Okay, okay, but you asked me if I was sure? So yeah, I'm sure. Herb pissed me off as he kept staring at her. And then I made him switch places with me, and then he got pissed off as I kept staring at her. Like I said, she was . . . Oh yeah, and her husband, he was something special too. I only saw his back for most of dinner, but when they got up to leave – wow. Herb told me I was drooling . . . Yeah, no I'm sure on the date. It was our wedding anniversary. Real special evening.

August 2012
Witness Statement
Luca Savelli, Capri Grand Hotel Manager

He was a good tipper. The dead guy. He's stayed here a few times. A few days ago, there was a bit of a misunderstanding with a waitress. I helped clear things up for him and he was grateful.

August 2012
Witness Statement
Luisa Edwards, Waitress at Giovanni's Restaurant, Capri

That piece of shit put his hand up my skirt. I freaked out and dropped the bottle of wine I was holding. He was disgusting. I'm glad he's dead. I mean, I didn't do it, obviously. I'm sure plenty would've loved to be the one to kill him. All the girls knew about him. We always drew straws on who had to wait his table. Management don't give a shit, as he's loaded. It's so depressing. Fuck, I need to get out of here. My mother was right. I just . . . Yes, that couple were there when it happened. I remember them. Who wouldn't remember them? They paid up and left before the shit did. Racing back to their suite, probably. Lucky cow.

August 2012
Witness Statement
Marie Bosanquet, Reception, the Pampelonne
Prestige. St Tropez

No, *they hadn't stayed here before. I would've remem-*
bered them. They were here for a thirtieth birthday party.
Some Russian guy's. Apparently his family are a big deal.
It all got a little crazy. I remember we had to charge their
damage deposit for at least one broken table. People
were dancing on them all night. And don't even get me
started on the mess in the . . . Well, no, I don't think that
couple were leading the trouble. Just, you know, normal
rich party guests. I think they left before check-out. She
was a redhead, not like your photo.

August 2012
Witness Statement
Dreya (No Last Name Given), Housekeeping, the
Pampelonne Prestige. St Tropez

I don't want any trouble. I don't . . . Okay . . . You're a
private investigator? . . . How much? . . . No, okay I
can help. Yes, I cleaned their room when they were
here . . . Any what? . . . No, no, nothing like that. Just
usual, you know . . . They were a couple who liked to be
alone in their room. You know . . . Happy couple.
Nothing else. I mean, there was a private problem. Big
stain on one of the towels. She said it was, you know,
woman's problem. It happens, you know. She was very
nice and apologetic about it. Not like usual guests who
trash everything and ignore me.

August 2012
Witness Statement
Alison Martin, Guest, the Pampelonne Prestige.
St Tropez

Oh god, I hated those two. They were in the next room to me. Made me want to puke. Yeah, so you're hot and into each other, bully for you. Why'd you have to go round rubbing it in our faces. Are they dead? Did he kill her? . . . No, no, I didn't see him be violent or anything. I was just hoping, you know, that no one can be as happy as that for real.

59

Haze

Getting glammed up to go to a black-tie masked ball at a stately home should have been fun, but the whole potential deadly threat of what lay ahead was putting a bit of a downer on things.

The usual pre-event jitters with heightened stakes.

Less worry about dying of boredom from a banker's bad chat, and more worry about actually dying.

I'd squeezed myself into a tight black Roland Mouret dress that hugged my curves in all the right places. My sheathed knife was strapped to my right inner thigh so as not to upset the lines of my dress – its fastening at the back could unzip upwards, releasing me to run, climb, fight. The three-inch Louboutin heels were perhaps a little impractical. But I really couldn't wear flats with this outfit.

We'd assessed it repeatedly and had concluded it would be unlikely that we were walking into an outright attack. If they wanted to make a scene, it wouldn't be at a home of national importance and in front of such polite society.

Social hand grenades only.

Tonight was the night we would hopefully once and for all

lift the shadow of the last year. We could finally come face to face – or, really, mask to mask – with The Chameleon.

Drake might have tried to warn us off, but he didn't realise that we had to go. We needed answers. We didn't hide from our problems; we confronted them head-on.

I came down to the kitchen to find Fox looking resplendent in his black tie.

'Hot,' I said to him.

'And hotter,' he said back as he kissed me.

We were absolutely nauseating, and I was totally into it.

Our masks were on the kitchen table. Mine was an elaborate peacock-feather one that hid most of my face. Fox's was the classic Phantom of the Opera.

Fox picked up mine and put it on me, gently tying the ribbon at the back. Then he put on his own and pulled it down. It was a little large for him, but that worked, as it hid more of his face.

'The masks are great.' Jenny walked in, gripping her laptop and a large Thermos of coffee. She always brought her own instant coffee, as she said our expensive coffee machine was overcomplicated and underwhelming. 'You're nearly unrecognisable.'

Jenny had insisted she was up to manning the fort: babysitting Reggie and Bibi and scanning the relevant local police channels. And she was the only person we truly trusted to be with our kids on a night like tonight. We didn't know what might happen. We just knew we didn't want someone in our house who would ask questions when we returned, whatever state we were in.

Frank and Sandy were at Jenny's house with Felix but on standby in case they needed to swoop in and take our kids. None of us had said it out loud, but we'd all felt more than a little guilty about potentially having to use them for child-care when they had enough going on. They had both insisted that if it was called for it would be no trouble. Just like Jenny had said when we'd questioned her that any distraction was a welcome one.

Having Jenny at base camp monitoring us and looking up anyone we wanted her to was the best course of action. If things went bad, really bad, we didn't want all three of us neutralised. She needed to be clear of it all, ready to come to our rescue. *Like in Ivrea.* I shook off the thought. Tonight was not going to be a repeat of that night.

Admits two. The Chameleon had made it clear he didn't expect Jenny to attend. We needed tonight to run smoothly. He needed to think we were playing ball, right up until we smashed him in the face with it.

Jenny placed her laptop and Thermos down on the kitchen table. Her hair was scraped back in a high ponytail. 'Your watches will make sure I know exactly where you are. Remember, if things look like they're going bad, ring me and I'll keep the line open so I can hear everything.' Balgray Hall was too far away for our headsets to connect to Jenny on our secure encrypted radio channel.

I checked my watch. 'We'd better go. The kids are asleep. The baby monitor is on the countertop, and the sharpest knife we have is the one on the chopping board.'

'Good luck.' Jenny looked between us both. 'I won't hug you, as I don't want to crumple you.'

Ours was the only minivan in the Balgray car park. We left Danny's gun in the footwell of the passenger seat. We couldn't risk being caught with one at the party.

The path towards the house was illuminated by a long line

of lanterns plunged into the ground. We joined the many other masked people walking towards the outline of Balgray Hall.

I held hands with my husband because I loved him, and because the gravel made it tricky to walk in heels.

The murmur of those around us talking, the masks, the dark grandeur of Balgray. It wasn't a particularly cold night, but I felt a shiver.

Inside the house, the entrance hall that had looked mundane by daylight had been transformed. Gone were the black partitions for queuing and the information desk with boxes of leaflets on the history of the estate. Now, huge floral displays adorned the staircase, and waiters and waitresses holding silver trays of champagne were accosting everyone as they arrived.

We entered the main reception room, which was already bustling. Fox pulled his mask up over his head. 'I can't see properly with this on.' He looked out at the sea of people. The majority of women had favoured feathers and lace for their masks. The men were in anything from animal masks to simple black-and-white ones. There was one joker who was wearing a *Scream* mask. A good percentage hadn't bothered at all, and more than a few already had their masks half off.

A tall man with foppish dark hair approached us, a jester's mask perched on top of his head. 'Nathaniel! Good to see you here, supporting the cause.' He gave Fox a hearty backslap. 'And this must be your wife?'

Fox tore his eyes away from scanning the room. 'This is Haze.'

'Benjamin Norwood.' The man gave me a firm handshake, his fingers gripping mine for just a moment too long.

'Wonderful to have you both here.' He was slurring a little.

This was Fox's big new client. The idiot who didn't realise Unique Events was using his little charity to launder money for gangbangers. There was already a large red wine stain on his white shirt.

'It's good to see you, Benjamin, but we're just looking for some friends.' Fox put a hand on my back and guided me forward.

'Good, good. Have fun!' Norwood stumbled off.

The room was so busy it was hard to take everyone in. Fox looked around. 'I'll head to the back. You check through to the library.'

I pulled his mask back down. 'We're avoiding Drake, remember.'

Our headsets were in. We could keep talking to each other as long as we were within radius.

I walked through the party.

One figure stood out. Diana Morgan, in a white jumpsuit, was holding court in the centre of the room, surrounded by several masked partygoers. She hadn't ruined her hair or hidden her perfect make-up with a mask, instead wearing just one feather on a hairband. She caught me looking at her and smirked as she glided over.

'What are you doing here?' she asked. 'I thought you'd be like Cinderella. Stuck at home, busy with council paperwork.'

'That would make you the evil stepmother.' I had nothing to lose by pushing her. If she was here, it wasn't a stretch to believe she was involved with The Corporation. It was her law firm that had set up the company they were hiding behind, after all. 'I see that Backhouse Dunne had a hand in Unique Events. So much for lawyers abiding by the law.'

She shrugged. 'It's technically legal.'

I couldn't believe she was so blatant. 'Is that what you say to yourself so you can sleep at night?'

Her brow furrowed. 'A tax break is not a crime. Rich clients are always looking for deductibles – and why not something that means you get to go to a fabulous party in a grand location?'

I took in Diana and her immaculate ensemble. She was a successful lawyer. She cared about her appearance, her son and her money. Fun parties, exotic holidays, beautiful interior design. Nothing as complicated and seedy as gangsters and assassins and The Corporation.

It was suddenly very clear to me that she would never dirty herself with all that. Why would she? Reputation was everything to someone like her. She wouldn't risk putting little Ted through the humiliation of his mother being arrested for being involved with criminal gangs.

She wouldn't take such a risk – but we were happy to, apparently. I shook off the thought.

If I believed what Diana was saying, that meant that Unique Events was just a tax dodge. But we were so sure it was The Corporation. It all fitted. What could it mean?

'You'll have to try harder to find something to pin on me, Hazel.' She swept off, waving at a handsome bearded man on the other side of the room.

A woman with cropped pink hair was weaving a little as she made her way through the crowd, clutching a glass of champagne. Her mask was pushed up on to her head. She looked familiar. Where did I . . .?

Razia. Danny's PA. Danny still hadn't been reported missing yet. Clearly, no one cared about him enough to notice he'd been off-grid for nearly two weeks.

I stopped her. 'Hi! Razia, isn't it?'

I lifted my mask a little. She looked at me and tilted her head. 'Oh, the pretty one. You were at my office.'

'Is Danny here tonight?'

She frowned. 'Who's that?'

Danny had lied. No surprise there. But why? Was he pretending to have a PA to seem like a bigger deal? Or was it something else?

'Danny. The man I was in a meeting with when you came in.'

'Oh, him. I've no idea.'

'He doesn't . . . he doesn't work for Unique Events?'

'We let out those meeting rooms to local creatives. I thought you guys worked together.' She spotted a waiter brandishing a bottle of champagne and headed for him. 'Oh, here, please!'

I tried to make it make sense. Danny did not work for Unique Events. He'd had no part in organising this party.

Danny was here at Balgray Hall that first day because he knew we were coming. That chance meeting had not been chance at all. The Chameleon wanted us to think we were getting one step ahead of him. But we weren't. He knew about my history with Danny. As soon as Danny told me about the party, he knew I'd use Danny to find out more.

Everything we'd seen, he'd wanted us to see.

Fox crackled in. *'I'm at the seating plan. Something's not right. All the names from the guest list are different to the names up here.'*

The guest list. That had come from the booklet I took from Danny. They could've written anything they wanted in it. There were no elderly clients who only liked printouts. If something was too easy, there was usually a reason for it.

Those booklets had just been sitting on a desk, waiting for me to take one.

The guest list was fake. Criminal names had been put in to make us think something big was happening. And the Joe Jones name was planted to make us go to the Airbnb.

Unique Events wasn't The Corporation. It was just an events company Backhouse Dunne had set up as a tax break.

Diana Morgan was just a vicious school mum.

This wasn't a great criminal get-together of all the big players. This was . . . just a party.

Blood was pounding in my ears. Every instinct was telling me this was a trap.

Just like Ivrea.

We'd gone charging into that apartment thinking that it was the perfect place to kill the target. We'd been so busy thinking about attack that we hadn't thought about defence.

And now he'd done it again.

At the Airbnb, The Chameleon had showed us he had evidence on all our past kills. He'd used that as leverage to make us come here tonight.

But why?

He'd had people following us. He could've got us at any time at home.

It must be because he didn't *want* to get us at home.

Was it because our children were there, always with us? Maybe he wanted us here to get us alone?

Did he want us here, without our children, so they wouldn't be harmed?

Or—

Did he want us here, without our children, so they *could* be harmed?

I felt my handbag vibrating. I took out my phone.

Jenny.

I answered it without speaking. I knew whatever she was

going to say would be bad. I braced myself, but I still fell to my knees when she got the words out through her racking sobs.

Bibi.

He'd taken Bibi.

His last big job wasn't happening at Balgray.

It was at our home.

Him taking Bibi was what all of this had been leading up to.

With all this running around we'd been doing, we'd thought we were chasing him – but he'd been drawing us in.

We'd done exactly what he wanted. And now he had our daughter.

My heart was breaking.

Everything was spinning.

I couldn't breathe.

My worst nightmare was coming true. My child was in danger. And it was all our fault.

60

Fox

'*Fox!*' Haze's voice came through my headset. But she didn't sound right.

I walked back into the main hall, trying to find her. I spotted her at the other side of the room, her shoulders stiff, her phone gripped to her ear. I watched as she fell to her knees, her right hand still gripping her phone.

I ran to her, pushing past people in my way. I scooped her up off the floor and propped her up on my shoulder.

'Bibi . . . Bibi . . . She's gone.' She managed to get the words out.

We'd been set up.

He'd got us out here so he could get to Bibi.

Why?

She was just a child. What did he want with her?

Leverage.

That must be it.

I couldn't let my mind go anywhere else. He'd taken her to make us do whatever he wanted. And he was right. We would.

Her little face. Was she scared? Was she trying to be brave?

It took everything I had not to roar at the thought of my baby being sad and us not being there to help her.

Her smile. Her little pigtails. The way they swung when she skipped down the road.

This couldn't be happening.

If he hurt her . . . I couldn't even finish the thought.

The sounds of the party. The music. Glasses clinking. People laughing. It was closing in on us. It was too loud. All of it. We needed to think. I half led, half held Haze, and walked us towards the exit.

We were nearly there when a loud trumpet sounded. We both jumped and looked around. The brass band was starting up. A cheer went up from the crowd as they launched into a loud, energetic waltz. The people around us moved towards the music as we moved against them, towards the door.

As soon as we got out into the fresh air, I took the phone from Haze and listened to Jenny. Haze pulled off her mask and threw it to the ground. The tears were still flowing, but she was silent. I made Jenny repeat everything twice before hanging up.

The air was crisp, and the sounds of the party inside carried from an open window. Music and laughter.

I hated the people in there. Oblivious. Enjoying their evening as our world was crumbling.

Haze couldn't stand still; she was walking in circles, her hands to her head. I stopped her and gripped her by the shoulders.

'Haze!'

She wouldn't look at me.

'Haze.' I shook her gently. 'I need you. Bibi needs you.'

Her eyes finally flicked to mine.

'She needs you angry, Haze. She needs you furious.'

Haze nodded, and then crouched over as she took several deep breaths. When she looked back up at me, her eyes were clear and focused. She was back – and she was terrifying.

'Let's go get her.' She took off her shoes and we ran back towards the car park. She didn't cry out as the gravel cut and bloodied her feet. She didn't even seem to notice.

I was running faster than her.

'You go!' she shouted at me. 'Pick me up!'

I went full pace. Within a minute, I was at the car. I jumped into the driver's seat.

Haze was still running, a good ten feet away. That's when I saw them. Two men. Big men, dressed in black tie. Running towards her.

'Haze!' I shouted. 'Faster!' She didn't look back; she would've known what was coming. I started the engine and opened the passenger door. They were gaining on her. She wasn't going to make it. I accelerated towards her, my lights on full beam. Nearly there. Nearly. I slowed down enough to let her get in.

She slipped into the passenger seat, but a man with a shaved head was right there. He hung on to the door, not letting her close it. I started to speed up. He flung himself on to her, just as she plunged her index finger into his right eye. He howled, and then she did the same to his other eye. She punched him in the head and pushed him out of the car. There was a crunch as I drove over his leg.

Haze was already grappling for the gun in the footwell. She leaned out of the door and fired two shots at the other man, who was still running towards us.

He dove to the ground.

We screeched down Balgray's drive and towards the motorway.

Minivans were not designed to drive at speed.

I was struggling not to slam my foot down on the accelerator, to slam it down until it could go no further, until the doors rattled, until we were back home, back to Reggie, back to Bibi's empty bed.

I gripped the steering wheel and tried to keep my speed to eighty miles per hour. We couldn't afford to be stopped. We couldn't afford to die in a fiery crash. We needed to get our daughter back, and we needed to wreak vengeance on those who had dared to take her.

61

Haze

Fox rang Jenny on loudspeaker. I didn't know how he was able to drive. It was taking everything I had to not scream, and keep screaming until my daughter was back in my arms.

'We're both here now, Jen.' Fox kept his eyes on the road.

'*I'm so sorry. It's all my fault. I should—*'

Fox cut her off. 'Jenny, stop. You know who we're dealing with. If he decided he wanted Bibi, he was going to get her, no matter what.'

If Jenny had happened to come across him taking her, he was a professional. He would've left with Bibi regardless; Jenny wouldn't have stood a chance.

'Tell us again what happened.'

Jenny's voice was low but steady. She'd cried it all out too. The steely focus was back. '*I last checked on Bibi an hour ago. She was in her bed, asleep. I went down to the kitchen. I was on my laptop at the kitchen table. A dog started barking, then howling. Loudly. I thought maybe there was an injured dog in the garden. The sound was so loud. I went to the back door and looked out. There was nothing there. I then—*'

'That's when he would've exited through the front door with her.'

'*Agreed. I've already checked and the Ring doorbell is disconnected. No footage can be recovered.*'

Fox and I looked at each other. A well-organised kidnapping plan.

'*I wasn't sure she hadn't just decided to get up and go find you, or to give me a scare with a game of hide and seek. But then I found a Bluetooth speaker hidden in the garden. There was no injured dog – just a recording of one. If I was looking out of the back door, he knew I'd have my back to the front door.*'

I turned the scene over in my head. Something didn't make sense. And then it hit me.

'Sausage! She didn't she bark at the sound of the dog?'

'No.' Jenny paused. 'She's been asleep all evening.' Our minds went to the same place and, before I could ask, Jenny cut in. 'I'm holding her now. She's very floppy and tired, but she's fine.'

There was no doubt Sausage would've heard or smelled a stranger in the house. The kidnapper had drugged her.

He had taken my child and fucked with my dog.

There weren't enough superlatives to describe the level of pain I was going to put him through.

I got out my phone and tried to get my fingers to stop shaking enough to tap out a message.

> *What the fuck have you done?*
> *Why have you taken her? What do you want?*

A ping came back immediately: undeliverable. He'd blocked me. He'd taken what he wanted, and he'd blocked me.

All the texting to make me feel we were building a rapport. All bullshit.

A thought hit me. 'Are her school shoes there?' I asked. 'Or her school trainers?'

Jenny switched to FaceTime as she approached our front door. The shoe rack came into sight. Bibi's black school shoes and blue school trainers were both there. Her pink trainers were missing.

'Fuck! He took the one pair that didn't have a tracker in.' He wasn't just prepared, he was immaculately prepared. I slumped back in the passenger seat.

Fox looked at me. 'If The Chameleon took Bibi for leverage, why hasn't he contacted us with his demands?'

It was the same question I'd been wrestling with.

The Chameleon had tried to kill us once and failed. And now he'd taken our child. If he wanted to do something worse than killing us, then that would be hurting our child. Did he know that? Was that his plan? Did he know that hurting us was nothing compared to how crushed we'd be if he hurt Bibi?

'*The call will come. Maybe he's waiting until you're back home.*' Jenny tried to sound reassuring.

None of us wanted to think about what it would mean if the call didn't come. None of us could entertain the idea that taking Bibi and hurting her was the end plan.

I shook my head to myself.

He was a professional. This wasn't vindictive. He didn't have an issue with us; his bosses did.

Then it all became horribly clear.

I spoke calmly. 'I know what he's going to say. He'll want us to surrender ourselves to him, in exchange for Bibi. He wants to hand us over to The Corporation.'

We were his final hurrah. His last job. This was his grand finish – the two of us delivered to the gang who wanted us dead.

No fuss, no mess, no bloody shoot out that would capture the attention of the authorities. The Corporation were discreet. That was their reputation. They didn't want the drama, the news headlines. The Chameleon had planned to take us quietly in Ivrea. If I hadn't escaped, if I hadn't come for Fox, he would've succeeded.

The Chameleon had planned this to perfection.

We would go quietly. We would do anything he asked. Because he had our child.

It was our fault.

We'd been too distracted. If we'd come closer together after Ivrea, and not spent the last year disagreeing over how best to handle Fox's trauma, we could've protected our children. We should've seen this coming.

Fox reached over and squeezed my hand as Jenny spoke again.

'*I've been looking at the traffic cams and CCTV of the street, and I've got a car leaving your street two minutes after the dog barking got me out of eyeline of the front door. The timing fits to be our guy.*'

'What kind of car?' asked Fox.

'*Just zooming in, I think I can . . . Got it. A grey Ford Fiesta.*' Jenny groaned.

'What? Why's that bad?'

'*The grey Ford Fiesta is one of the most popular cars in the UK. I won't find one – I'll find ten. And then we'll need to work out which one is right.*'

Our child was out there alone. We didn't know where and we didn't know with who. We had failed her.

'Do we know it's definitely The Chameleon?' Fox said.

I turned to look at him. 'Who else would it be? Who else would take our child to spite us?'

'I just mean, do we have anything directly linking him to this?' Fox was clearly in shock and not thinking properly.

'You mean, apart from a convoluted plan to make sure we attended an event over an hour away from our children, enabling him to take one of them?'

'*Yes, it has to be him.*' Jenny sounded as confused as I was. '*Mum is on her way to come get Reggie. We thought it'd be safest for him to be at theirs?*'

Fox and I looked at each other. Every instinct made me want to strap Reggie to me and not let him out of my sight. I wanted to keep him safe so much it ached.

But what we were going to do to get Bibi back was not exactly going to be baby-friendly. The safest place for Reggie was with Sandy, in a house for which The Chameleon hopefully did not have the address.

I nodded at Fox.

'Yes, that makes sense,' he said. 'We'll be home soon.' He clicked off.

We were both silent the rest of the drive back.

Should I be grateful The Chameleon had only taken Bibi, and not Reggie too? Our baby son was still safely at home.

Why?

Was it that he didn't have the balls to handle two kids at once? Or was he scared that Reggie's cries at a stranger holding him would've given him away?

He had been here in our house. Standing outside their bedroom doors.

Our children had been in danger, and we hadn't been there for them.

These last few months, we'd been struggling. Desperate to have it all. Trying to pretend we could. But look at us!

We'd *had* it all – and we'd lost it. We'd lost Bibi. We were kidding ourselves to think we could continue with this life and keep our children safe.

62

Fox

Bibi.

My little Bibi.

I knew I had to say something. Just in case. I couldn't risk keeping quiet. My Bibi was at stake, and there was nothing more important.

I waited until we were back in our kitchen. Haze was already changing into the clothes Jenny had laid out for her. Danny's gun was on the kitchen table. Haze had been gripping it the whole drive back. She was standing there in her jeans and bra, and I couldn't keep it in any longer.

'There is someone else who might have taken her. I should've told you. I just didn't think she would ever . . .'

'Fucking spit it out!' Haze stared at me.

'Sally.'

'The therapist?' asked Jenny.

'She was pretty unhinged when I told her I didn't want to see her any more. Talked about all she'd done for me. Said she needed me to value her, as she'd been so understanding. Lots of crazy talk. I think . . . I think she's in love with me.'

Jenny started tapping at her laptop.

Haze was completely silent.

It was more terrifying than if she'd screamed at me.

When she finally spoke, her voice was quiet and steady. 'So much in love with you that she'd steal your daughter as a twisted revenge for your rejection?'

I tried to weigh it up. 'No, I don't think . . .' I remembered the flash of Sally's face, the way her eyes had narrowed. 'Okay, maybe.'

There was one more beat of ice-cold calm Haze before all hell broke loose.

'You fucking idiot!' She came at me. 'How could you not tell me? I'm going to fucking kill you if—'

'Not helping!' Jenny shouted her down. 'Fox, I've got Sally's home address from when I did a deep dive into her. You can go to her house to make sure she's got nothing to do with this.'

Haze's hands were shaking. 'If she *is* involved, I swear I will fucking lose my mind. You invited that woman into your life, and she's a psycho!'

'I was trying to do the right thing! I was struggling and I got help. How was I to know she was an unstable stalker?'

'Because you should always think the worst of everyone!' Haze's arms dropped to her sides. 'Isn't that what this has taught us? Never trust anyone!' Her voice cracked. 'We've got to find her.'

'We will. Of course we will.' I put my hands on her shoulders. 'We're going to get her back. She's going to be fine.'

Haze looked up at me. Her body rigid. A beat. And then she collapsed into my chest. I held her close.

'We need to move.' Jenny stood up from the table.

We unravelled from each other as Haze reached for her jumper.

'I've got two Ford Fiestas leaving this area in the right timeframe. I've got the numberplates of each, and the last location sighting on CCTV. Haze, you're on the one with a numberplate ending in OGE.'

We had a plan. And we had each other. I had two knives on me. Haze had one in her back pocket, and Danny's gun in her waistband. Jenny picked up the knife from the chopping board.

We were ready to get Bibi back.

Sally lived half an hour away from us in Surrey. I hadn't known she was that close. Close enough, I realised with a creeping dread, to easily come and spy on us.

Weaving through traffic on my motorbike, the loud thrum of the engine was doing little to drown out the thoughts going round and round in my head.

One question kept coming back. How had she known to call me Fox?

This trip was just to rule her out. Just because she'd developed what was clearly an unhealthy fixation with me didn't mean she'd take my child.

She lived in a terraced house on a long street of identical houses. Her small back garden overlooked a footpath. I charged down it and climbed over the fence.

From the end of the garden, it looked as if Sally was sitting watching television. I could make out her outline in a fluffy dressing gown in an armchair. A bowl on her lap. If you'd just kidnapped someone's daughter, it was doubtful you'd be so relaxed. But she could be a sociopath who didn't think anything of it. I needed to get closer.

I creeped up to the garden door just as a security light came on, illuminating me. Sally turned towards the light, saw me and screamed.

I opened the door and walked in. 'Shush! Sally, it's me.'

She half swallowed her scream and spoke with a quivering voice. 'Why are you here? How did you get this address?'

She stayed stuck to her armchair, the remote control gripped in her hand. I saw her glance at her mobile phone, which lay on the coffee table.

I was aware now of how it looked. I was a patient, turning up at my therapist's unlisted address. At night.

'My daughter is missing.'

'And . . . and you want a therapy session?'

'No! I'm checking she's not here.' I took another step towards her, and she cowered further into the armchair. 'Just walk around your house with me and then I'll be gone.' I beckoned her with my hand.

She got unsteadily to her feet. 'Why would *I* have her?'

I took her by the arm and led her through to the hallway. It wouldn't take long to ascertain if Bibi was here.

'You were clearly upset about me quitting our sessions.' I checked the small bathroom off the hallway. Empty. I led her up the stairs.

'You thought I'd take your child as revenge for you quitting? How does your mind work?'

The first bedroom on the landing was a small double. I walked in and led her round as I checked inside the wardrobe and under the bed.

'You seemed kind of . . . obsessed with me.'

Her jaw dropped. 'We should talk about your inflated self-esteem.'

I led her out of the bedroom and into the room next to it, which she seemed to use as an office. There was nothing but a desk and an armchair.

'You kept giving me compliments and being rude about my wife!' I snapped.

I headed back on to the landing. The bathroom. The last place to look. I opened the door and went to the bath, flinging back the shower curtain. Empty.

Sally shook her head. 'You weren't prepared to talk about whatever had really happened to you. Fobbing me off with this whole fake-mugging story. I thought if you weren't going to be honest, I might as well use you to get this grant I've been angling for.'

'What grant?' Was she bullshitting me? Had she still got Bibi, but just stashed her somewhere else?

'I'm doing a thesis on coercive relationships, and you were a good candidate for a case study.'

'But I'm not *in* a coercive relationship.'

'I don't think you realise you are.'

'So you were encouraging me to think my wife was evil and controlling to get a grant?'

'Look, the stuff you were saying was close enough that I could fudge the data a little, but I had to have proof of you attending sessions – so you totally screwed me by quitting.'

I took this in.

Sally shrugged. 'I've had a few problems in the last couple of years. Patients who got the wrong idea. Complaining about silly stuff. I needed this grant to get back on track.'

I could see how that could make her desperate enough to try and claw back her professional reputation. What calibre of therapist had I expected to find via junk mail? Why hadn't I checked her out before I started offloading my problems to her?

'If you're not obsessed with me, how do you know I go by Fox?'

Sally frowned. 'Jesus, your ego! You were only useful to

me for my career. And please – whenever you do an impression of Haze and put on an English accent, you're all, "You need to get over it, Fox." '

That did sound like me.

'And the pills you gave me? I know there was something bad in them!'

Sally chewed her inside cheek. 'I gave you a perfectly harmless SSRI. It has been reported it may cause increased anxiety before they take full effect.'

'I had blackouts! Waking up and not knowing how I got there.'

Sally held her hands up. 'I couldn't have known that would happen!' She paused. 'Okay, so with those particular pills occasional blackouts have been reported. But it's very rare!'

She'd never mentioned the pills' potential side effects as she wanted me to think it was all me and my PTSD. She needed me to feel like I was really suffering to make sure I kept seeing her.

I didn't have any more time to waste on her. Not when my daughter was missing.

'You've been completely unethical. Criminal, actually! And if you don't mention all this' – I motioned towards myself, being in her house, uninvited – 'I won't report you to your board.'

Sally folded her arms. 'Fine.'

As I rushed down the stairs, she called after me.

'You do clearly need help, though!'

I texted Jenny and Haze.

She's got nothing to do with it.
I'm coming to you, Haze.

63

Haze

Sally was a bust, and Jenny had updated us to say that five teenagers had just got out of the car she was following and piled into a house party. Our one remaining lead was the car I was trying to find: a Ford Fiesta with a numberplate ending OGE.

OGE had gone down this road less than ten minutes ago. I had to find it. I had to. We had no other leads. If I didn't, that would be it. She'd be in the wind. At the mercy of a madman. I couldn't let my mind go there. I couldn't. Not while we still had hope.

Jenny had now parked up and was trawling CCTV. She'd confirmed that there was no sign of the Fiesta leaving the area. If he'd parked up somewhere and taken Bibi on foot, we'd have no idea where they were headed. I couldn't let myself panic yet.

I went to Cherry Lane. Nothing. I turned right into Hawthorne Avenue. A grey car was parked up ahead. My heart rate sped up. I got close enough to see the numberplate was wrong.

Fuck.

I kept going. I looked around. I knew this area. I'd just been here yesterday.

When my boot was overloaded with boxes of toys.

I paused.

I had to make a decision – and fast.

No sign of OGE – but then, if I knew where it was headed, what did it matter? I swerved into a parking space and got out of the car.

The charity shop was on the opposite side of the road.

The blinds were down, but the lights were on.

I didn't believe in coincidences.

And I didn't believe there was any reason anyone would be in a charity shop at 10pm.

I rang Fox and Jenny. 'No sign of OGE, but I'm going to check out the charity shop here. I was there yesterday, and there was something off about this guy Freddie who was working there. It looks like there's someone in there now.'

They reacted as I expected.

Jenny: '*Looking up the CCTV around the shop now.*'

Fox: '*I would tell you to wait for me, but I know there's no point.*'

I saw a shadow of someone walking past the blinds.

'I'll keep the line open.'

'*The shop has a back entrance that takes you into a narrow alleyway that leads out on to Hawthorne Terrace,*' Jenny said. '*The alleyway has no CCTV, so he could've parked up and gone into the shop that way.*'

The charity shop was on the corner of a quiet street. I was going to have to break in, and doing that at the front door would draw too much attention. If the kidnapper had gone in through the alleyway, I'd do the same. I got out of the car and headed into the alleyway – and came face to face with Alain Drake.

'What are you doing here, Mrs Cabot?'

I had a second to work out what to spin. And I couldn't get my brain to cooperate. I couldn't think of anything to say except the truth.

'My daughter is missing. I think she's here.'

'Why didn't you call the police?'

I paused. 'I don't want them to know.'

Drake observed me in silence. 'This does not surprise me.' He nodded towards the charity shop. 'I've tracked the man I've been chasing here.' He took a gun out of a holster inside his jacket. 'You get reunited with your daughter, and then you can tell me everything.'

'Yes. Fine. Anything once I get her back.'

I could face the Drake problem another time. The only thing that mattered now was getting Bibi back into my arms.

I watched as Drake leaned down to the back door lock with a couple of small silver tools. He fiddled with them and then tried the handle. It opened.

I pushed past him and walked in.

Bibi was sitting on a display table in the middle of the empty shop. She was wearing pink rabbit pyjamas. Rabbits were her second favourite animal. A large McDonald's milk-shake was in her hands.

I longed to just run to her, but I had to be careful. Alert. I must've made a noise without realising, as she turned.

'Hi, Mama.' She was okay. And she wasn't afraid. Thank god.

I looked around. No one was here.

Was she really alone? Or was this the trap? Was Bibi the bait? But I couldn't think of anything else other than getting her out of here. I went to her and held her close. 'Bibi, it's okay. We're going to go home now. Before the man who took you comes back.'

Bibi frowned. 'What you mean? He's already here.'

She was looking over my shoulder. At Drake.

I reached slowly for the gun in my waistband.

He smiled at me. 'Let's not get carried away, Mama.' He tapped his jacket, indicating where his gun was. 'I'd like your phone, please.'

What choice did I have?

I took my phone from my pocket, ending my call with Fox and Jenny without him seeing. How much had they heard? Enough to work out what was going on?

'And your . . . toys. Both of them.' He motioned to my waistband and my back pocket. Of course he knew where my weapons were. He knew everything.

Bibi was back to slurping on her shake. I handed him my gun and knife without her seeing.

Drake was The Chameleon.

It was the perfect cover.

An Interpol agent could travel freely. He had the best contacts. The best databases. He was a powerful ally to turn. He could find out information on anyone. His credentials gave him access to anywhere he wanted to go.

For fuck's sake. Even the name. The Chameleon. He fitted in wherever he was. An assassin. An agent. He adapted to be whoever he needed to be.

How the hell was I going to get Bibi away from him without scaring her?

She was still noisily sucking on the straw of her milkshake, getting a sugar spike when she should be tucked up in bed, fast asleep. She stopped and looked up. 'You want some, Mama?'

I shook my head.

She didn't know how much danger she was in, and for that, at least, I was grateful.

Bibi's long brown hair was perfectly straight. She hadn't been asleep long enough to get it into her usual knotted mats. I chewed on the inside of my cheek. He'd plucked her out of her bed. He'd taken her while she was sleeping.

It had been so well planned, so masterfully executed. He was a professional, after all. He'd taken her when she was sleeping because he knew we'd have a tracker on her during the day. That was the problem when you came up against someone who thought like you.

I had to get her out of here, away from him, alive and not so traumatised that her life was ruined in another way.

I was desperate to inflict pain on the person who'd dared to take my child.

It was going to be hard to rein it in.

There really wasn't a PG way to kill a man.

How long would it take for Fox to get here? I tried to remember where he'd said Sally's house was. And Jenny. How far away was she?

'Can we go now, Mama?'

I needed to think. And fast.

'Give Bibi my phone,' I said. 'We need to talk, and she loves watching *Octonauts*.'

Bibi had no idea anything was wrong. I wasn't going to change that. My priority was getting her out of here safely – and preferably with no idea she had ever been in danger.

'*Octonauts*! Yayyyyyy!' Bibi spun round to look at Drake.

He took a few steps forward and handed my phone to me. He watched me as I tapped a few buttons and the *Octonauts* theme tune blared out. I turned up the volume and handed the phone to Bibi, then led Drake a few feet away from the table. Away from my daughter.

'What do you want from us?' I kept my voice level.

Drake folded his arms. 'Last year, I was given a keyring with a set of keys on it to unlock a safety deposit box. Inside it was my final payment, my goodbye bonus. The amount I needed to retire.'

'What the hell has this got to do with us?'

'I thought the keyring could've had a locator inside it. I took it off the keys and planned to hide it in someone else's vehicle to throw them off knowing my actual movements.' Drake shook his head. 'But I made a mistake. The keys were the decoy. The keyring itself was the key.'

I was still no closer to understanding how any of this was our problem.

'When I realised I needed the keyring, I went to get it from my car. But it wasn't there. My employers said it was my fault I'd lost it, and I could only have the duplicate if I did another job for them.'

Was I meant to feel sympathy for him on hearing that he'd been screwed over by his gangster bosses?

'Back in Italy, I drove you and Bibi to the hospital. Bibi found the keyring and took it.'

'Don't accuse my daughter of being a thief! She—'

'It would've looked like nothing. It's just a small metal ball. It might've still had the chain attached to it.'

A keyring without its chain. A broken pendant. Bibi's penguin had been wearing it round its neck.

'Last month, I finally tracked down security footage from the hospital. I saw Bibi playing with something small and silver.'

'You came to England for the keyring? And you took Bibi just to ask her where she'd put it?'

'I know who you are, Haze. I know what you are.' He stared at me silently.

I stared back. This couldn't be happening.

'I wanted Bibi to give it to me without involving you,' he said. 'I didn't want you to keep the keyring for yourselves.'

'You really think we'd run off with some piece of kit we don't even know how to use? To try and cash it in at some unknown location?'

'I would never underestimate you. I've seen your victims.'

And there it was.

He knew us; he knew our work. He was law enforcement, but he was dirty. A child kidnapper and a mercenary. And he was judging us. A couple of serial killers who only ended bad men. There was black, white and grey – and that was us right now.

'Don't judge us,' I hissed. 'You're the worst of the worst. Pretending to be a good-guy agent, pretending you care about the greater good – but look at you! Anyone's for a quick buck! It's all about the money.'

Drake shrugged. 'I like nice things, Haze. There's no shame in that. I am good at what I do. I deserve to get paid well for it.'

I looked around the shop. 'Bibi told you the keyring was here?'

'She had no idea what I was talking about, but said, "Mama gives all my precious things to charity shop."'

'That's not true!' Jesus, why was I defending my parenting to this maniac?

'I checked the surveillance logs and saw this place was on the list of where you'd visited. But it's proving a little tricky to find.'

The logs. He was admitting he'd had people watching us.

'Bibi didn't know where it was because she doesn't think of it as a keyring.' I turned to her. 'Bibi, where's Pinga's pendant?'

She spoke without tearing her eyes away from the screen. 'He didn't like it any more, so I gave it to Dodo Dolly.'

I looked at Drake. I knew exactly where Dodo Dolly was.

The Chameleon had come after us for the keyring. He'd taken Bibi for the keyring. If I gave it to him, then what? The Corporation wanted us dead. And here was their pet assassin, holding us at gunpoint.

Every step of the way, this man had outmanoeuvred us. Everything he'd done had brought us to this moment. He'd made it very clear that he was the professional, we were the amateurs.

How was I going to get us out of this alive?

64

Fox

Hearing Drake's voice through the phone threw me. Any hope of getting Bibi back and getting out of this unscathed was diminishing fast. We'd done well to escape Interpol's attention for this long, and now this was it.

I listened as they entered the charity shop.

I had to remind myself to breathe. And then I heard it. Bibi's voice! She was okay. My baby girl was okay.

Everything else, we could face.

And then it turned.

'He's already here.'

The line went dead.

My heart was going crazy. I accelerated. I needed to get there. I was fourteen minutes away. Fourteen minutes too many.

Drake was The Chameleon.

My wife.

My daughter.

Being held by a madman.

65

Haze

I stared at Drake. I had no way of getting the better of him. I was outmatched. I had no weapon, and my precious daughter was in his potential firing line.

'I know where the keyring is.' I took a step towards him. 'If you let my daughter go, we can go get it.'

Drake shook his head.

He knew Bibi was the best leverage he could get.

'I know what you're planning. You take the keyring, and then . . .' I sliced my finger across my neck.

Drake smiled. 'I don't want you dead.'

'The Corporation want us dead. You work for The Corporation.'

Drake's eyes kept flicking between the shop's two doors.

How far away was Fox now? And was he even going to be up to saving us?

'The Corporation were convinced you were working for a rival gang. Killing you in Ivrea was going to send a message that no one should get involved in their business.'

'But you failed.'

Is this why he'd been so interested in us? Failing to kill us had hurt his ego? His professional reputation?

Drake shook his head. 'I saw the kill order go out, and I told them I'd do it. I took control of the operation. You were never meant to die.'

'What do you mean?'

'The men who took you were under strict instructions to not touch you. But then you escaped through the window anyway.'

'I was meant to live – but Fox was meant to die?'

I tried to understand it. If we'd attracted attention for our killing work, then wanting Fox dead but me alive didn't make sense. We came as a pair – unless they were sexist enough to think I wouldn't be a threat without my man? God, it was exhausting always being underestimated.

'Why would The Corporation want him dead and me alive?'

Bibi snorted. 'Jumping jellyfish!' We both turned to look at her. She was still transfixed by the screen.

Drake leaned closer to me. 'They wanted both of you dead. 'I wanted you to live.'

I huffed. 'You have some morality clause about women? God, how noble.'

He was looking at me funny.

'What? They didn't pay you enough to take us both out?'

'Blood is thicker than gold.' He paused. 'I wasn't going to let anyone hurt you.'

What was he saying?

'I've been trying to help you,' he went on. 'I thought you'd see that.'

What the fuck was he saying?

I kept my voice calm. 'What are you talking about?'

'You know what.'

'No.'

I stared at him. He stared back.

A jolt – a snap of recognition. Something in the curve of his nose.

He took a step towards me. 'I've tried to teach you patience. I've tried to make you see threats everywhere, to question everything. I've tried to make you better at what you do.'

My head started spinning.

Our early texts.

Your parents never taught you patience?

They never taught me anything.

'Twelve years ago, an alert came up that a DNA sample taken at a murder scene had enough alleles in common with mine to be my offspring.'

He was saying he was my father.

My actual father.

The Chameleon was my father.

Not Mike Martin.

Alain Drake.

'Until then, I never knew you existed. And it didn't take me long to realise what you were up to.' He smiled. 'You clearly took after me more than you did your mother.'

Twelve years ago. One of my very early kills. Pre-Fox days. A bad man who'd hit me – before I hit him back. With a skillet pan. He did draw blood. I just hadn't had the sense to make sure it was all cleared up.

'Last year when I got an alert that your DNA had been registered at Find My Heritage, I thought you were trying to find your father. It was a good opportunity to make contact.'

This wasn't making sense.

'Why did you create Mike? What was the point?'

'I wanted to get to know you, although it soon became clear it was Fox pretending to be you. And I wanted to see if you were interested in getting to know me.'

'So you created a perfect grandfather with a twee, wholesome life?'

'It didn't matter who I was pretending to be. You turned up that day. Before you realised that Mike didn't exist, you were going to meet him. You wanted to meet your father.'

Everything I'd felt when Fox first told me he'd found my father was still there. I wanted to know more about my history. About where I came from. Now, I was just trying to work out how I felt knowing that he was a violent gun-for-hire working for a shadowy criminal organisation.

I kept looking at him, trying to determine if I could see any of myself in him. Was this even true? Could he just be some bullshit artist who got off on lying?

The Chameleon.

How often had I thought of myself as the same thing? Playing up whichever side of my heritage I figured was going to help me fit in more. Mine was an identity that could be changed whenever I needed it to.

I could see it now. I did look like him. He was a little darker than me, but I could see it.

The Chameleon. He could adapt to whatever surroundings he was in. Interpol agent. Assassin. And his hard-to-identify heritage. He'd used it all to his advantage. No one could ever quite work out what I was, and he'd been afforded the same privilege.

I thought of 'Mike's' messages with Fox. The way he wrote, the things he said. It was all so believable. Nothing gave away that English wasn't his first language. The multi-lingual

Chameleon. It was all part of being able to be whoever he wanted to be.

'Where did you meet my mother?'

'In a bar. She was very beautiful, but troubled.' A polite way of describing a messy fucking drunk. 'We only spent a few nights together. The last time, she told me she was pregnant. But how was I to know she wasn't lying? How was I to know it was even mine?'

'And you realised she'd been telling the truth when you discovered someone you shared DNA with was out there committing murder?' If I'd been more careful when I'd killed that first bad man, Drake would never have found out about me.

Drake nodded. 'It was easy to find you. I read all the childhood records on you, and then followed police reports with certain details. A male victim, usually with a history of assault against women. A violent yet poorly thought-out attack. A kitchen knife or other household object used as a murder weapon. It wasn't hard figuring out which were yours.'

My father. Reading up on me.

'You never thought to introduce yourself? Like a normal person?'

Drake threw his hands in the air and raised his voice. 'I was doing the best parenting I could from afar. Cleaning up your mess! Making sure you kept your freedom.' He took a step towards me. 'I'm not a good person. I don't care about others. What could I ever offer you? I stayed away for your sake.'

I didn't excuse him, but I understood him. 'You've been watching me all this time?'

'You made mistakes in the early days. The skillet pan

kill; I had to encourage a neighbour to forget seeing you. The bar kill; I had to make sure the hairs you left behind got misplaced.'

I thought I'd been out there on my own, that killing men and getting away with it was a sign that I was an avenging angel with good luck behind me, that it showed I was doing good work. But I'd just had my dad hovering over me, clearing up my mistakes?

'Fox was a good influence at first. He was careful. Maybe not as good as me, but he was methodical. I respected that. But even before The Corporation's kill order came in, it had become clear that Fox was going to be your downfall. He was the one pushing for the big names, the ones that were going to get you caught or killed. He needed to be stopped.'

'You were happy to let Fox die?'

'Once I'd found you, I did a good job of protecting you. I made sure you got away with all your crimes. I'd trusted Fox to do the same. And then he let you down. Unforgivable.'

I shook my head. 'When Ivrea failed, how did you convince them to not try again?'

'I said you'd been given a big enough scare that you'd rethink your choices. I said I would monitor you and step in if necessary.' He looked at me as if he expected praise for this. 'When I realised what the keyring was, and that Bibi had it, I put you under surveillance. I had to be sure you hadn't managed to cash it out. That you weren't part of a bigger infrastructure, a bigger gang.'

I started pacing. 'We're a family! We just have an unusual little sideline. That's all we've ever been!'

Drake shrugged. 'I couldn't understand why you'd take all that risk – for what? This naïve attempt to make the world a better place? But with every surveillance report I received, it became clearer and clearer it was just the two of you and your little detective friend. I was about to call it all off, but then you took Clark Dixon.'

'We thought he was just a random wife-beater! We had no idea he—'

'He was working with The Corporation. They were going to buy Boltons.'

Bibi laughed hysterically at my phone. 'Silly Peso!'

I dropped my voice further. 'You thought us killing him was a sign we were working for one of your competitors?'

'Losing him killed The Corporation's carefully engineered takeover plan – and then they saw how much Fox made from shorting on the Boltons stock.'

Drake was The Chameleon. Drake was my father. Drake had been trying to save us from The Corporation. Drake wanted cash. Drake wanted Dolly Dodo.

What the actual fuck was going on?

Something else hit me. 'Danny, Kristoff, Barry – they all died because of you?'

'Danny needed to die because he knew too much. I was meant to be meeting him there, but Fox beat me to it.'

Danny had been standing there waiting for Drake, not Fox. He would've ended up dead either way – just at my father's hand, not my husband's.

'I never even knew Danny was a criminal.'

Drake snorted. 'He was very small-time. A little drug-dealing here and there. I enlisted him to help because of your history with him. But he was an idiot who got ideas above his station. Started strutting around, thinking he was a big deal.'

That did sound like Danny.

'Kristoff was a threat to your career. The reputation you had built. He was an entitled idiot. And Barry was too nosy for his own good. I saw him taking photos of me when I was in my car. I couldn't risk him handing anything in to the authorities. I wasn't going to let some nobody be the one to unmask me.'

'But why did you kill him at our house?'

'To confirm Jenny was working with you. Watching how she helped make his death look like an accident was very interesting.'

I tried to take in everything he was saying.

My father had been watching me for twelve years. Twelve years!

He'd been trying to help me.

He wanted me alive.

But he wasn't so bothered about Fox.

66

Fox

Jenny patched in. 'Fox, *if you can hear me, I'm getting to Haze as fast as I can, but I'm still ten minutes away.*'

My GPS told me I was four minutes away.

The roads passed by in a blur. I had to stay focused on driving.

I watched the time tick down.

I pulled up close to the charity shop. I had my knife. I was prepared to do whatever it took.

The glass windows at the front had their blinds pulled down. I could hear the low murmur of voices. I crept up to the windows and listened.

I heard what sounded like: 'Peso!'

I recognised that name. *Octonauts* was playing.

What the hell was going on? An attempt to calm a hysterical, terrified Bibi?

The blinds blocked my view. I couldn't see anything inside. I crept round to the alleyway and the back door that I knew Haze had entered through. I tried the handle. It turned. I heard raised voices from inside. Things were escalating.

I crept out into the main shop. Drake had his back to me,

standing in front of my wife and daughter. Bibi was sitting on a table, staring down at Haze's phone. I couldn't hear what Drake and Haze were saying over the noise of *Octonauts*.

I gripped my knife harder and charged at Drake. I threw myself at him, toppling him to the ground.

'Dada!' Bibi had turned towards the noise and was grinning at me. 'What you doing?'

I wanted this man dead. But not in front of my daughter.

'Playfight! That's fun, isn't it?'

Drake was rubbing his head as I patted him down and took his gun, tucking it into my waistband.

Haze went over to Bibi. 'We're going to have a little grown-up talk, and then we're going home.' She turned up the volume further on her phone and came back to us.

Drake tried to sit up. I pushed him back with my foot and turned to Haze. 'Where are we going to do it?'

My adrenalin was spiked. I was ready for this. For once and for all putting the hell of the last year behind us.

'We're not.' Haze folded her arms. 'We're letting him live.'

Of all the things I'd expected my wife to say, that was not it.

'Tell me why we aren't going to kill the man who took our daughter? The man who tried to kill us? He is The Chameleon, isn't he?'

'He is The Chameleon.' Haze took a deep breath. 'But he's also my father.'

I looked between them both. Haze's father?

How? What? *Why?*

Oh, god. This man was my father-in-law?

I looked between them. I could see it. I could goddamn see it. A resemblance.

I tried to focus.

The Chameleon had been tasked with killing us.

He was our enemy.

'If he's your father, then what happened to familial loyalty? Everything we've gone through this last year was because of him!' I pushed my foot down harder, pressing it against Drake's chest.

'It's a fair point.' Haze shrugged at Drake. 'But he claims he's been trying to save us from The Corporation. And it feels a bit icky killing my dad.'

'*Save* us? What about Ivrea?'

Haze and Drake looked at each other.

'Well, that's complicated,' is all Haze would say.

'I told you to not go to Balgray!' Drake was staring up at me. 'The Corporation somehow found out you were going to the party. They were going to kill you there.'

I shook my head. 'Wasn't everything you were doing set up to make us *go* to Balgray?'

Drake pushed my foot off his chest and sat up. 'That was before I realised what The Corporation had planned. I wanted you to leave Bibi at home so I could talk to her. She had something of mine.'

I looked at Haze. She nodded.

'I was never meant to take her. I was going to make sure you had no idea that I'd even been there. But when I heard The Corporation were going to kill you there, I tried to warn you not to go. You didn't listen so I had no choice. I took her and made sure you knew about it, to get you out of there.'

'You kidnapped Bibi to save us?' I scoffed.

'It worked, didn't it?' Drake looked up at me as he got to his feet. 'I knew nothing would get you out of there faster than thinking your child was in danger. I knew the men there would be no match for you when you were in such a state.'

'You expect praise? After everything you've put us through?' I didn't want to shout. But this was it. I was finally face to face with The Chameleon, yet I couldn't unleash the hell I wanted to. 'What was wrong with just coming to us? Explaining everything? Like a normal human being?'

'I had to be sure!'

'Let's stop the shouting! There's a child—' Haze was cut off by Jenny charging through the front door, holding our kitchen knife.

'Hi, Jen-Jen,' said Bibi, still staring at Haze's phone.

Jenny took in a totally unfazed Bibi, and the three of us standing, facing each other.

'What is going on?'

67

Haze

We were driving back home together. Fox had left his motor-bike at the charity shop. He didn't want either of us out of his sight for a moment.

Bibi had fallen asleep as soon as he started the engine.

Fox was gripping the steering wheel. He'd muttered. 'I just don't understand,' at least three times.

Drake was following us in his car.

'We give him the keyring he's been so desperately wanting, and then he's once again out of my life,' I said.

'You don't want to try and . . .?' Fox trailed off.

'What? Form some kind of relationship with him? God, no. He gave me his excellent bone structure, and that's about all I'm grateful for.'

'You sure?'

'I don't think any good can come from having him in our lives.'

It was quite something to grow up without a father, and then find him and be so brutally disappointed. Not about the killing part – clearly, I understood that. It was the total lack of morality. He was The Chameleon, a man who could play both sides. He could adapt to whoever he was with to get what he wanted. He was all about the money. There was no sense of him trying to do the right thing. I could see that I might have got the whole not-every-life-is-sacred feeling from him, but he was a greedy, gun-for-hire killer.

We might share certain similarities, but we were not the same.

We all made our own path. Our own rules. We got to be our own people, and parent in our own way. We could find totally new ways to fuck up our kids.

I might have inherited my father's killer instincts, but I was using my low regard for human life to take out bad men, and bad men only. I had a strict moral code and a righteous mission. He just wanted cash

We got home, and Fox plucked a sleeping Bibi out of her car seat. He held her close to him as we walked into the house, and we went upstairs together. He transferred her gently into her bed as I reached for Dolly Dodo on her bedside table. Jenny was on her way to us with Reggie.

I heard Drake's car pull up outside.

I took off Dolly's necklace and went back out. Drake was leaning against his car. I handed him the keyring. He stared at it, smiled to himself and put it in his pocket.

'Who are The Corporation?' I asked.

Drake shook his head. 'How do you think I've lasted so long in this business? I don't ask questions. I don't try and uncover information that could cause me trouble. We had a special channel to communicate through, and they always paid me. That was all I needed to know.'

'What are you going to do now?'

'Enjoy retirement. I've used up my nine lives. To leave this job rich and breathing is all I've ever wanted.' He put a hand on my shoulder. 'I didn't want it to go like this.'

I looked down at it.

Click-click.

Drake turned at the noise. A tall man with black hair was photographing us. He clocked us looking, and ran to a parked black moped. He hopped on it and sped off.

'Do you know him?'

A black moped. The man following Fox the other day.

'Mario. He works for The Corporation.' Drake got into his car and started the engine. 'He shows them the photos, and this is bad for us both.'

He accelerated away before I could ask him what he was planning on doing.

Jenny arrived with Reggie fifteen minutes later. I put him to bed after several kisses all over his sleeping head, and joined Jenny and Fox at the kitchen table. Two glasses of whisky and a Bailey's were waiting. I pointed out that, as no one was actually dead, this was technically against Fox's rules. He shrugged and downed his drink.

I shook my head. 'I can't be half French.'

'I can believe it,' said Jenny.

'You have that, you know . . .' Fox trailed off.

Jenny butted in. 'That haughty air? That sense that you think you're better than everyone else? That way of saying no just to be difficult?'

'*Merde.*' I took a glug of whisky.

68

Fox

We had a busy couple of days. Jenny wiped any CCTV showing any of us anywhere near the charity shop. She'd also arranged for an incredibly generous cash donation to be left there with a note 'for the damages'. Freddie, the volunteer I'd wrongly been so suspicious of, had raved all over Facebook about the mystery benefactors. We were good people. We made a mess. We cleared it up.

We looked back over the last month and were able to make everything make sense.

Drake had come to the UK for the keyring. That was all he'd wanted. And then we'd killed Clark Dixon, and The Corporation was back to wanting us dead.

I knew now wasn't the time to mention it to Haze, but Drake was impressive. It was no wonder he'd had such a long, illustrious career. For more than a year, he'd been behind the scenes pulling the strings like some kind of chess Grandmaster. And he'd succeeded. We were alive and he'd got his retirement fund.

Throughout, he'd had people watching us. Logging our movements. Proving to himself and to The Corporation that we were just a couple with a penchant for killing. No big boss. No gang affiliation. I should've seen this sooner. I remembered the constant yelling of, 'Who are you working for?' by the men who took me in Ivrea. That was all The Corporation really cared about – that we weren't working for the competition.

The people Drake had watching us were good enough that we'd never noticed them. They were individuals who'd been able to merge into the background and not arouse our suspicions. Everywhere we went, people looked at us, assessed us, judged us; how were we meant to know who was doing it for money?

When The Corporation began to suspect that Drake's motives didn't align with their own they hired the useless Rob and then Mario and his black moped.

The mystery of Frederica and her husband had been solved by Jenny, who frequently did image searches for us in case we'd been captured anywhere we didn't want to be seen. A photo of us taken at a school fete had come up on a private swingers' website. Someone had been catfishing, using our image to look for 'like-minded local couples wanting excitement away from the status quo'. Frederica must have been taken in by it.

Despite everything, it still wasn't over. It was hard to know how much we could trust my father-in-law. The men who'd chased us at Balgray had clearly wanted it to be the last party we ever attended. We still needed to convince The Corporation to back off and leave us to live in peace.

Everything felt in limbo. We were going through the motions of everyday life, but were braced for impact.

I was making dinner when the doorbell rang. Haze was putting the kids to bed.

'I'll get it!' Haze shouted from upstairs.

69

Haze

I opened the door to find my father standing there with a suitcase. Was he coming to say goodbye? Or moving in, so we could bond?

Drake motioned towards the suitcase. 'I got you this. To apologise for the whole taking-Bibi thing.'

'New luggage?'

Drake frowned. 'No. Mario.'

I looked again at the suitcase. Great. Another dead man. I thought of how big Mario had been, and how small the case was in comparison.

'He was taller than—'

'Not any more.'

'Right.'

What the hell was wrong with this guy?

'Couldn't you just get me a bottle of perfume? Some flowers?'

Drake shrugged. 'He saw too much. I'm cleaning house. You need to be more ruthless.'

My father was aware of how many men I'd killed. Yet this was his takeaway?

'I'll bear that in mind,' I said.

'I need to get a flight back to Brussels. So I don't have time for . . .' He tapped the case.

It wasn't going to be easy disposing of another body, but I figured we had no choice but to fit it in.

'I will send you the details I use to contact The Corporation. Maybe you can find a way to track them down. I tried to make them understand you're not a threat. But I worry they have discovered our genetic connection. Despite my history, they might fear I've gone soft.'

'Don't worry, Dad. I'll let them know you kidnapped your granddaughter and threatened to kill me if it turned out I was working for the rival gang.'

He nodded. He might speak five languages, but he didn't seem to understand sarcasm. 'I've done all I can. You need to stay alert. They still want you dead.'

My first pep talk from my father. I wondered how I would've turned out if he'd claimed me back when I was a motherless child. Was there any good in him at all? I wasn't one to be giving out parenting advice, of course – and besides, where the hell would you start with this guy? But it could be argued he had been trying to be a good parent. In his own deeply fucked-up way, he had been looking out for me. In Ivrea, he'd arranged to save me, but not Fox. Fathers often believed a daughter's love interest wasn't good enough – they just didn't always take that to the extreme of thinking that meant it was fine to let them be killed by a pack of gangsters.

'You get your money?'

Drake smiled. 'The keyring served its purpose.' He handed me a small box from his pocket. 'This is a thank-you gift for Bibi. For keeping it safe.'

I opened it. Inside was a necklace with a silver pendant in the shape of a penguin. It was covered in diamonds.

'You got this for a four-year-old?'

'She can sell it for sweets money,' he deadpanned.

'Next time you want to know how we're all doing, can you just call me? No more sending people to watch us. It's creepy.'

'Okay.'

'Okay.' We nodded at each other. 'Goodbye.'

'Bye.'

I wheeled Mario inside and closed the door.

Fox came out of the kitchen. 'That was like listening to two robots malfunction. At least we know where you get your inability to express emotions from.'

'I've also learned he's not good on presents.' I motioned towards the suitcase and the necklace. 'I guess I really didn't miss out on much growing up without him.'

'You don't have to welcome him into our lives, but you can still ask him things you've always wanted to know: who his parents were, where he grew up, if we should be aware of any predisposition to genetic illnesses.'

'Next time he's in town, we'll do lunch.' I kicked the suitcase. 'Now, what do we do about him?'

'Let's drop him at a secure location until we can find a permanent resting place. I've got a lead on The Corporation.'

Fox parked our minivan outside the Brentford branch of You Pay, We Store!. Drake had given us the details of the website he'd used to communicate with The Corporation. Drains-RUs.com had a chat forum where people could discuss their top tips for clearing drains. Once Fox had logged on, there was a back-end weblink that took him through to a secure page where orders were given and received. Jenny had been able to track it to a host server that was masking The Corporation's IP address.

If we could get to the server, we had a chance of getting the IP address, which would then lead us to the device The Corporation was using. A long, painful dance, but one we needed to do.

We'd spent the last month trying to get to The Chameleon, and now he was helping us get to The Corporation. You want to stop the snake, you have to cut off its head.

DrainsRUs.com had a registered storage locker at You Pay, We Store!, a facility that was open 24/7. We put on our baseball caps and walked in, heading straight to Number B36 on the second floor. Our hope was that the server was being stored inside this locker.

There was no one else here. Which was understandable at 4am.

The lock was easy enough to break.

Surprisingly easy, really. Something was jangling in my mind as we pulled up the locker door. Inside, it was empty except for a stack of blocks with a bundle of wires, and a timer that was counting down at lightning speed.

Tick-tock, tick-tock.

Ding.

Fox and I looked at each other. This couldn't be it. This couldn't be how it ended.

Part 5
Love

'We start every day by telling our children we love them, and we tell them every night when we tuck them in. Love makes the world go round, and love makes my family soar and be the best versions of themselves.'

Bells Brightley, parenting blogger (MommaKnowsBest) and bestselling author of *Reason for Being: Blessed to Be a Mom!*

'Kids might blow up your life, tear it apart to the point where you barely recognise yourself, but fuck it, it's worth it. You'd die for them. Kill for them. That is family. People you love no matter what. Until your last breath, they're the ones that matter, no matter how much they drive you fucking nuts. You're stuck with them, and they're stuck with you. The beautiful, inescapable, suffocating bond of unconditional love.'

Hazel Matthews, mother

70

Ten days later

Jenny

I stood up and tried to ignore my legs shaking. The church was cold. I straightened my shoulders and walked towards the lectern. I was glad I was wearing loafers. I didn't know why I'd even considered heels. I could hear Haze's voice in my head: '*Because you need to try and elevate that god-awful trouser suit that does nothing for you.*'

I bit my lip.

Talking in front of people was easy when it was my colleagues in an incident room and I was barking orders. There, I could find my voice with no problem. I knew what had to be done. This was new territory. But this was how we honoured our dead, and I was going to do my job. I was going to hold it together.

Bibi was in the front pew in a pretty navy dress. Felix sat next to her in his school uniform shirt and trousers, the smartest clothes he owned. They'd insisted on sitting together. '*I want to help, not be sad.*' At the age of four, it was already clear how important it was to be there for your friends.

I looked out at the people filling the pews of this old church. Reggie was in a pram, being rocked by my mother's constantly moving foot.

I placed the cue cards on the lectern. I knew what I wanted to say by heart, but they were there if I stumbled. I looked out at all the faces staring back at me.

I would channel Haze and Fox, take inspiration from them and their bravery. Say everything I needed to say without crumbling.

I took a deep breath, and then the church doors creaked open. Bright light filtered in. I squinted at the two figures who stood framed in the doorway. Everyone turned to look.

Haze and Fox, backlit by the sunlight behind them.

Both in black suits. Both wearing sunglasses. Haze had red lipstick on. Her bandaged hand was the only hint of the trouble they had managed to stumble away from.

They gently closed the door behind them and slipped into a pew at the back. They kept their sunglasses on. To the many members of the congregation still staring, it would've looked like they were famous. I gave everyone another minute to settle. To try and turn back to me. To the main event. I wasn't upset. I understood it. Haze and Fox were the bright, glossy peacocks in a sea of pensioners' M&S knitted cardigans and orthopaedic shoes.

People looked at them and didn't realise that their beauty and money didn't protect them from the ups and downs of parenting, from the mind-numbing frustrations of mundane daily life. They were just like us – they just had a special glow that drew your attention. Even now, I couldn't shake it off. Whenever we were out together, I still felt it – that I was lucky to be sitting at their table. They needed me, but I needed them more. I had been destined for a sad, quiet, beige life until Haze had steamrollered her way into it. They had shown me how different life could be when you dared to really live it. Don't coast – soar.

Dad had understood it. I had told him everything. He had shaken his head and chuckled, asking if what he was hearing was really true, or if the morphine was messing with him.

Then his sharp eyes had become clear for a final time. 'Sounds like those men all deserved it.' He'd clasped my hand. 'You make me proud. Everything you do.' He'd told me how much it had hurt him to see me with Bill, knowing he wasn't a good man. He'd always known I hadn't told him the truth about what had happened to Bill, but he'd wanted to wait for me to tell him the real story when I was ready. He told me how strong I was, and how glad he was that I was happy and safe. He could go easy now, knowing I could face anything life threw at me.

It was everything I could've hoped for.

We'd broken through that English reserve that so often keeps our tongues from saying what the heart really feels.

Home had always been my favourite place. My parents made me feel safe and loved, and it was everything I'd ever needed. Moving back in with them with Felix when my life had hit rock bottom was not how I'd meant for things to be, but they'd never judged me. They'd looked after me, like they always did. Made sure I was eating right. Fussed over me. There, I got to be a kid again: just turning up for mealtimes, getting my laundry done, having them checking what time I'd be home.

And then, sometime over the last few months, it had changed. Their home had stopped being a place I went to be looked after; it was somewhere I went to look after them. I was checking their fridge, making sure they had enough food, fixing things they'd let slide. Dad was getting sicker, and Mum was worrying about him, not remembering things like she used to. It broke my heart. But I was grateful that I could be there, that I could show them my love through my actions, like they'd always done for me.

Dad had slipped away with Mum and I sitting by his bedside. He was ready, and I wasn't.

Last week, I was standing in Tesco, crying at a box of chicken Kievs. They were the same brand we used to buy on the first night of every holiday we took to Cornwall in my childhood. An easy dinner after a long drive. I was crying because it was a happy memory I'd never realised was happy. It was so mundane. Chucking a box in the trolley. Eating them and laughing at our garlic breath. My phone had rung, then, and when I'd answered it, mid-sob, a voice had told me that I'd been matched to a little baby girl. It was the call I'd been waiting for.

She'd be coming home with me in a couple of weeks. I was going to call her Frankie. I didn't care what anyone else thought, I knew she was a gift from my dad up above. He always knew better than anyone what I needed.

I smiled over at Mum; she was gripping a tissue to her nose. Bibi and Felix sat together, kicking their feet.

I cleared my throat and began.

'Frank Dennis Needham was a good man. The best man. I was lucky to have him as a father. No matter what age I'd lost him at, it always would've been too soon. There's never enough time with those you love the most.'

I let myself slip into autopilot. I didn't want to let myself truly feel the words. I just wanted to say them without breaking down. I needed to honour him, to say everything that needed to be said. I could do this last thing for him.

As I talked, I looked across at Haze and Fox. They were holding hands and nodding me on. My friends. My family. My future. I might be their back-office pigeon, the support act to their starring roles, but I was happy with who I was. Not everyone needed to be shining out on centre stage. They were different to me, not better. We were all trying to do the best we could with the lives we'd been given. I was going to celebrate everything I was, not focus on what I wasn't. I was choosing happiness.

71

Haze

Jenny spoke so beautifully about Frank that I was glad I was wearing sunglasses. She was hurting so much, and I hated the fact there was nothing we could do to make it better.

I'd seen a lot of death.

I'd caused a lot of death.

Knives. Blood. Slit throats. Crushed skulls. Spilt guts.

But nothing beat the utter savagery of the natural death of someone much loved.

We either had to watch the people we loved die, or they had to watch us die. There was no avoiding that pain. It was inevitable. How the hell did everyone walk around with that knowledge without wanting to scream?

What had we been hardwired with that allowed us to live without constantly dwelling on the pain and futility of our existence? Was there some specially designed microchip within each of us that helped us to get up each day, despite knowing that one day the misery of losing those we loved most was going to happen – and that the only thing we could do to avoid it was die first?

It was all a cruel joke. You search for – you *long* for – love, connection, people who make your life better. Yet the more you love, the more pain there is to come.

How was Jenny going to get through losing him? How did anyone?

I'd never had a father. That was my story, and I was sticking to it. Better to be in the fatherless group than admit to having one who had swooped back into my life only to try and kill my husband and kidnap my daughter. Wow, did I luck out there.

Frank was a real father. He had worshipped Jenny, and wrapped her up so tightly in his love that she never questioned it. He'd been there for her when she needed him, and even when she didn't. He'd wanted to make her life better, easier, and nothing was ever too much trouble.

I squeezed Fox's hand. I had chosen a man who would be exactly that kind of father to our children.

I might have inherited certain physical features from my parents, they might have given me their genes, but that was all they had passed down. I had never felt supported, understood or loved by them. They made me, and then they left me. I was long past resentment.

Some people weren't meant to be parents. The sacrifices were too great.

Cowards run. Heroes stay.

It was easier to disconnect and break away.

I brushed a bit of soil off Fox's elbow.

I knew how lucky we were to be alive.

The bomb had annihilated the storage locker and the six surrounding it. As soon as we'd seen the timer and the flashing lights we'd turned and run. Luckily, the locker next to the blast had been owned by someone storing five superking-sized mattresses, which had taken the brunt of the blast. We'd been able to escape with bad cuts and bruises.

Drake had been right. The Corporation clearly weren't finished with us yet. We just needed to get through today, and then we had a plan for how to deal with them.

Jenny finished speaking. I wanted to give her a standing ovation, but Fox quietly pointed out that funerals didn't really have that as an option.

The music started up and the coffin was gently carried out, with Jenny, Sandy and our children following behind it. Bibi and Felix walked together, pushing Reggie's pram. Jenny stopped at our pew and took me and Fox by the hands. We all walked out together, Frank leading the way.

We lined up around the gravesite to say our final goodbyes. I stood next to Jenny.

'Everything okay?' she whispered.

Fox and I had done a final check of the perimeter once everyone else had filed into the church.

'Yes.'

We both watched as the coffin was lowered into the ground.

'You sure he won't mind having company down there?'

Jenny smiled. 'He'd be glad to help. It would give him a good chuckle. One last favour for a beloved daughter.'

I looked around at the gathered mourners. Many of Frank's old police colleagues were in attendance. It was undoubtedly the first – and hopefully the last – time we'd buried a body knowing a good number of law enforcement would be at the site the next morning. A loving goodbye to Frank. A 'fuck off for good' to Mario.

Our family might be a little less conventional than the others in the suburbs around us, but I couldn't imagine it any other way.

72

Fox

The village fete was in full swing, with laughing children and parents gripping Styrofoam cups of very average coffee.

We found who we were looking for by the bouncy castle.

'Go on, Bibi. We'll wait right here.'

Bibi kicked off her shoes and was clambering into the castle before I'd finished my sentence.

Benjamin Norwood was standing watching his daughter charging around the bouncy castle at full pelt, her plaits swinging.

I walked up to him. 'Lovely day, isn't it?'

He turned to look at us, his eyes immediately flicking to the nearby bodyguard who was doing his best to blend in, despite his dark glasses and thick jacket.

We knew The Corporation would've had a presence at the Balgray Hall. Someone there to do the job. Someone there to watch us. Jenny had obtained security footage of the party.

'Not here,' Norwood said.

'Absolutely here. It's good to remind you what's at stake.' I nodded towards the two laughing girls. Then I spoke fast. 'We are nobodies. Independent. We have a hobby. It's a little different to other parents' hobbies. And there might be simi-larities with your work – but to us it's not work. It's not a career choice. We are not trying to take over anything.'

'We're just having fun.' Haze attempted a smile.

'This is what The Chameleon told me too.'

'But you didn't believe him?'

Norwood shrugged. 'He was so emphatic, so desperate to get us off your case, it made me think he was in business with you both.'

'I understand you see threats everywhere. Everyone is out to get you and take over – but that's not what's happening here.'

Reggie started crying. Haze leaned down and plucked him out of the pram, bouncing him on her hip. 'We're parents, first and foremost. But we need a little something to keep us going. Something more.'

Norwood looked at Haze. 'Pilates and online shopping not enough for you? That did it for my ex.'

'We all choose our own ways to help us be the best we can be. The key is finding what works for you' She smiled up at him.

A surprisingly Zen response from Haze considering that he'd just asked her why stretching and working out her credit card didn't keep her quiet.

Norwood observed us both. 'You two just have a "hobby". There's no bigger plan?'

'No,' we said in unison.

'Dave is a part of my organisation,' Norwood said.

I remembered the drug-dealer with the coasters.

'He vouched for you both,' he went on. 'Said he'd tried to hire you, and you refused.'

'As we've been saying, we're not in the business. It's purely a passion project.'

'And you won't come after any of my people again?'

I nodded. 'We'll make sure we stay in our lane, and only kill the nobodies. The bad men acting on their own bad thoughts. Not on someone else's orders.'

Norwood looked me in the eye. 'How did you know it was me?'

'We saw a video clip of you at the party, dipping your finger into a glass of red wine and smudging it on your shirt.'

'Bloody cameras everywhere. You never know when you're being filmed.'

'You wanted us to think you were a dumb drunk,' said Haze.

'The toff with nothing better to do is an easy stereotype to lean into.'

He'd played the part well; we'd fallen for it without a second thought. If it hadn't been for that small giveaway in the video footage, we might never have clocked it was him.

All the intelligence we had on The Corporation told us that they were a European gang with a new business model. That they had people working for them who were the best in their fields, regardless of nationality. Just because the majority of those doing the grunt work were Albanian or Bulgarian, it didn't mean the head of The Corporation was.

The shell company they hid behind wasn't Unique Events – it was Restore Glory, Norwood's charity that had supposedly been set up to help save England's stately homes. Those houses were such money pits that I knew how easy it would be for them to fudge accounts. Funds allocated for a new roof could be used to support a drug-importing venture. The parties themselves helped launder the cash they were getting from their enterprises. Of course, no one was actually spending £50,000 to sit at a table and eat boiled chicken and drink average wine. It was all for appearances – and to clean the money.

I looked at Norwood. 'You need to assure us that this is it. You're not sending anyone after us again?'

He shrugged. 'You can relax. You're off my shit list. You were a threat. An upset. We thought you'd been hired by a higher power to mess things up. Three of our most important men died at your hands.'

'They were terrible people,' said Haze through gritted teeth. 'We were going after them as individuals. Not you as a group.'

'Clark was a good friend. And one that was going to make me even richer. We had big plans for the future.'

'Clark was an unfortunate coincidence.'

'You can see my confusion. You were taking out my top brawn, and then not long after Ivrea, when you were supposedly scared of us, you went and took out my top brain. It looked like you were coming after my whole business.'

Bibi squealed as she bounced high and landed on her bottom. Norwood's daughter was lying beside her, laughing.

'It's a shame you don't want to join us. My model of using people based on ability not nationality is really bringing gang warfare into the twenty-first century. We're not hiding in the shadows, on the run from police. Most of us are out here living our lives, and people have no idea what we're capable of.'

It was a little galling to find out we weren't that special. We'd been out presenting ourselves as Mr and Mrs Normal, congratulating ourselves on hiding our dark side from the world. Now it turned out we weren't the only ones.

'You must know what it's like to work a stereotype to your advantage?' Norwood motioned at Haze. 'You get written off as a yummy mummy.' He patted my shoulder. 'You as some crass American finance bro.' He shrugged. 'And I'm just a posh twat with a stately.'

'We're on the side of good.' I sniffed. 'Of making the world a better place. You just care about making big money.'

'If you had heating bills like mine, you'd care about that too. And don't deny that money plays a part in what you do. It might help you sleep at night to say it's only about doing the right thing, but it's luxury Egyptian cotton sheets you're snoring soundly on.'

I bristled. 'You've got my number now. If you're worried about anything, pick up the phone – don't pull the trigger.' I motioned towards our happy daughters. 'It's high stakes for all of us.'

He nodded. 'Fatherhood changes you. We all have a line we won't cross. It's why no one ever came near you when the children were nearby.'

We killed only men, and only bad ones. He killed anyone, but only adults. We all had the rules we lived by, the things we needed to tell ourselves to prove we weren't monsters.

73

Haze

Finally, we could breathe easy. We had convinced Norwood we were just a quirky couple with a sideline in bad men. Independent contractors with no interest in branching out. The hit on us was officially off. We were leaving each other to it. A respectful truce.

It was freeing knowing the threat that had been lingering over us for the last year was finally gone. Yesterday, a woman in a green coat had kept staring at us. I loved the fact that I knew it was because she was judging me – Bibi was sucking on a lollipop and it was only 10.30am – and not because she was reporting to a higher power who wanted us dead.

Now, I could soak up stares, knowing they were filled with disdain or admiration and not deadly intent.

Green-coat woman might be thinking I was a slum mum spoiling my child and her teeth, but what did she know of what we'd been through this week?

I'd realised it didn't matter how your parenting looked to others; it was all about what you did when no one was watching. Bells 'Bullshit' Brightley had reminded me of that. It didn't matter if friends, strangers or three million followers thought of you a certain way, the truth was what was between you and your family. That was it.

We were out in the park *en famille*. Apparently, despite my French genes, my accent was still 'embarrassingly shit'. Thanks, Jen. It was a beautiful day. Our sunglasses were on. Bibi was on Fox's shoulders, while Reggie was strapped to me in a papoose. Sausage was circling us, his tail wagging. We passed by a couple who smiled at us as they walked hand in hand. We were the picture-perfect family, and we knew it.

Last night, Reggie had, for the first time, slept through the night. I'd bounced out of bed this morning. The end was in sight. Sleep was back on the table.

Drake was back in Belgium. He'd been in touch: a vague message about when he was next in town and whether he could come to see us. I had low expectations. It was a good place to start from. He hadn't exactly inserted himself into my life smoothly. Fox had been pretty relaxed about how Drake had been happy to let him die in Ivrea. He said he'd kind of understood, as if Bibi had a husband whom he thought was endangering her, he'd have done the same. There was some common ground we could all meet on: killing was acceptable when it came to protecting your children.

Fox set Bibi down, and she began chasing a pigeon, laughing. He squeezed my hand.

Parenting wasn't easy. We were still winging it. Learning on the job. But if our kids ended up fucked up, we could at least look them in the eye and say we'd done everything we could and then some. Yes, one may have been briefly kidnapped by a dodgy grandfather. But no one is perfect. We always had the best of intentions, and we were doing all we could to not let them down. It was a good pep talk to remember. *'Look, baby, we might not make every ballet recital, but if you ever get taken we will always get you back.'*

We had to keep everything in perspective. And if we could survive getting in the crosshairs of a violent international gang and getting blown up, we could raise a happy, functioning family.

Life throws all kind of shit at you, and we're all bombarded with ways to make it better. Ways to heal. But the self-help we needed, that really Fox needed, didn't come from books, affirmations, meditation or dodgy therapists. And certainly not from that bloody motorbike. It came from within and reigniting that killer instinct. Believing in ourselves. Believing in our skills.

Killers.

Parents.

We were doing our best at being both. We could do it. We *were* doing it.

'Could you ever live abroad?' Fox was looking at me.

'Why?'

'I used to think England would be our home forever.' Fox looked around the park. 'But I think I'd be okay with moving. Starting somewhere new.'

I waited to see how I felt. I didn't hate what he was saying.

He kept going. 'Look at how far we've come since Bibi was born. We've been through so much. And what's happened? We've adapted, every time. We're pretty good at this.'

He was right. I thought back to our first few months here. The abject horror I'd felt at the suburban life we'd signed up for. And now look at us. Just last week, I'd told off Fox for not counting out the plastic bags he was returning to Ocado.

We were used to always feeling like we never really belonged.

In that respect, being ex-pats wouldn't make us feel any different.

I knew why Fox was asking. The Corporation might be through with us, but we'd had a glimpse of the underworld that was ticking along beneath us. Who else was down there? Who else was going to one day worry we were competition?

We thought we were just a couple with a little sideline. We'd flirted with the dark side, killed men in cold blood and thought we could escape the bigger world it was all a part of. We'd been wrong. You didn't get to make the occasional foray into darkness and come out unscathed.

We'd believed we could live our dream of playing nice in the suburbs, keeping the criminals off the perfectly cut grass. But it was only ever a matter of time before our two lives collided. The marked line in the ground had long gone. It had been gone even before Bibi walked in on me covered in blood.

We were known entities now. People out there knew about us and what we did. What if they came knocking? The Corporation might be the biggest organisation out there, but it wasn't the only one. If anyone came after us, our family were at risk. That's what it came down to. We were all in this together, and no matter how much we tried to keep them apart from it, we couldn't.

We could live anywhere and be happy as long as we had each other. Life here worked for the moment, but if it didn't we could pack up and leave. Perfect houses, schools, galleries, jobs, victims . . . They were all replaceable.

Family wasn't. Family came first.

We weren't bound to a place. We were bound to each other.

And that was as comforting and delightful as it was downright terrifying.

'You okay?' Fox looked over at me as I stroked Reggie's head.

'Just peachy.' I reached for him with my other hand. 'You're right. Together we can do anything.'

He kissed the top of my head. 'Lucky that we'll never be apart.'

Bibi squealed as she came running back to us at full pelt and flung her arms round my leg. It wasn't luck that kept us together. It was hard work, determination, a whole lot of love and a whole lot of enjoying making bad men bleed. What could ever tear us apart?

THE END

Acknowledgements

For those new to my Acknowledgements – please note I always write them with a glass of wine in hand to help recreate the vibe of gushing acceptance speech.

Editors are incredibly important and clever people and I'm very lucky to have worked with a trio of truly great ones. Jack Butler at Wildfire, who is gone but not forgotten (to clarify, he's not dead – he just moved jobs). We started Haze and Fox together and were blissfully sympatico with everything I wanted for them. I'm doubly blessed that Rachel Hart, who took on the mantle from Jack, has been equally dreamy to work with. Over at Bantam the most excellent Jenny Chen has once again worked her magic at making this book better. I'm very grateful to you all.

To the team at Wildfire – Alex Clarke, Joe Thomas, Jo Edwards, Katrina Smedley, Rebecca Bader – I've loved working together for round two. Thank you for everything you've done for Haze, Fox and little old me.

Alice Lutyens. My devoted super agent. Even when you're on a beach with a martini in hand, I know you're still thinking about all you can do to make my life/career better. That is dedication. And because I never leave you alone. I'm needy but in a good way. Right? RIGHT?

I do particularly enjoy it when you fight over me with my other very impressive agents – Camilla Young and Katie Battcock – about whether I should be writing books or television next. You guys are the best and I will keep trying to do both – you're so lucky I have no social life.

For me Acknowledgements are the perfect chance to immortalise in print the people who make my life so much better. So here I go spreading goodwill and never-ending thanks . . .

Four books in and these four wonderful women have made an appearance in this section in each one. I've nearly run out of things to say about them. But here goes.

Rebecca Thornton. A very brilliant author who I've known my whole life and without whom my whole life would fall apart.

Georgia Tennant. An incredible friend. An incredible annoyingly multi-skilled everything. But above all an incredible audiobook narrator . . . In fact, Robert Burns said it best (it definitely needs to be read in a really authentic Scottish accent to truly capture the meaning of his words). '*Oh would some power give us the gift to see ourselves as others see us.*' I bet you did that brilliantly (evil laughter). Please don't kill me.

Caroline Barrow and Lara Smith-Bosanquet. I remain totally indebted to the unfailing support, ginger biscuits and map-reading you bring to our friendship. And for understanding I will always be a passenger princess.

Theodore Backhouse. Seeing your name in print helps me pretend you're still here annoying me. So I'll keep doing it.

Lou Hill, I remain forever grateful for everything you do. Leading lights of Team Chiswick – Zoe Flower and Simon Byrt for the last-minute wine, kebabs and dog walks, Niall Murphy at Four Leaf Coffee for the very best caffeine fixes with the very best pre-big-meeting-pep-talks. Raza Jaffrey for his heroics saving us from burglars (true leading man behaviour).

Fergus Glenapp. You get a special mention for being the best half first cousin once removed a girl could hope for.

To teachers who have spotted their names in this book – congratulations for both coping with teaching my kids, and them liking you enough to request you be included. I remain grateful and in awe of your skills and deeply embarrassed by my own lack of knowledge (including grammar – which pained copy-editors can attest to).

To the friends who were hoping to get a mention and have upped the friendship game accordingly. Bravo. I've acknowledged some of you by adding you in as character names . . . Yes, this is a cunning plan to make sure you actually read the whole book and don't just skim to this bit looking for glory.

To my beloved parents. What a year we've had! It's been an honour looking after you both. Being a daughter to you in your later years is bringing me back to being a mother to the kids in their early years. Getting to grips with complicated mobility devices, panicking over every little cough, worrying about what you eat – but most of all staring at you while you sleep being so grateful you're here. Dad, if I have a fraction of the grace and good humour you've shown in what you delightfully call 'the fag end of life' I'll feel very lucky. I owe you everything – and your dedication to my writing, extending to giving feedback on a first draft of this book while in the back of an ambulance, will never be surpassed. Thank you for it all.

To the many people who've helped us – your jobs all might be very different, but your hard work, kindness and care towards my parents has been the same. Thank you, Ari

Johar, Charles Go, Chiara Hunt, Christina Middleton, Emil Cretoiu, Fernando Ruiz, Kathleen Abuel, Sarah Zimmerman.

And now to my very own home team. Andrew Trotter – my partner in crime and kid wrangling – I know it's annoying having to constantly repeat 'it's not based on us' every time someone mentions Haze and Fox, but I'm sure it's giving us street cred (and, let's face it, driving a minivan means we need the edge). Tavie, Arlo, Gus and Silva – you are absolutely the very best bit of life (when you're doing exactly what I ask you to).

Tavie, I thought long and hard about dedicating this book to you – not because you don't deserve it (I'm so embarrassingly proud of everything you are) – but I knew it would mean squeezing out another three books so you couldn't claim gloating rights over your siblings forever more. So that's it. I've committed myself to keeping going. Gulp.

If people can gush about their children online even when their kids don't have social media, I reckon I'm allowed to gush about my dogs in a book even though they can't read. Reggie and Richard thank you for being the cuddliest lap warmers as I write. You're the very best doggies.

Finally to anyone who read all the way through to this very last sentence, did you know that every time you rate a book five stars on any public forum sparkling rainbows fill the sky, fluffy bunnies and cute puppies leap with delight and a writer weeps that it was all worth it and rewards herself with chocolate cake, wine and five minutes to herself? Bring joy. Change a life. Too much?

Asia Mackay is a Chinese Scottish author and mother of four based in London. Asia studied Anthropology at Durham University and began her career in television. She moved to China, presented and produced lifestyle programmes in Shanghai before returning to London where she worked for the likes of Ewan McGregor and Charley Boorman, and subsequently completed a Faber Academy course. *A Serial Killer's Guide to Marriage* was shortlisted for The Radio 2 Book Club Award 2026 and her debut novel *Killing It* was the Runner Up in Richard and Judy's Search for a Bestseller competition and Runner Up/Exceptionally Recognised for the Comedy Women In Print prize.

Dear Reader,

We'd love your attention for one more page to tell you about the crisis in children's reading, and what we can all do.

Studies have shown that reading for fun is the **single biggest predictor of a child's future life chances** – more than family circumstance, parents' educational background or income. It improves academic results, mental health, wealth, communication skills, ambition and happiness.[1]

The number of children reading for fun is in rapid decline. Young people have a lot of competition for their time. In 2024, 1 in 10 children and young people in the UK aged 5 to 18 did not own a single book at home.[2]

Hachette works extensively with schools, libraries and literacy charities, but here are some ways we can all raise more readers:

- Reading to children for just 10 minutes a day makes a difference
- Don't give up if children aren't regular readers – there will be books for them!
- Visit bookshops and libraries to get recommendations
- Encourage them to listen to audiobooks
- Support school libraries
- Give books as gifts

There's a lot more information about how to encourage children to read on our website: **www.RaisingReaders.co.uk**

Thank you for reading.

hachette
UK

---

[1] OECD, '21st-Century Readers: Developing Literacy Skills in a Digital World', 2021, https://www.oecd.org/en/publications/21st-century-readers_a83d84cb-en.html

[2] National Literacy Trust, 'Book Ownership in 2024', November 2024, https://literacytrust.org.uk/research-services/research-reports/book-ownership-in-2024